"I'd have been happy to help."

Lavinia set the figurine down and pinned Henry with a steely gaze. "Has it occurred to you I might not want your help? This party is my undertaking, my opportunity to show you that—" She clamped her lips together and turned away.

"To show me what? That you're determined to win the children's affection? I know that. I just don't think you're going about it the right way." *Ugh!* How tactless could he be? "What I mean is—"

"I know what you mean." She whirled around, her dark eyes flashing. "You think you can do a better job caring for them than I can, that because I've led a sheltered life I don't have the necessary skills. You think you're going to show me that they belong here with you. But you're mistaken. I'm more capable than you give me credit for."

"I think you're more capable than *you* give yourself credit for."

"I appreciate your kind words, but if you think plying me with compliments will make me give in, you're mistaken."

Award-winning author **Keli Gwyn**, a native Californian, transports readers to the early days of the Golden State. She and her husband live in the heart of California's Gold Country. Her favorite places to visit are her fictional worlds, historical museums and other Gold Rush–era towns. Keli loves hearing from readers and invites you to visit her Victorian-style cyberhome at keligwyn.com, where you'll find her contact information.

Books by Keli Gwyn

Love Inspired Historical

Family of Her Dreams
A Home of Her Own
Make-Believe Beau
Her Motherhood Wish
Their Mistletoe Matchmakers

KELI GWYN

Their Mistletoe Matchmakers

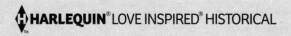

Recycling programs
for this product may
not exist in your area.

LOVE INSPIRED BOOKS

ISBN-13: 978-0-373-42548-8

Their Mistletoe Matchmakers

www.Harlequin.com

Printed in U.S.A.

And whatsoever ye do, do *it* heartily,
as to the Lord, and not unto men;
Knowing that of the Lord ye shall
receive the reward of the inheritance:
for ye serve the Lord Christ.
—*Colossians* 3:23–24

To my bright, beautiful daughter, Adriana,
who loves Christmas more than anyone else I know.

Chapter One

November 1860
Sutter Creek, California

The ominous crack of the large oak tree branch overhead sent a chill racing down Lavinia Crowne's spine. Despite her mad scramble to get out of the way, she lost her footing on the slippery path and fell backward.

The jarring impact as she hit the ground was nothing compared to the thunderous roar as the limb came crashing down. She gasped, certain that her terror-laced breath would be her last.

To her surprise, she found herself trapped beneath a bend in the branch, staring at the stormy sky above. Her arms were pinned to her sides, but she was alive.

Thank You, Lord, for Your protection.

"Help!" Surely someone would hear her.

Bitter cold seeped through Lavinia's clothing. The swollen gray clouds that had gathered throughout the day had begun unleashing their burden only minutes ago, quickly turning the yard into a muddy mess. Raindrops fell fast and furious, running off her cheeks like a fountain of tears. If only she'd attempted her dash to the shed earlier.

"I'm on my way!"

Lavinia recognized the man's voice and groaned. Of all the people who could have come to her rescue, why did it have to be *him*? She had no desire for Henry Hawthorn to see her in her present state. When she faced her recently orphaned nephew and nieces' uncle, she'd planned to be in her best form. Instead, she was a muddy mess.

The front gate banged against the wrought iron fence surrounding the corner lot, obviously thrown open in haste. A second shout penetrated the downpour, louder and closer than the first, confirming that the man whose boots were thudding across the soggy ground toward her was indeed Henry. "Hold on! I'm almost there."

She hadn't heard him speak since their one and only meeting at the wedding of her sister and Henry's brother ten years before. Unlike his late brother, Jack, who'd embraced his heritage wholeheartedly, Henry had worked to lose his Scottish burr. The hint of the strong *R* she'd heard that day remained, though, giving his rich voice an undeniable appeal—even if it was the last one Lavinia had wanted to hear in response to her cry for help.

When she'd arrived in town eight days before, her sister's friend, who lived next door, had been watching the children. Since Norma had three little ones of her own, she was happy to leave the job of caring for Jack and Pauline's three children to Lavinia.

Henry had returned to Sutter Creek earlier than expected, having left for Marysville a day before Lavinia's arrival. He'd told Norma not to expect him back until the day before Thanksgiving. That would have given Lavinia ten days to get to know her precious nephew and nieces on her own. But Henry was here now, cutting short her time alone with them by two days. Although the youngsters had been anxiously awaiting their uncle's return, she wasn't eager to face him again.

The irksome man had a knack for showing up at the most inopportune times. What he'd witnessed at Jack and Pauline's wedding reception all those years ago was nothing compared to her present state. She must look a fright. No doubt, her silk gown was ruined. Thankfully, she'd brought several more when she'd come west—along with the boots to match each of them. Some might see that as frivolous, but what lady didn't fancy fine footwear?

From her vantage point beneath the broken branch, all she could see when she turned her head were a pair of leather boots and the bottom of a stylish overcoat worn by the purposeful man headed her way. The downed limb blocked everything else.

Henry covered the short distance from the white clapboard house at a jog. He leaned over her, confusion creasing his broad brow. Rainwater poured from the brim of his top hat. "Lavinia! What are *you* doing here? I left the children with Norma."

The fact that he recognized her was a good sign. Her face must not be covered with as much mud as she'd feared. It also meant that even though so much time had passed since they'd met on that memorable but melancholy day his only brother had married her beloved sister, Henry hadn't forgotten her. Then again, how could he after the spectacle she'd made of herself at the reception afterward?

Although she'd been just sixteen at the time, she'd known better than to behave like a petulant child. It wasn't his fault that his brother, Jack, had robbed her of her only sibling and best friend, whisking Pauline off to the Wild West. Not that Henry had shown much sympathy. Lavinia could still hear his mild reproach. *They're happy. Why can't you be happy for them?*

He'd neglected to mention the gulf that had separated Jack and Pauline—a poor blacksmith and the daughter of a man who owned a hotel empire—which had become an obstacle that had led to discord, hurt feelings and, now, a bone-deep sorrow. Henry's younger brother and her older sister had gone to their heavenly home two months ago following a boiler explosion on the steamboat taking them to San Francisco for their tenth anniversary, leaving behind three adorable children.

Lavinia squelched the desire to toss out a sarcastic reply to Henry's question. That's what she'd done when she'd met him at the wedding—not one of her better moments. But she was older and wiser now. "Despite my best efforts, I couldn't free myself. I thank the good Lord you came along." She'd stretched the truth a bit since Henry wasn't her choice of a hero, but she *was* grateful he'd heard her cries for help and come to her aid.

He stared at her a moment, disbelief clouding his sky-blue eyes, and shook his head, sending water droplets flying. His businesslike manner reappeared. "I'll get this off you, and then I'll fetch the doctor."

"I don't need to see a doctor. I'm fine."

"Perhaps, but you should still be examined." He stood and gripped the branch with his gloved hands. They were fine leather gloves, not those worn by a smithy, such as he'd been in his days spent working with his brother in their shop back in Philadelphia.

Lavinia appreciated Henry's concern, but God had

been looking out for her. As far as she could tell, she hadn't suffered any injuries.

The downed tree limb was large and must weigh a lot, but Henry hefted it with ease and dragged it out of the way. She attempted to rise onto her elbows, but the soggy ground made the task difficult.

"Don't move!" He dropped to his knees beside her, heedless of the mud puddle that had formed, and rested a hand on her shoulder. "I need to check you over first. You can lift your head, which is a good sign, but what about the rest of you?"

"Nothing appears to be broken." She'd done a quick test earlier, relieved to find that everything seemed to be in working order.

"If you'll permit me, I'll perform a cursory examination. Once I'm satisfied that moving you won't be a problem, I'll take you in the house."

She wasn't a hothouse flower in need of special treatment. "I appreciate the offer and would take you up on it, but—"

"You don't want the help of a man like me. I understand. You made it clear that my family doesn't meet your exacting standards, but I'm not the lowly no-account you seem to think I am."

"I never said that." All she wanted to do was get out of the rain, not recall memories of an unpleasant encounter she'd spent years trying to forget.

"You didn't have to. Your behavior that day spoke for you." Although his tone was level, the underlying hurt that had crept into his voice flooded her with remorse.

He made a valid point. She'd behaved badly, but now was neither the time nor the place for a discussion on that. "Fine. Check me over if you must, and then can we get out of the rain? I'm drenched, and you will soon be, too. I'd like to spare you that."

Despite their charged exchange, his hands were gentle as he ran them along her arms and legs, twisting them to and fro until he was satisfied. "From what I can tell, nothing's broken, so I'll get you inside."

Before she realized his intentions, he had scooped her into his arms and started for the house. "You don't need to do this. I'm perfectly capable of walking. Besides, I'm covered in mud. I'll get it all over you."

"I don't care about that. I care about you."

His kind words, spoken with sincerity and that rich rolled *R* of his, robbed her of speech. Henry meant nothing special by them, but aside from the servants who were paid to see to her needs, no one back home had cared about her in years—not since her mother had passed on.

Her father certainly didn't care. The drive to expand his hotel empire consumed him. Paul Crowne had used her unexpected trip to California to care for his orphaned grandchildren to his advantage. He'd assigned his latest protégé, Stuart Worthington, who had served as her traveling companion and protector, the task of assessing San Francisco as a suitable location for another of his hotels, the Golden Crowne.

Not that she was surprised by her father's callousness. He hadn't spoken of Pauline or Jack in anything but derogatory terms since the happy couple had headed west. Lavinia's request to pay them a visit after the birth of their son, Alex, had been flatly denied. She'd attempted to bring up the subject a second time when Jack and Pauline had welcomed their first daughter into the world, but her father had made it clear the subject was not open for discussion.

Lavinia hadn't brought it up again until Henry's letter arrived with the tragic news. To her surprise, her father had granted her permission to make the journey, proving he wasn't as unfeeling as people seemed to think he was. If only he would wholeheartedly embrace the faith that her beloved mother had instilled in her daughters. He attended church and even made contributions, but he rarely spoke about spiritual matters, leaving Lavinia to wonder if he really loved the Lord as she did.

Eager to ease the awkward silence that had descended on them as Henry carried her toward the house, she asked the question that had occurred to her as she'd lain flat on her back with nothing shielding her from the pelting rain but bare branches and a massive clump of mistletoe high in the tree. "What would make a limb come down suddenly like that? It's not as though the tree was struck by lightning, and the winds aren't that strong, although they seem to be picking up."

"It happens with oaks, especially after the hot, dry summers we've had the past few years. If a tree can't support all its branches, it will shed one to survive. A falling limb usually occurs during the heat, but it can happen any time of the year. I'm just glad you weren't hurt when that one came down." He inclined his head toward the fallen branch.

"You and me both. I thanked the Lord posthaste."

Her face was so close to Henry's as he cradled her in his strong arms that his profile filled her vision. He'd already been good-looking at twenty, but the ensuing decade had done remarkable things for him, transforming him into a strikingly handsome man. With his angular jaw, aristocratic nose and arresting blue eyes, he must have turned the head of many a lady over the years.

And yet, from what Pauline had written, no woman had turned his.

He reached the back porch, tromped up the steps and glanced at her. His eyebrows shot toward his hairline, and his well-formed lips lifted in a winsome smile.

She averted her gaze. How could she have been so foolish as to let him catch her staring at him? He might be a feast for the eyes, but he wasn't the type of man to capture her attention. Like their late siblings, she and Henry came from different worlds.

And yet it appeared his situation had improved. His waterproof top hat, made of high-quality beaver, provided a sharp contrast to the shabby slouch hat he used to wear. Her head rested on his chest, the wool of his alpaca overcoat soft against her cheek. The coat, one every bit as fine as her father's, had to have cost Henry a small fortune.

"Since my hands are full—" he winked "—could you open the door?"

Her many years spent schooling her emotions enabled her to hide her surprise. Barely. The gentlemen of her acquaintance would never have behaved in such a familiar manner, but in her experience, Henry only conformed to the social mores when it suited him. "You could put me down, you know."

"I will. When I'm ready. The door, please." He inclined his head toward it.

Obstinate man. "Are you always this insistent on doing things your way?"

He grinned. "Only when I'm carrying a lovely lady in my arms."

Her manners failed her, leaving her mouth gaping. She snapped it closed and grappled for a suitable response, delivering it with playfulness on par with his. "Might

I point out, kind sir, that I'm a muddy mess and don't qualify for any special treatment?"

"This isn't special treatment. I make it a point to come to the aid of anyone who tangles with a broken branch or—" his pleasantly full lips twitched "—a wayward piece of cake."

He remembered? Of course he did. How could he forget that mortifying moment when she'd stumbled and sent her slice of Jack and Pauline's wedding cake sliding down her front?

Henry had hustled her off to the kitchen after the unfortunate incident and helped her remove the bits of white frosting clinging to the silk. She'd done her best to ignore him up to that point—not an easy task since he was the best man—but he'd repaid her with kindness. Aside from that rather pointed remark about begrudging Jack and Pauline their happiness, of course.

"Very well. I'll do your bidding." Lavinia leaned over, twisted the knob and pushed open the door.

He entered the kitchen, set her down in front of the cook stove and rested his hands on her shoulders. "You're not dizzy, are you?"

"No. Just a bit chilled." She turned out of his grasp and held her hands toward the heat, reveling in the warmth.

"Where are the children?"

"Alex and Marcie are in school. I sent Gladys to meet them with umbrellas since the weather took a turn. Dot asked to go, too, so I let her." She'd had such fun getting to know her nieces and nephew over the past week. The youngest girl loved her older siblings and missed them when they were gone. Since they were all Dot had left of her immediate family, it made sense.

Henry leaned back against the dry sink, his arms folded. "Who's Gladys?"

"My maid, er, the housekeeper."

"You brought a servant all the way from Philadelphia? Why?"

She preferred his playful side to his drawn eyebrows and pursed lips. She'd dealt with more than enough disapproval from her father over the years. She didn't need it from Henry, too. "To care for the children, of course."

"You don't have to care for them. I am."

"How can you? You still live up in Marysville, don't you?" In his Miners' Hotel, which he'd opened a few years back, if she had her facts straight. Pauline's friend Norma said he'd made the trip down to Sutter Creek as soon as he'd received word of the steamship accident that had claimed Pauline and Jack's lives, among many others. Although Henry's concern for the children was laudable, he couldn't leave his business for too long. Could he?

"I did live there, but I'm here now."

Norma hadn't elaborated on his plans. "For a visit?"

"To stay. The children need me, so I've put my place up for sale. That's why I had to go back up there and wasn't here when you arrived."

He wasn't making sense. "Are you saying *you* intend to take them in?"

"Yes."

That one word, uttered so matter-of-factly, robbed her of her breath. He wasn't going to raise the children. She was.

She needed to set him straight. Now.

The last thing Henry needed was the children's meddlesome aunt interfering, but that determined look in Lavinia Crowne's chocolate-brown eyes spelled trouble.

"I was clear in my letter. Father sent me here to—"

"What letter?" He hadn't received one.

"The one I mailed the day we set sail. Didn't you get it? I understood the Pony Express to be quite reliable."

"Where did you send it?"

"To your hotel in Marysville."

He nodded. "It would have arrived there when I was here in Sutter Creek. I asked my clerk to forward everything. The letter's probably on—" he swallowed "—on Jack's desk." Two months had passed, and yet he still had a hard time saying his brother's name without a stab of pain.

"I s-see." She was rubbing her arms and clenching her teeth to keep them from chattering.

"We can talk later. You need to get out of those wet things. I'll get some water heating so you can bathe, and then I'll see about stretching a tarpaulin over the shed before it gets any wetter inside."

"Wh-what happened to the shed?" She rushed to the window overlooking the backyard. "Oh! The branch destroyed a good bit of the roof, didn't it? That's too bad."

"Don't worry. I'll fix it once the storm's past."

"I'm glad I wasn't inside. I was g-going out there to get more kerosene."

"I'll bring some when I come back." He moved closer, attempting to capture her attention, but it remained riveted on the storm's damage. "Do you need anything else before I go?"

She twisted a mud-coated curl around her finger. Her parted mouth and glassy-eyed stare gave her the look of someone who was lost. "I never thought about death much until I lost my mother. First Maman and now Pauline and Jack. Life's a fleeting thing, isn't it?"

He wasn't sure what she wanted to hear, so he waited to see if she would continue. Thankfully, she did.

"Do you miss them?"

"I do." He stared out the window, remembering the last time he'd seen Jack and his doting wife. It had been a hot September day. They'd been sitting on a blanket in the shade of that very oak tree, having a picnic lunch with the children. Laughter had flowed as freely as the lemonade.

"My brother and I had our differences when we were younger, but once we got a few years on us things improved. Pauline helped smooth Jack's rough edges. She tried to help smooth mine, too, but according to her, I'm a—" he formed quotation marks in the air "—'diamond in the rough.'" The memory of her saying those words in that playful way of hers made him smile. He turned to find Lavinia gazing at him, a look of wonder on her lovely face.

"I'm glad you got to know her. She was w-wonderful. I m-miss her so much it hurts." She dragged in a shuddering breath, blew it out and squared her shoulders. "I should get changed. It wouldn't do for the children to see me looking like this."

"They were happy, Lavinia."

She nodded, but her attention was on her soiled dress. "Yes. You've mentioned that before."

He had—ten years ago. She hadn't believed it then, but if she did now, it might bring her some comfort.

"I'd better see to the tarpaulin. Be sure to bolt both kitchen doors so you have your privacy. I'll come in the front and entertain the children when they arrive."

She spun to face him, her chin lifted in regal fashion,

all business once again. "That's not necessary. Gladys can see to them until I'm ready."

Lavinia's clipped dismissal didn't sit well with him. He was the children's uncle, and he knew them far better than she did. At least she cared about them—unlike her father. Paul Crowne had shown no interest in them, a fact that had grieved Pauline greatly. How could a man ignore his own grandchildren and deprive their only aunt of the right to visit them as he had? Pauline would have loved to have seen her sister again. From what she'd said, Lavinia had begged their father to allow her to come to California repeatedly, only to be met with his steadfast refusal.

Henry chose not to challenge Lavinia. He could clarify things later, once she was clean and dry.

He headed to the shed and surveyed the damage. It wasn't as bad as he'd feared. He tacked a tarpaulin in place, a task that took longer than expected due to the brisk wind.

There. He put down the hammer and checked for leaks but found none. That should keep out most of the water. Once the rain stopped, he would see to the repairs. He grabbed the kerosene tin and hurried toward the house. The children should be home soon, and they'd give him those delightful hugs that threatened to turn him into a pile of mush.

He'd arrived in California back in '52 just in time to welcome his nephew into the world. The surge of emotion that had come over him when he held the squirming, squealing bundle of boy for the first time had nearly bowled him over. If being an uncle brought such joy, he could only imagine what it would be like to hold his own child one day.

His smile faded. To become a father, he would have to

find a wife. Not an easy task. When he'd first set foot in the Golden State, men had outnumbered women nine to one. There was now one woman for every five men, but only a small fraction of those females were God-fearing ladies. An even smaller fraction were single. Of those suitable ladies who had come, even fewer had stayed.

Life in California wasn't easy, but it certainly wasn't boring. Each day was an opportunity to meet new people, experience new things and increase one's knowledge. Pauline had been a rare breed, supporting her husband's dreams and wholeheartedly embracing life out west.

Finding a courageous, spirited, supportive woman of God like his late sister-in-law had proven to be a challenge. He'd tried, but the handful of ladies like her that he'd met had been snatched up before he could say *competition*. The one time he'd believed that he'd forged a friendship with an eligible lady, she'd headed back east, offering him only a cursory goodbye.

He'd surrendered his dream of having a family to the Lord. Due to the steamship accident that had claimed the lives of Jack and Pauline, he had one now. Ever since losing their parents, Alex, Marcie and little Dot had turned to him for love and support, and he wouldn't have it any other way—even if it meant putting down roots. Those three youngsters meant the world to him.

The sound of childish chatter sent Henry hurrying up the front steps, taking them two at a time. Despite his eagerness, he slipped inside as quietly as possible, yanked off his gloves and removed his rain-soaked coat and hat.

He opened the door to the parlor and stepped into the room. "You're back, I see."

"Uncle Henry!" the children cried in unison.

The two girls flew at him. Six-year-old Marcie flung

her arms around his waist and gave him a sound squeeze. Four-year-old Dot grabbed hold of his thigh and wrapped her feet around his ankle. Eight-year-old Alex followed at a leisurely pace, attempting to look more mature than his sisters.

Henry ruffled Alex's hair and stooped to kiss the top of Marcie's head. She released Henry, and he took off in a lurching trek across the parlor with Dot still clinging to his leg. Her giggles filled the room.

A throat cleared. He turned toward the noise. An older woman with folded arms and a frown stood in the doorway. He hobbled over to her with Dot in tow and held out a hand. The housekeeper stared at it with a curled lip. Memories flooded in of others hesitating to shake his hand, Lavinia among them. He dropped it to his side and offered her a smile instead. "You must be Gladys. I'm Henry."

"So I heard. Lavinia said you'd shown up and pulled that tree off her. I can't believe you kept the poor dear talking as long as you did. Her teeth were chattering something fierce when we got back from the school. I poured her a bath straightaway. She's almost ready, so she sent me out here to watch the young'uns—like I've been doing the past eight days."

Evidently, Lavinia had told her maid-turned-housekeeper that he planned to care for the children, as was Jack and Pauline's wish, and Gladys had taken offense. "And doing a fine job of it, too, I'm sure."

The prickly woman scoffed. "Flattery won't work on me, young man, so you can save your breath."

She was outspoken for a servant and not at all the type of woman he would have expected Paul Crowne to have accompany his daughter. Perhaps he'd had a hard time finding a woman willing to make the trip west, despite his wealth. The conditions on board a California-bound steamship were reputed to be lacking, even for those traveling first class. Worse yet was the train trip across Panama. Although that leg of the journey only took about six hours, the exposure to disease had taken its toll. Three miners who'd rented rooms from him during the years he'd run his hotel had contracted yellow fever or malaria shortly after they'd arrived. They'd suffered terribly. Sadly, the diseases claimed all three victims in the end.

"I don't say things I don't mean, ma'am. The children are healthy and happy. That tells me they've been well cared for."

She stepped closer and lowered her voice. "But you think you can do better, I hear. You? A man, alone? I reckon you believe that to be true, but I have my doubts."

He had his, too, but he'd made a pledge to Jack and Pauline. Honoring it required him to make significant changes and to give up his dream of running a restaurant one day, but he'd do whatever it took to ensure a good future for the children.

Gladys pinned him with a searing gaze, turned on her heel and left. A hushed exchange took place in the entryway, and then Lavinia appeared, looking every bit the refined lady she was, from the mass of damp curls piled on top of her head to the dainty leather boots that matched her dress. The cranberry red, while not customary for a woman in mourning, complemented her fair complexion and dark brown hair.

"Uncle Henry." Dot let go of him and beckoned with a crooked finger.

He leaned over, resting his hands on his knees. "What is it, Dimples?"

She grinned, revealing the reason for the nickname he'd given her. "You said you miss my kisses when you go 'way, so here's one." She smacked a kiss on his left cheek.

"Come here, you." He hefted her into his arms and pressed a kiss to her forehead. Dot beamed.

Marcie tugged on his sleeve. "I have a kiss for you, too."

"I'm glad to hear that, Muffin, because your kisses are as sweet as sugar." He leaned over and received a buss on his right cheek.

He swiped a finger across his cheek, stuck it in his mouth and pulled it out with a pop. "I was right. Sugary sweet."

The rustle of skirts drew his attention to Lavinia once again. She'd entered the room and stood by the settee. She caught him looking at her, and a shy smile lifted her lovely lips. Her eyes held a hint of...approval? From Lavinia Crowne, the woman who'd looked down her dainty nose at him during her sister's wedding reception? Nice to know she found something in him to like now, whatever it was.

He tore his gaze from her and gave Alex his attention, struck once again by his nephew's resemblance to Jack at that age. Henry swallowed the lump in his throat. "How did things go at school today?"

The quiet boy shrugged. "It was all right."

Marcie, the talkative one of the trio, scoffed. "It was a real good day. He got the highest marks on his whole grade's arithmetic examination. He knows his multiplication tables all the way to fifteen."

Henry clapped a hand on Alex's shoulder. "That's great, Buddy. I'm proud of you."

Lavinia joined the conversation. "I am, too. I know how hard you studied for the test."

Alex scuffed the toe of his boot over a swirl in the worn rug. "Thanks."

Dot tapped Henry's cheek.

"What is it, Dimples?"

"Can we have some hot cocoa? It was awful cold outside."

"Yes, you may," Lavinia answered. "Just ask Miss Gladys nicely if she'll make it for you."

"I'll ask her instead. She likes me best, so she'll do it for me." Marcie patted her thick, curly hair. "I'll even ask her for whipped cream on top."

Alex scoffed. "What are you talking about? Miss Gladys doesn't like anyone."

"She does, too," Marcie countered. "She said I'm a flibbertigibbet. Isn't that a fun word? Flibbertigibbet."

Alex burst out laughing. Henry kept a straight face, but he couldn't keep his lips from twitching. Aside from merriment dancing in her dark brown eyes, Lavinia kept her amusement under control. She shot Alex a pointed look. He covered his mouth, but his shoulders still shook.

Marcie jammed her hands onto her hips and faced her brother. "What's so funny?"

"You are," Alex shot back. "Do you even know what a flibbertigibbet is? It's a person who talks too much."

"Well, Mister Smarty, at least I talk to Miss Gladys. You hardly say anything. Just please and thank you. That's boring."

"Come now, children." Lavinia draped an arm across Marcie's shoulders. She reached a hand toward Alex and let it hover for a moment, as though waiting for him to welcome the contact. When he didn't, she pulled her hand back. "Go into the kitchen and get that cocoa. And no more quibbling, please."

Henry set Dot down, and she trooped after her siblings. As soon as they were out of earshot, Lavinia laughed. "Marcie is really something, isn't she? Even though I've just gotten to know the children, it took no time for me to see how similar Marcie is to… Pauline." She blinked rapidly to clear her misty eyes. "I'm sorry. It's just that I miss her so much."

"I understand. I miss her, too. She was so full of life."

"She was the best thing in mine. I love how she saw everything as an adventure—even coming out here. I can't believe I'll never see her again. I should have come sooner, but…" She heaved a sigh.

"But your father forbade it."

"She told you?"

He nodded. Paul Crowne hadn't gone to his daughter's wedding. Ten years had passed without a word from him. Pauline had never given up hope that his heart would soften one day, but he'd shut her out completely. "He didn't even realize he had grandchildren until he got my letter with the sad news, did he?"

"I told him, but he—" Lavinia toyed with the button on her sleeve. "He rarely mentioned them."

The admission had cost her. Henry softened his tone. "He has no idea what he missed, but it's too late."

"It's not. He's going to meet them. Quite soon, in fact."

His jaw dropped. "Your father is actually going to come out here after all this time?"

She shook her head, dislodging a curl. The spiral drooped over her left eye. "He can't get away. Business, you know. That's why I'm here. I'm going to see that the children have a special Christmas celebration, and then we'll be going home."

He raised an eyebrow. "You and Gladys?"

She brushed the loose curl aside. "Yes, plus Stuart and—"

"Who's Stuart?" The question had slipped out before he could stop it.

"Stuart Worthington is one of my father's competent young managers. He accompanied us all the way to Sutter Creek before returning to San Francisco. He's there now and will come back here at the end of the year to escort all five of us back to Philadelphia."

Henry stared at her in disbelief. "You're not seriously thinking of taking the children, are you?"

"Yes." Lavinia's too-sweet smile was at odds with the determination in her eyes. "I am."

"Let me make myself clear then. You're *not* taking them. They're staying here with me. I'm their legal guardian, as per Jack's will, and I won't be relinquishing that right to you, your father or anyone."

Chapter Two

Henry was their guardian? What could Jack have been thinking? Henry couldn't raise a child on his own, let alone three of them.

Or could he? Her brother-in-law had obviously thought so. Lavinia couldn't deny that Henry was good with the children. It hadn't taken long to see that they doted on him, and it was clear he loved them deeply in return.

It appeared he had the means to provide for them—at least their basic needs anyhow. Although his frock coat, shirt and trousers appeared to be ready-made, his hat, overcoat and silk cravat were of the highest quality. His hotel in Marysville must be doing well, enabling him to hire a housekeeper, if he chose to.

But the children deserved more than the simple life they'd been living. Her father could give them that. He was determined to do so, which spoke well of him. Alex, Marcie and Dot would live in a lovely home, go to the finest schools and have opportunities beyond their wildest dreams.

Gaining the right to take them back with her might involve a legal challenge, but it wouldn't be hard for a

knowledgeable lawyer to overturn a will. Her father had
waged far more difficult battles in the past and won.

Lavinia took a seat on the bright red settee and arranged her skirts, giving her time to form a suitable
response. Henry meant well and deserved respect. Perhaps she could convince him that she'd be a more fitting
guardian. He might even welcome the opportunity to
relinquish his obligation. No doubt, he hadn't expected
to assume the role when he'd agreed to be named. "I admire your willingness to see that the children are cared
for, but surely you realize what kind of life they would
have back home."

He gave a dry laugh. "Of course, I do. They would
be taught to disparage people like their hardworking father, and I won't have that. Jack might have fallen short
of your father's ideals, but he was a good man, and he
was good to Pauline."

She ran a hand over the arm of the well-worn settee.
Like most of the items in the house, it had seen better
days. At least there was a piano. Pauline had loved to
play. "He couldn't give her what she would have had if
she'd heeded Father's counsel and remained back east."

"Jack couldn't give her what she had as a girl, no, but
he gave her what mattered most. She had a husband she
adored and who loved her deeply, and they had three
wonderful children. As I said earlier, Pauline was happy
here. Anyone who knew her would tell you that."

Norma had said much the same. "Be that as it may,
I'm sure you'd agree that the children deserve to have the
best we can offer them."

Henry studied her for the longest time before taking a
seat in the leather armchair to her left. He slipped a finger under the collar of his white dress shirt and tugged

at it, loosening his cravat in the process. "I've worn one of these fancy things every day for the past five years, and I'm still not used to them. Some of society's conventions sure can be restrictive."

His attempt to make a point wasn't lost on her. Her father had worked hard and done well for himself. His position required him to adhere to social mores, but he didn't consider them to be restrictive. Perhaps that's because he was used to them. He'd dressed in fine clothes as far back as she could remember.

"And yet you wear one," Lavinia said.

"I've made concessions. A businessman is expected to present a certain image. I've learned that first impressions are what matter most, so I invested in the trappings necessary to make a good one."

"Your hat, overcoat and cravat." They did lend him an air of distinction. Of course, with his thick, wavy wheat-colored hair, bottomless-blue eyes and muscular build, he'd probably look good in grubby miner's wear.

Henry nodded. "Men give other men a quick once over, and then they look each other in the eye, so a nice hat, a silk cravat and a clean collar are what's important. Once a man has formed his opinion, the rest doesn't matter as much."

"So you're saying my father looked down on Jack because he didn't have those things?"

"What do you think?"

"I doubt they would have made much difference." She mentally kicked herself. She'd just admitted that her father had disliked Jack on principle.

"You see my point, then?"

All too clearly. "Father had his reasons." He'd shared them freely, loudly and often. She could hear him now, his booming voice filling his spacious study. *Jack Haw-thorn is nothing but a presumptuous smithy. Imagine a man like that asking my daughter for her hand in marriage when his are filthy. Has the interloper no sense of how things are done?*

"Such as?"

What had they been talking about? Ah, yes. Her father's reasons for rejecting Jack as a suitable suitor for Pauline. "Does it matter? Haven't you formed an opinion of my father based on outward appearances, too? You don't really know him or what kind of man he is."

"I know enough about him to do whatever it takes to keep the children here where they belong."

This conversation had dredged up things she'd rather not think about, gone places she didn't want to go. She loved her father and wouldn't allow anyone to speak ill of him, but his treatment of Pauline had left something to be desired. Taking another tack seemed the wisest choice.

Lavinia grabbed a sofa pillow and toyed with the fringe. "We can discuss this after Christmas. You obviously love them and want them to be happy, as do I. For now, I'm here. I think we should strive to make the holiday season as pleasant as possible for them." That would give her time to assess the situation, locate a lawyer and overcome this unexpected obstacle.

He rubbed his chin, and in the quiet room she could hear the rasp of his thumb over the golden stubble dusting his jaw. "What did you have in mind?"

"To begin with, Gladys and I have been working on a menu for our Thanksgiving dinner. It's going to be quite a feast."

His former antagonism fled, replaced by genuine eagerness. "Really? What will you be serving?"

"The traditional dishes—turkey with cranberry sauce, ham, roast beef, an assortment of vegetables, fresh bread and, of course, a chicken pie. It wouldn't be Thanksgiving without one, would it?"

"That's a lot of food for six people."

"It is, but I want the meal to be special."

"I'm sure it will be." A wagon rumbled past out front, drawing his attention. He looked from the window to her. "That reminds me… I only have a satchel with me, but my trunks should arrive in the next day or two, so you can expect to see the freight wagon show up."

She blinked in disbelief. "You're having them delivered here?"

"Of course. This is where I live now."

Her surprise turned to shock. "You can't. I mean, I know you have been, but you can't continue to do so, not with me staying here. It wouldn't be proper. Besides, I've given Gladys the downstairs bedroom, and I'm staying in the spare one upstairs."

He leaned forward, resting his hands on his knees. His calm tone was at odds with his rigid posture. "Let me see if I have this straight. First, you announce that you intend to take the children back east, and now you're saying I can't even stay in my own brother's house?"

Put that way, she came off looking high-handed, which she wasn't. At least, she hadn't meant to be. "This isn't how I intended for things to happen. If only the letter had reached you before I arrived." She'd spent hours getting the words just right.

"You made the same deman—er, requests in your letter, I presume?"

"I did, but I was more gracious." She'd taken pains to state her case as tactfully as possible.

He released his breath in an audible sigh. "Perhaps we could reach a compromise."

She didn't see how that was possible, but she owed him the courtesy of hearing him out. "What do you have in mind?"

"Since it would be safer for you and Gladys to stay here in the house, given that men greatly outnumber women, I'll take a room at a boardinghouse. For the time being."

"That's kind of you." But that wasn't the compromise. It obviously had to do with the children. Something told her Henry wasn't going to give in as easily when it came to them. "And regarding the other part of the compromise?"

"Let's start by finding our common ground, shall we? Am I correct in thinking you want the children to remain together?"

"Yes, of course! They shouldn't be separated."

He nodded. "Good. Would you agree that keeping them in one location rather than dividing their time between here and Philadelphia would be wise?"

"By all means. Uprooting them repeatedly would be quite disruptive. Children need stability. Not only that, but the journey is fraught with dangers. There's the risk of shipwreck or disease. And now that Lincoln's been elected…" She couldn't bring herself to complete her thought.

"War is imminent, so traveling the waters along the southern states isn't wise."

"Exactly. That's why Father wanted me to turn right around when I got here, but I convinced him that allowing the children to spend one final Christmas season in their own home instead of at sea would be a compassionate gesture. He saw my point but insisted we begin our journey by the end of the year. I assured him we would."

There. She'd let Henry know where things stood and had shown that her father could be reasonable. He was, on rare occasions anyhow, although she rarely challenged him for fear of enduring his slights. In fact, that was only the third time she'd done so. Christmas had been Pauline's favorite holiday. Her children deserved to have the best one possible.

Henry rested his left elbow on the arm of his chair and leaned away from Lavinia, putting as much distance as possible between them. He clasped his hands, lifted his gaze to the ceiling and closed his eyes, giving her the impression he was praying for patience. His shoulders rose and fell three times before he opened his eyes. They held conviction coupled with…compassion. An odd mix.

"It appears we're at an impasse. You loved your sister and want to do what you think best for our nieces and nephew. I loved my brother and Pauline, too, and want to do the same. They entrusted the children to me, which makes their choice of guardian clear."

Jack might have named Henry as guardian in the will, but Pauline had said long ago that if the unthinkable happened and the Lord took her and Jack home, she wanted Lavinia to care for the children. And she had the letter to prove it!

Henry leaned toward her once again. "Let me ask you this. What do you think the children want?"

He had an annoying habit of asking questions she didn't care to answer. He knew what the youngsters would say. He'd been an important part of their lives since they were born, whereas they'd only met her eight days ago. She couldn't permit him to question them on this point. Not yet. Not until she had an opportunity to let them know what wonderful things awaited them in the east.

But how could she do that? They couldn't begin to imagine how different life would be there, how much fun they would have. If only she could show them.

An idea struck her, filling her with hope. She *could* show them. By creating a Christmas like those she and Pauline had enjoyed when they were young, the children would see what their lives would be like in Philadelphia and why she was eager to take them there.

Showing what she could do for the children would also help strengthen her case should Henry refuse to relinquish his rights, forcing her to take legal action. She prayed he would have a change of heart before that, but she had her doubts.

"I think what they want is to know they're loved and will be well cared for. As I said before, we can start by doing all we can to see that they have as enjoyable a Christmas season as possible, considering the circumstances. Wouldn't you agree?"

Wariness creased his brow. "I can tell by the determination in your eyes that you're up to something. What is it?"

"Just what I said. I'm going to make this Christmas extra special."

"And after that?"

Another probing question. But she'd anticipated this one and had a ready answer. "We'll discuss the children's future then. It makes no sense to do so now. You and I have only had two brief interactions. Postponing the conversation will give us time to get better acquainted and determine which of our situations would be best for the children. Not only that, but if we put off the matter and focus on the children at present, they won't witness any petty quibbling on our part. Not that you'd engage in any, of course," she said with playfully exaggerated sincerity.

A slow, easy smile lifted Henry's lips and eased the tension in his face—his very handsome face. "My dear Miss Crowne, I've underestimated your talents. You're quite the diplomat."

She returned his smile. "And you, Mr. Hawthorn, are a worthy adversary. If you're in agreement with my plan and are willing to wait until December twenty-sixth to revisit the matter then perhaps you'd be willing to shake on it." She extended her hand.

He stared at it a moment before taking it. His grip was firm but not overly so. To her surprise, he didn't pull his hand back right away. Although she welcomed the reassuring gesture—and the resulting warmth that flowed through her—the resolve in his eyes gave her cause for concern. "I appreciate how much the children matter to you, but don't expect me to change my position."

She didn't, which was why she would work hard to show her nieces and nephew why they'd be better off with her—and gain custody of them.

Lavinia closed her bedroom door behind her and inhaled deeply. The tantalizing scent of pies filled the air—apple and pumpkin, with more to come. Gladys had spent the previous afternoon in the kitchen, and she'd be there again today, getting things ready for tomorrow. Although this Thanksgiving meal wouldn't be as sumptuous as those Lavinia had enjoyed around her father's table, it would give the children their first taste of what life would be like when they reached their new home.

She rapped on Alex's door. "Good morning, my favorite nephew. Are you awake?"

"It's too early," he grumbled.

"You'd better hurry, or the girls will beat you downstairs." She'd discovered that a friendly competition helped get the children moving in the morning. The one who reached the kitchen first got an extra slice of bacon. Marcie had earned that honor the past two days. The sound of feet hitting the floor told Lavinia that Alex intended to have it today.

The door to the girls' room opened, and little Dot peeked her head out. "I'm up, Aunt Livy, and I'm gonna get dressed real fast so I'm the firstest."

"I heard that!" Alex hollered from behind his door. "But I'll be there before you!"

Lavinia smiled. Another day was underway. She descended the stairs, ready for breakfast. After her frightening ordeal yesterday afternoon, followed by the draining conversation with Henry, her appetite had fled. She'd eaten little at supper and, consequently, had awoken hungry. She could almost taste Gladys's crispy bacon, but—she sniffed—she couldn't smell it.

She hurried to the kitchen to find Gladys hunched over the cook stove. The wiry woman's movements were stiff and slow. "What's wrong?"

"My rheumatism is acting up again, so wrestling with all these buttons took a while." She swept a hand over her bodice. "Don't you worry, though. I'll get that bacon going right away." Gladys placed several thick strips in the bottom of a frying pan and plunked it on the burner.

"I'm sorry you're hurting. I'd be happy to help."

Gladys turned and studied Lavinia. The older woman's

face was pinched with pain. "I reckon you mean well, Miss Lavinia, but what do you know about cooking?"

Very little, but she wouldn't let that stop her. "I'm a quick learner."

"Then put on an apron, and you can take over."

Lavinia grabbed a knee-length red apron that looked good against her green dress. The colors reminded her of Pauline. Her sister had rarely worn any others. "What do I do?"

Gladys handed her a pair of tongs. "Watch the bacon, and turn it every now and then. Keep your face back 'cause it splatters. I'll fry up the eggs." She reached for a second frying pan, but the heavy iron skillet slipped from her grasp and crashed to the floor, narrowly missing her feet.

"Are you all right?"

"I'm fine. My fingers are just being a mite troublesome this morning."

Lavinia picked up the frying pan, which had landed right side up. "Why don't you have a seat at the kitchen table and instruct me from there?"

"Maybe I should rest my poor hands a bit. They've got a lot of work ahead of them the next two days." Gladys gave Lavinia a quick lesson in how to fry an egg and sank into the nearest chair.

Lavinia's mind raced, going over the many items yet to be prepared for tomorrow's feast. She couldn't ask Gladys to work when she was in such pain, but without her help, the meal was in jeopardy.

A rap on the back door startled Lavinia. She rushed over, saw Henry through the window in the upper half and yanked open the door. "What are you doing here so early?"

"I've been eating my meals with the children. That won't be a problem, will it?"

Technically it wouldn't be. They had plenty of food, but she had no desire for him to witness her first cooking lesson. What choice did she have, though? He was the children's uncle and had a right to spend time with them. A legal right, thanks to the will he'd shown her after their conversation on Monday. Not that she'd let that stop her. A will could be contested.

She produced a polite smile. "Come in and take a seat. I have to see to the bacon."

He glanced at her apron and back again. "You're cooking?" His voice held a note of disbelief. Not surprising, since he knew her father employed several servants, but discouraging just the same. Although she might be uneducated in certain areas, she wouldn't let that serve as an obstacle. She'd learn whatever skills she needed to care for the children, and it appeared cooking would be the first.

"Gladys isn't feeling up to preparing breakfast today, so I've taken over." Lavinia hurried to the stove where the bacon was sizzling, turned the strips and added a dollop of butter to the second frying pan.

She took an egg out of the basket and rapped it against the edge of a bowl as Gladys had instructed her. Something went wrong, and the slimy mess oozed over Lavinia's hands. A groan escaped her.

Gladys clucked her tongue. "Don't hit it so hard, Miss Lavinia."

"Here you go." Henry held out a damp cloth.

"Thanks." She wiped her sticky hands, grabbed another egg and tapped it on the lip of the bowl, doing her best to ignore the handsome man leaning against the counter. Her efforts resulted in a jagged crack. She positioned the egg over the frying pan, careful to get it close enough, and gently pulled the shell apart. The egg plopped into the pan with the sunny yellow yolk intact. So far, so good.

As she held the spatula and watched the white part cook, trying to determine the right time to flip the egg, the thundering of feet on the stairs announced the children's imminent arrival. She turned just in time to see the three of them racing through the dining room.

"I'm going to win!" Alex hollered.

"Oh, no you're not." Marcie shot forward.

They reached the kitchen doorway at the same time, with Dot right behind. The little girl darted between them, tripping Marcie in the process and bumping into Alex. The three children toppled over.

Alex dragged himself out of the heap and huffed. "I was first."

"No you weren't. I was." Marcie popped up and glared at her brother.

Dot sat on the floor with her lower lip puffed out in a pout. "You're wrong. I'm the winner, aren't I, Uncle Henry?"

"From what I saw, six arms and legs were tangled up together, so that makes it a three-way tie."

Lavinia smiled. "He's right. You're all winners and get an extra slice of bacon."

The bacon! She spun around, grabbed the tongs and flipped the sizzling strips.

Gladys helped Dot to her feet and dusted her off.

Marcie sidled up to Henry. "It wasn't really a tie, was it? You just said that so Dot wouldn't cry, right?" The precocious girl didn't miss much.

Henry ruffled Marcie's mass of dark curls that Lavinia had yet to wrestle into a braid. "I saw three young Hawthorns burst through that door at the same time, and I couldn't be prouder. My nieces and nephew know how to go after what they want. If I'd known there was extra bacon to be had, I'd have been racing here, too."

Lavinia slid the spatula under the egg and attempted to turn it over, but the slippery thing slid off before she was ready. The yolk broke open. Gladys made preparing breakfast seem easy, but the task was harder than it looked.

Marcie made a choking sound. "I'm not eating that egg."

Alex wandered over and peered into the pan. "Why are you cooking and not Miss Gladys?"

"She's not feeling well, so I'm taking over."

He glanced at the kitchen table, where Gladys sat holding Dot, and back again. "What's wrong with her? She doesn't look sick."

"It's just my joints." Gladys held up her bent fingers. "They get stiff every now and then."

"Then let Uncle Henry cook," Marcie said. "He's good at it."

Henry placed his hands on Marcie's shoulders and turned her toward the table. "Your aunt would have an easier time of it without you children getting in her way. Take a seat, and your breakfast will be ready soon."

They obeyed him without the usual objections Lavinia encountered. Henry came alongside her and lowered his voice. "If you'd like, I could fry the eggs."

The last thing Lavinia needed was for her first attempt at cooking to result in total failure with Henry watching. She could ask Gladys for another egg-frying lesson later when she didn't have a room full of young critics.

"You'll need this." She held out the spatula to him.

He chuckled. "And here I thought you'd turn me down."

She probably should have. Working side-by-side was more disconcerting than she'd expected. She was all too aware of Henry's powerful presence. His muscular arm brushed hers as he attempted to salvage the sorry egg, sending a jolt of electricity through her.

Taking her cue from him, she adopted a playful tone. "I considered refusing, but since we're running behind schedule this morning, I decided to let you come to my rescue." Again. This was their third interaction—and the third time he'd found her in a less than flattering situation.

He leaned so close that his breath warmed her cheek. "I only come to the rescue of pretty women with piles of curls." He tugged on one of her curls that had broken free of her pins, let it go and smiled as the spiral sprung back into place.

Had Henry just flirted with her? The idea seemed preposterous but strangely appealing. Since she had no idea how to respond, she remained silent and focused on her task.

Several minutes later, they all sat around the table. Every plate boasted crispy strips of bacon and, with one exception, expertly fried eggs that would have made even the finicky chef at the restaurant inside her father's Royal Crowne Hotel in New York City happy. Henry had taken the remains of her failed attempt. He speared a bite of the egg and ate it with as much relish as the children did theirs.

He looked up, caught her staring at him and winked. Merriment danced in his blue eyes. It seemed he was just toying with her. She'd been a ninny to think he was drawn to her. Oh, there were sparks between them, however, they weren't fueled by attraction but by their adversarial relationship. They might have deferred their discussion regarding the children's future until after Christmas, but it was on her mind. No doubt it was on his, too.

Alex and Marcie left to walk to school with their next-door neighbor, Norma, a short time later, lunch pails in hand. Dot went to her room to watch her siblings as they headed down Church Street toward the schoolhouse on the west side of Main, which doubled as the church while the small congregation worked to raise the funds needed to construct a building of their own.

Gladys began to gather the dirty dishes, but Lavinia stopped her. "I'll see to those. You need to rest."

"I'm not one to shirk my duties. If I rub on some liniment, I'll be fine. Thanksgiving is tomorrow. There's a meal to be prepared, and I aim to do it."

"Now, Gladys," Henry began, "I'm inclined to agree with Lavinia. Bustling around a kitchen for the next two days when you're already hurting is likely to make things worse. What you need is someone who could work under your direction. I'm available."

Gladys studied him through narrowed eyes. "You can fry an egg, but there's a lot more work involved in fixing a feast. Are you sure you're up for that?"

He nodded. "Provided Lavinia has no objections..." He turned to her. "What do you say?"

Why must he be so agreeable? And helpful? And adorable? With that boyish eagerness in eyes, she was powerless to resist him. "It appears I don't have a choice, but it would ease my mind if I knew you'd be able to follow Gladys's directions."

"Ah." He flashed her a winsome smile and continued, his lovely rolled *R* a bit more pronounced than usual. "You're wondering if I can cook. The answer is yes. I'm a long-time bachelor and know my way around a kitchen. Besides, I'll have Gladys there to make sure I don't make a mess of things."

His confidence eased the tension in Lavinia's shoulders. "Very well. I'll leave the meal in your hands then."

"Don't worry. It will be a feast you'll remember for years to come."

Chapter Three

The blast of pumpkin-scented air that escaped as Henry opened the oven door that afternoon made his mouth water. He could almost taste the rich filling. Plunging a butter knife into it and marring that smooth surface wouldn't be easy, but he had to know if the pie was fully baked. He stuck in the blade and quickly pulled it out. Clean.

Gladys lay on the settee he'd moved into the kitchen and watched as he set the pan on a trivet in the middle of the table. "If that tastes as good as it smells, we're in for a treat. The custard is smooth, and your pie crust turned out quite flaky. I never heard of keeping the ingredients on ice before, but I'm going to try that next time."

"I think every kitchen should have an icebox. I'm surprised Mr. Crowne's doesn't."

She snorted. "He's not one to think about making life easier for his household staff. It's a different story when it comes to his hotels and restaurants, though. I hear they have all the modern conveniences."

Henry wasn't surprised. From what he'd seen, Paul Crowne put his hotel empire before everything else, even his own family. They were expected to do his bidding, just as his employees and vendors were. Henry had seen that himself when Jack landed the contract for the iron work at the Crowne Jewel Hotel in Philadelphia. Mr. Crowne had barked orders at Jack. The domineering man had been just as demanding with Pauline, whose artistic bent had earned her the right to plan the hotel's décor.

To her credit, his eldest daughter hadn't cowed under the pressure. Pauline had stood up to her father regarding the work. She did so again when she fell in love with Jack and chose to marry him against her father's wishes. She'd held her head high at the wedding, even though her father had refused to come and forbade his wife from attending, too.

At least Lavinia had shown up. Whether she'd chosen to defy her father or not, Henry didn't know. She was understandably reserved that day, glossing over the matter of her parents' glaring absence with well-rehearsed comments. Despite her aloofness, he'd detected a note of sadness in her bearing and pain in her eyes.

His attempt to make her feel more welcome at the wedding had resulted in disaster. She hadn't heard him coming and had started, causing her to drop the piece of cake she'd been holding. Her mortification led to a temporary collapse of the barrier she'd erected. In that moment, he'd seen a joyless young woman trapped in a lonely existence.

If only she could break free, as her sister had. But from what he'd seen so far, Lavinia was more deeply entrenched in the ways of her father's world than before. Worse yet, she wanted to whisk the children away and immerse them in that life, too, which wasn't going to happen. They deserved to be happy. So did their devoted aunt, who was trying hard to prove that she was capable of caring for them.

Henry smiled at the memory of Lavinia staring at the frying pans that morning with determination befitting a military commander facing a ruthless foe. If only she could bring that stoutheartedness to bear in her dealings with her iron-fisted father.

"Don't be daydreaming, Mr. Henry," Gladys chided. "This meal won't fix itself."

He roused himself from his musings. "You're right."

"At least you took a pleasant journey, judging by that smile."

The front door opened, and childish laughter filled the entryway. Lavinia and the children had returned. With school finished for the day, the holiday recess was officially underway. Despite the terrible losses they'd suffered the past year, they would celebrate with a meal sure to help ease the heaviness in their hearts.

Dot burst into the kitchen first and flung herself at him. "We're back, Uncle Henry."

"I see." He scooped her into his arms. "It must be cold out there. Your cheeks are rosy, and your nose is red." He popped the tip of it with a finger.

The little girl giggled. "The hot cocoa will warm us up. Is it ready?"

"It will be. I just have to fill the mugs."

"And put whipped cream on top, right?"

"By all means. I can't imagine cocoa without it."

Marcie and Alex arrived, followed by Lavinia, who greeted Gladys, plumped the pillows behind her and pulled up the throw that had slipped off the side of the settee. "How are you feeling?"

"A bit better."

"Helping Henry isn't too taxing, is it?"

Gladys glanced at him and actually smiled. Her gruff exterior didn't fool him. He'd seen the longing in the housekeeper's eyes when he'd joked with the children. Not that he let on that he'd been watching her. If he had to guess, he'd say that the longtime servant had faced difficulties in the past, which had left her hardened. How sad. Life was meant to be enjoyed not endured.

She returned her attention to Lavinia. "I'm not much help, other than keeping him company and serving as his taster. Mr. Henry is a far better cook and baker than I'll ever be. Just wait until you sit down to the meal tomorrow."

He eagerly awaited Lavinia's response. He'd poured himself into the preparations in the hope that she'd see how supportive he was of her plan to make this year's holiday celebrations the best they could be. The fact that he was enjoying himself immensely was a bonus. He embraced any excuse to spend time cooking. His opportunities to do so were few and far between, but one day…

No. He wouldn't be opening a restaurant after all. He'd been granted the privilege of caring for the children, and working well into the night wouldn't fit with his new role in their lives.

"I'm sure I'll enjoy it." Lavinia's words lacked conviction, and her smile appeared forced, which was puzzling.

Marcie bounded up to him. "I'm going to eat lots, Uncle Henry."

"Me, too," Alex added.

Henry shifted Dot to a more comfortable position on his hip. "How about you, Dimples? Are you going to fill your plate?"

She nodded so enthusiastically that her curls bounced.

"And what will be on it?" Henry asked.

"Food."

Laughter erupted all around him, but he managed to keep a straight face. "What kind of food? Turkey? Stuffing?"

"She doesn't like stuffing," Marcie informed them. "But I do. Mama's stuffing tasted *so* good." The normally exuberant girl's shoulders drooped, and her voice took on a sorrowful tone. "I wish she was still here to make it."

"I miss her, too, sweetie, but I know she'd want us to be happy." Lavinia wrapped an arm around Marcie and drew their niece to her side. "I think a cup of cocoa would be just the thing to cheer us up, and I heard your uncle say he'll have it ready for you soon. Why don't we get you out of your coats so you're ready for it?"

The children trooped after Lavinia and returned shortly—without her. "Where's your aunt?"

"In the parlor," Alex said, "putting another log on the fire."

"Very well. If you'll take a seat at the table, I'll serve you."

They clambered into their chairs on the side opposite the pies and awaited their treat. He prepared the drinks with his back to them, carried over the steaming mugs and set one in front of each of them.

Dot clapped and squealed. "It has whipped cream *and* chocolate curls."

Marcie smacked her lips, and Alex nodded appreciatively.

"I made a cup for you, too, Gladys." He handed her one.

"Why, thank you. It's right fancy."

"What about Aunt Lavinia?" Dot asked. "She likes cocoa, too."

"I'll take her some while you stay here and keep Miss Gladys company."

Moments later, he entered the parlor, mugs in hand. He held one out to Lavinia, who was seated in Pauline's favorite chair, gazing at the fire. "Here you go."

"Thank you." She took the cocoa and stared at it. "You don't do anything halfway, do you?"

"What do you mean?" He sat in Jack's wingback armchair and sipped the tasty beverage.

"This isn't an ordinary cup of cocoa."

"I thought the children would appreciate that."

"I'm sure they do, but…" She set her mug on the side table and turned to face him. The sadness he'd seen all those years ago had returned. She must have been thinking about her sister. "You could have told me you know how to cook."

So that's what this was all about? "What difference does it make?"

"You said you know your way around a kitchen the way a bachelor does, but it's obvious you know a lot more than that. I saw the pies you made. They're not the work of a novice. Have you worked in a restaurant or something?"

He'd spent as much time as possible in the one inside his hotel, but he didn't advertise that fact since many men thought of cooking as women's work. The miners he served appreciated a man who could broil a steak or whip up a mess of beans, but they didn't come west expecting to eat white fricassee chicken or ragout of onions. If they knew he was a trained chef, he would become a laughingstock.

"I don't see why it matters, but I received some instruction."

"Where?"

She was certainly persistent. That trait could serve her well when she encountered obstacles. He'd have to remember that, since she seemed to consider him one. "Back in Philadelphia. I made some wrought iron railings for a widow who'd been a student at Mrs. Goodfellow's cooking school when she was young. She paid for the materials, but I offered her free labor in exchange for lessons."

"Why did you want to learn? Few men would."

He rubbed the chair's smooth wooden arms. "I happen to enjoy cooking."

"It's certainly a useful skill. You've proven that." She picked up her mug and took a sip. A bit of the whipped cream remained on her upper lip, but she swiped it off with a finger and popped it in her mouth. She pulled out her finger, stared at it and blushed. The heightened color did nice things for her fair complexion. "Forgive me. That wasn't very ladylike."

"We're practically family. You don't have to pull out the company manners for me."

She gave him a look that made him wonder if he was sporting a whipped-cream mustache himself. "Although we share the same wonderful nieces and nephew, you and I are most definitely not related."

Her formal tone, the same one she'd used at the wedding, grated on him. "I realize I'm not up to Crowne standards, but I'm a decent fellow."

She took a sudden interest in her mug, running a finger around its rim. When she finally looked at him, the stiffness was gone. "I'm sorry. I didn't mean it as an insult. Like you, I'm aware that we come from different worlds—and different places. That's put us at odds, whether we like it or not. But I meant what I said yesterday. I'll work with you to see that the children are as happy as possible throughout the holidays."

"They're looking forward to Thanksgiving."

She nodded. "You've seen to that."

Her statement sounded more like an accusation than a compliment. Could it be she was jealous of his relationship with the children? If that was the case, she had no cause for concern. He would see that they wrote to her once she returned to Philadelphia. In the meantime, he had to do something to make her feel more welcome. "Gladys shared your menu with me, but is there anything special you'd like me to make?"

His request earned him a hint of a smile. "Since you ask, did the woman who gave you lessons teach you how to make lemon meringue pie?"

"Of course." Mrs. Goodfellow had been known for that particular pie. "I'll whip one up right away."

Lavinia stood, mug in hand, and he shot to his feet. "I'll go see how the children are doing." She crossed the room, paused in the doorway and turned to face him, wearing a warm smile. "Thank you, Henry."

"My pleasure." He liked seeing her happy. She would only be here a few weeks, but perhaps he could add a little joy to her life—before she faced the future and the difficult parting that was to come.

A tempting assortment of savory scents filled the air the following afternoon. The dining room table, although much smaller than the one at which Lavinia had eaten her Thanksgiving dinners back home, was groaning under the weight of the dishes already on it as Henry carried in yet another.

Clad in a black cutaway coat, white shirt and white silk cravat, he looked as fine as any waiter in her father's restaurants. He'd even draped a white linen cloth over his arm. The children, their eyes as big as their dinner plates, delighted in his performance.

She had to admit he'd impressed her, too, both with his cooking and his appearance. More than once, she'd caught herself staring at him, which wouldn't do. He might be an incredibly handsome man, as well as a talented one, but he was also the man intent upon exerting his rights as the children's guardian.

He found a spot to squeeze in the gravy boat, surveyed the spread and nodded at her. "All's ready for your dining pleasure, milady."

Dot tugged on Lavinia's sleeve. "Why did Uncle Henry call you that?"

Alex answered before Lavinia could. "It's what a waiter in a fancy restaurant calls a fine lady."

"How do you know?" Marcie asked. "You've never been to a place like that."

"My friend Frankie went to San Francisco, and he told me."

"Frankie fibbed. He's never been there. His sister told me so." Marcie gave her head a toss and stuck her pert little nose in the air.

Gladys put a finger to her lips and frowned. "Shh. Children in fancy restaurants don't squabble."

Henry removed the cloth from his arm and took his place at the head of the table.

Lavinia waited until the children were quiet to speak.

"Your uncle put a lot of work into this meal. What do you say to him?"

The children chorused their thanks.

She sent Henry a smile. "I'll add my thanks to theirs. Everything looks and smells great. Would you like to say grace?"

"I'd be happy to." As soon as all heads were bowed, he began. "Thank You, Lord, for this meal we're about to enjoy and the special people around this table. We think of two loved ones who are no longer with us, and we thank You that they were in our lives for as long as they were. Be with us in the year ahead, guiding us in the paths You would have us take. In Your name, I ask these things. Amen."

Silence followed, broken by sniffles from the girls. Even Alex swiped at his eyes. Lavinia struggled to breathe, which was not an easy task given the ache lodged in her chest. Unable to speak, she grabbed the nearest bowl, scooped some mashed potatoes and helped Dot do the same.

Henry picked up the serving fork and carving knife. "Who wants a drumstick?" His well-timed question dispelled the fog of grief that had descended. Excited chatter soon filled the room.

They lingered over the meal, enjoying the delectable dishes. Lavinia sampled each one. Although everything tasted good, she agreed with Marcie. Stuffing was her favorite, and Henry's was the best she'd ever had. His cooking was on par with that of the chefs her father hired for his restaurants.

To Lavinia's surprise, Gladys was the last one done. She dabbed at her mouth and laid her napkin on the table.

"You outdid yourself, Mr. Henry. Everything was delicious."

He smiled. "I'm glad you liked it. I noticed you tucked in a fair amount."

"I reckon that's because food tastes better when someone else fixes it."

He acknowledged Gladys's compliment with a wink. "Is anyone ready for dessert?"

Alex shook his head. "I'm too full."

"Me, too." Dot patted her stomach, producing three resounding thumps as evidence.

"I can squeeze in one more bite of stuffing." Marcie forked a bite, ate it and licked the tines.

Lavinia overlooked the informality. It's what the children were used to. There would be time enough to teach them proper etiquette when she got them back home. "I suggest we wait awhile. It's a clear day. Perhaps the children would like to play outside, provided they put on their coats first."

They voiced their approval of the plan and darted out of the dining room.

Gladys hopped up and began clearing the table, prompting Henry to stand as well. The children raced through the room and headed for the back door, with Marcie in the lead.

Lavinia rose and reached for Dot's plate.

"You don't need to do that, Miss Lavinia. I'm feeling a bit better this afternoon, and I want to help. It's the least I can do after Mr. Henry did all the cooking. You two go on out and enjoy watching the children romp around."

Lavinia wasn't eager to spend time with Henry after their talk the day before. Following the startling revelation that he was an accomplished cook, she'd left the kitchen to collect her thoughts. Before she could, he'd shown up in the parlor bearing the prettiest mug of hot cocoa she'd ever seen with artfully carved chocolate curls on top of creamy white whipped cream. If she wasn't mistaken, he'd even added a pinch of cinnamon to the steaming beverage.

She still couldn't believe that he was trained by a student of Mrs. Elizabeth Goodfellow, the renowned cooking instructor who'd run the most highly regarded cooking school in the country, conveniently located in Philadelphia.

And she, Miss Lavinia Hélène Crowne, daughter of a highly successful hotelier, couldn't even fry an egg. If only she'd been allowed to learn some basic cooking skills, as many of her friends had, she would be able to provide meals for the children. Henry could do so, but she had to rely on Gladys.

Henry was quick to thank Gladys for her offer of help. "I put the block of ice in a pan at the base of the pie safe and covered the door with some towels, so you can store the leftovers there."

Gladys sent him one of her rare smiles. "You made us an icebox? How clever."

He laughed. "You haven't seen it yet. It's not pretty."

"If it keeps the food from spoiling, I don't care what it looks like." Gladys entered the kitchen with a dish in each hand, leaving Lavinia alone with Henry.

An awkward silence descended on the room.

"Do you want—"

"I'll go fetch—" she said at the same time.

He nodded at her. "Ladies first."

"I was going to say that I'll get my cloak and head out back. And you?"

"You answered my question. I was going to see if you wanted to join the children."

He waited in the dining room while she retrieved her cloak. They passed Gladys on their way out.

The late November day was clear but chilly. A breeze sent crispy brown leaves from the massive oak tree somersaulting over the ground. The large limb that had trapped her was nowhere to be seen.

"When did you find time to move the branch?"

"I saw to that while you and Dot went to the grocer's to pick up the spices I needed yesterday. It's behind the shed, waiting to be cut into firewood. I'll get the lumber and shingles tomorrow and repair the shed on Saturday, provided the weather holds."

The children were involved in a rousing game of tag, zigzagging across the backyard. Marcie chased after Alex with Dot not far behind. How they could run after all they'd eaten was a mystery.

Lavinia took a seat on the porch swing, sitting to one side so there would be room for Henry. He inclined his head toward the open spot as if asking permission. She nodded. He sat and promptly pushed his feet against the floor, setting them rocking.

She leaned back and closed her eyes, relishing the soothing motion of the swing. The children's laughter helped drown out the distant rumble of the stamp mill at Leland Stanford's Lincoln Mine north of town, which operated around the clock, even on holidays.

The quest for gold drove the town and many of its inhabitants. Although Mr. Stanford's formerly fledgling mine was now doing well, most of the men who'd come west in the hope of striking it rich had little to show for their efforts. She'd been happy that Jack had come to

California prepared to ply his trade, knowing a black-smith's services would be in high demand. He'd done all right for himself and built a nice home for his family, a larger one than she would have expected.

Lavinia stood and ran a hand along the wrought iron railing with its decorative pattern. The front porch had a matching railing, but the one on the staircase inside the house was even more beautiful. "This reminds me of Jack and Pauline. I can see my sister's creative flair in the twists and curlicues, along with your brother's fine workmanship."

Henry smiled. "Pauline did have an eye for design. She wanted something even more elaborate, but I had to remind her that there was a limit to my, er, a blacksmith's abilities." He looked away, but not before she saw his lips pressed firmly together, obviously regretting his slip.

"I see. He was the salesman, but you did much of the work. Your talent is evident here as well as at the Crowne Jewel. Father might not have been happy about hiring Jack and having him win my sister's heart, but he's pleased with the job you did. Whenever he gives a tour of that hotel, he points out your artistry."

The swing's chains attached to the balcony overhead creaked rhythmically as Henry kept the swing in motion. "I appreciate the compliment, but I haven't practiced that trade in years. Long enough for these to come clean." He held up his hands and turned them so she could see the palms and then the backs. "I can offer to shake a lady's hand these days without offending her sensibilities."

She hadn't thought about his coal-stained hands since the wedding, but his comment caused a memory to rush in. He'd held out a hand to her when she'd arrived at the Hawthorns' home for the wedding, but she hadn't been sure whether she should shake it or not. "My hesitation that day had nothing to do with your appearance. My mother had taught me that it was a woman's place to make the offer, so yours gave me pause."

He frowned. "I see. It wasn't the stains then but my lack of manners. It must have been hard for you to be among so many common folks who don't put as much stock in minding their p's and q's as those in your social circles."

She straightened to her full height and lifted her chin. "You don't know me as well as you think you do, Henry. I wanted to be at Pauline's wedding so much that I went up against my father. He pushed back—hard—but I stood my ground. Even though I knew I'd be walking into a situation where people would pass judgment and whisper about me and my family, I didn't let that stop me. I was prepared to stand by my sister no matter what. And I did."

She drew in a calming breath and released the fists she hadn't realized she'd formed. She'd spoken without thinking, but she didn't regret her outburst as much as she ought to. The record needed to be set straight. She might have a wealthy father, but she wasn't unfeeling.

"I'm glad you came. Pauline put on a brave front, but your father's decision not to attend the wedding crushed her. I was ready to give him a piece of my mind, but she made me promise not to. She knew if I did, he wouldn't let you come, and she wanted you there very much."

Her vision blurred, and she blinked to clear it. "She wasn't just my sister. She was my best friend. I can't believe I'll never see her again."

"Why didn't you come for a visit in all these years?"

"I wanted to."

"But your father wouldn't agree to it? That's what Pauline told me when I asked her."

She turned away, gripped the railing and fought to keep the rush of memories at bay. Many times, she'd stood at the door to her father's study with the intention of going inside and making another request, but any mention of Pauline resulted in a heated rehashing of all the ways his eldest child had failed him and a reminder that as far as he was concerned, he only had one daughter. Lavinia spun around. "If I'd had the means, I would have come."

Henry nodded. "Even if it meant defying him?"

"I'd have found a way."

He stared at her for the longest time, his gaze passing from her head to her feet and back again. "I'm not an expert on etiquette, as you well know, but I've wondered about something. Your dress is pretty and reminds me of the cranberry sauce we just had. Most women who've lost a close family member wear black, but I've yet to see you in it. Why is that? I know you loved Pauline deeply, so I figure there must be an explanation."

She returned to the swing, sat and faced him. Although she wasn't about to tell him how her father had insisted the entire family go into mourning after Pauline left, she could tell him how she'd chosen to honor her sister now. "She loved Christmas more than anyone I know. The tree wouldn't even have been removed after one party, and yet she'd start talking about her plans for the next—which friends she would invite to Father's party, what she'd wear, who she'd have make her gown. I could count on one thing, though. Her dress would be red, green or a combination of the two. She loved those colors so much that she wore them all year long. I'm wearing them in remembrance of her."

"I understand your reasons and admire your decision, but how will you deal with those who might question you?"

"I'll tell them what happened when I arrived in Sutter Creek wearing a mourning gown. I'd only been here an hour when Dot asked why I was dressed in black. Alex told her it was because their mama and papa had died. The poor dear burst into tears and sobbed for a good ten minutes, soaking my shoulder and ripping my heart to pieces. She begged me not to wear the dress ever again. I took her to my room, opened my trunks and let her go through them and pick out what she wanted me to wear. She chose the dress I have on."

He brushed a hand over his sleeve. "I don't wear a black armband for similar reasons. Dot made a fuss when I did, so I took it off. No one seems to have noticed. They haven't mentioned it anyhow."

"My color choice raised some eyebrows when we went to the school for the church service this past Sunday, but to their credit, no one has said anything to me or to the children."

He nodded, his bright blue eyes shining with approval. "It appears the lovely Lavinia Crowne has more gumption than I gave her credit for."

Her? Lovely? With her unruly curls and pointed chin? She wasn't, but it was nice to have a handsome gentleman say so. "I might not be as courageous as my adventure-seeking sister, but there are times when I'll go after what I believe is right."

"I've seen as much. I do the same."

She knew that all too well. He had every intention of keeping the children here, and so far, he'd presented a stronger case than she had. A judge was sure to rule in his favor.

But that was about to change. She was going to show Henry, the children and the people of Sutter Creek how a Crowne celebrated Christmas. When they witnessed the party she had planned, they'd realize she was capable of offering the children far more than their small-town uncle could.

Chapter Four

"Uncle Henry."

Henry dragged his gaze from the guest room window on the second floor where Lavinia had stood moments before, her eyes riveted on him as he knelt on the shed's lean-to roof two days later. He focused his attention on his nephew, who had accepted his invitation to help with the repairs. "What, Buddy?"

"Did I do it right?" Alex looked up, a plea for approval in a pair of blue eyes so like his father's.

Henry felt the familiar stab of pain that came whenever he thought of Jack. The girls had taken after Pauline with her curly brown hair. Alex's resemblance to his father was striking, although the boy's thick wavy locks were a shade darker than Jack's, more coriander-colored than cumin. "You've done a great job lining up the lower edge of the shingle with the others in this row, but we need to leave a little room between them on the sides."

"Why? Won't the roof leak if we do that?" Alex was as inquisitive as he was conscientious.

"That's a good question. The space allows the shingles to swell when they get wet and keeps them from buckling. Since we offset the shingles in each row, there's another shingle underneath the gap in the two above it—a second layer of protection."

Alex smiled. "I didn't think of that."

The back door opened. Lavinia flew out of the house, marched across the yard and stopped a few feet from the shed. She raised a hand to shield her eyes from the sun, which was shining so brightly that Henry had shed his jacket and rolled up his shirtsleeves.

"What are you doing?" she asked, clearly vexed.

"Repairing the roof."

"I can see that, but what is Alex doing up there with you?"

The same thing, but evidently that wasn't what she meant. "Helping me."

"Do you think that's wise? He's only eight."

"He's quite safe. I wouldn't have invited him up here otherwise." It wasn't as though they were on the steeply pitched roof of the two-story house. They were all of ten feet off the ground on a roof with a minimal pitch. "You could come up and see for yourself if you'd like."

To his surprise, she nodded. "I think I will." She covered the few feet separating them in no time.

Henry scooted closer to the edge of the roof, grabbed the ladder to steady it and watched as Lavinia placed a foot on the bottom rung. Was he imagining it, or did her dainty boots match her strawberry-colored dress? If so, that meant she had two pairs of red boots. Most of the women he knew were content with one serviceable black pair. But they weren't the daughter of a man with more money than most men would earn in several lifetimes.

She climbed slowly, watching her feet as she went.

With her full skirt and fancy footwear, he could see why she was being careful. "You're doing fine."

"This would be a far easier feat in trousers."

"I didn't expect you to accept my invitation."

She sent a smug smile his way. "You underestimate me."

He liked seeing this spunky side of her. He'd have to challenge her more often.

Moments later, Lavinia's shoulders crested the roofline. She stayed at that level and looked around. "The view is nearly the same as the one from my bedroom window, but—" he detected a waver in her voice "—it's different seeing everything from here."

"I know just what you mean, Aunt Livy," Alex said. "Sitting up here makes me feel like I'm on top of the world."

"Indeed." She focused her attention on their nephew. "Would you show me what you're doing?"

"Sure." Alex positioned a shingle and nailed it into place, talking through the steps as he worked. "That's how you do it."

"You explained that quite well. You'd make a fine teacher." She followed her compliments with one of her cheery smiles that transformed her from merely attractive to outright beautiful.

Alex beamed. "Can I finish the row on my own, Uncle Henry?"

"Certainly."

Lavinia praised Alex's work as she watched. And watched. He'd completed the task, and she was still there. "Well done."

Henry nodded his approval. "Your aunt's right. You'd

make a fine carpenter, too. In fact, I think you could succeed at whatever profession you chose."

"Why choose just one? Your uncle didn't." Although she wasn't smiling, something shone from her eyes. Was it merriment or something else?

Alex looked from Lavinia to Henry and back again. "Are you teasing?"

Henry eagerly awaited her answer.

"Not at all. Your mama told me in her letters some of the things your uncle's done. He was a blacksmith when I met him at your parents' wedding, but he's been a carpenter, a hotel owner and who knows what else. But I know what he wants to do most of all."

No! He didn't want the children to hear about his dream of running a restaurant. They might feel bad if they thought they were keeping him from it. He caught Lavinia's eye and gave his head a small shake.

She forged ahead as though she hadn't seen him. "What your uncle Henry wants—" her smile shifted from friendly to calculating "—is to see that you children are happy and well cared for. That's what I want, too, which is why I have a plan that—"

"That she plans to discuss with me first." Henry didn't like cutting her off, but they'd agreed not to subject the children to any heated discussions or disagreements. He had a feeling both were about to take place.

Lavinia angled her head, lifted one side of her mouth and an eyebrow and shot a wordless rebuke at him. Not that he cared. She was the one who'd been on the verge of going back on their agreement, which came as a shock. Although he didn't know her well, he felt certain she wasn't the type of person who made promises she didn't intend to keep.

She cleared her throat. Loudly and pointedly. "As I was saying before I was interrupted, I have a plan that's one of my best."

Alex leaned forward, eagerness widening his eyes. "What is it?"

"I can't tell you yet. I came out to get your uncle's opinion first." Her declaration was followed by a toss of her head and a smirk. Rather than looking irritated, as she'd no doubt intended, she looked...cute.

The mass of springy curls piled on her head caught his eye, especially the one that had broken free of her pins. He reached out to sweep it behind her ear, brushing her petal-soft cheek in the process. The shock reflected in her chocolate-brown eyes mirrored the surge of it coursing through him. What had he been thinking? He yanked his wayward hand back. "I'd love to hear your plan."

Her eyes grew even wider.

What was happening? First his hand had acted of its own accord, and then his mouth had followed suit. "That is, I'd like to hear it."

"You would?" Her expression softened, but her gaze remained fixed on him. Confused, curious and...captivating.

He scrambled to remember what they'd been talking about. Ah, yes. Her plan. "By all means. Alex is ready to try a few shingles on his own, so we can go down and talk if you'd like." He sent his nephew an encouraging smile.

Alex's mouth went slack. "Really, Uncle Henry? You're going to let me do it all by myself? Do you think I can?"

"I wouldn't have said it if I didn't. Just take your time and remember all I've taught you."

Lavinia's gaze bounced from Henry to Alex and back

again. She scraped her lower lip between her teeth, a most distracting gesture, and then opened her mouth to speak but snapped it shut instead. Thankfully, she'd chosen not to challenge his authority in front of the impressionable boy.

Alex didn't miss much, though, as evidenced by the keen gaze he'd directed at his aunt. "You don't have to worry, Aunt Livy. I'll be careful."

"I know that. I'm just not used to boys. Your mother and I weren't allowed to climb on roofs and such. The only things we climbed were stairs."

Alex's brow furrowed, and then understanding dawned. He laughed. "You were joking, weren't you?"

"I suppose I was. Partly."

"So you've never climbed a tree or anything?"

Lavinia's eyes widened. "I should say not. A lady minds her manners."

"But you weren't always a lady. You used to be a girl, like Marcie and Dot."

"I was, true, but…"

Henry stifled a laugh at the unbidden image of Lavinia up a tree that popped into his head. "Some fathers don't let their daughters do everything they want to do." The words were barely out of his mouth when he realized his mistake. "What I meant to say was—"

"I know exactly what you meant." Lavinia shot a dark look his way and started down the ladder with far too much speed for a woman in high-heeled boots.

Henry clutched the side rails to steady it. "Be careful!"

"I'm fine." Her response came quickly, with an edge to it, but at least she'd slowed her descent.

As soon as she was safely on the ground, Henry scrambled down the ladder after her. He joined her under the oak a few feet away, far enough from the shed to give Alex a feeling of independence but close enough to rush to his nephew's aid if need be. Not that the careful boy would get into any trouble.

Unlike you, Hawthorn. He'd managed to insult Lavinia again. He'd had no intention of doing so, but he was a much better cook than he was a conversationalist. He could hold his own with the rugged miners who stayed in his hotel, but when it came to society ladies, he was out of his element. Unless the lady was talking about food. He'd gotten on fine with the woman who'd taught him everything she'd learned at Mrs. Goodfellow's cooking school.

"I didn't mean anything by what I said."

She studied him with narrowed eyes. "Didn't you? I know you don't think well of Father, but he was only trying to ensure our safety. A person could get hurt falling from a tree."

"Not if that person knew what he—or *she*—was doing."

"Perhaps, but I trust you have no intention of encouraging the children to climb trees, especially the girls. I couldn't bear it if anything were to happen to one of them." She shivered and rubbed her arms. "We've dealt with more than enough tragedy."

"I won't encourage them, but Alex's friend Frankie has been urging him to climb one, so I intend to show him how it's done. That way he'll know what to do should he give way to the pressure. I'll point out how far I'm comfortable having him go. Not that I expect him to climb too high on his own. He's a cautious one."

"I'm aware of that. I might not have spent as much

time with the children as you have, but I've gotten to know them quite well."

He'd trod into dangerous territory again. Best to avoid tricky topics altogether. "You said you had a plan. Care to tell me about it?"

Her wariness fell away, and the excitement he'd seen earlier returned. "Gladly." She watched Alex pound a nail after checking the shingle's position three times. "I want the children to see why Pauline loved Christmas as much as she did, so I'm going to throw a party like those we had growing up."

His sister-in-law had told him about the lavish affairs her father had hosted. "Wouldn't a ball be a bit much? The children are too young to dance."

Lavinia laughed and swatted his arm. "I know that, Henry."

He'd enjoyed the contact more than he should have, innocent though it was. Lavinia was a lovely lady, but she was a lady who had definite ideas about how things should be done. She was also the lady determined to take Jack and Pauline's children away from him. Not that he was concerned. She had no grounds for guardianship, whereas he had the law on his side. "What are you planning, then?"

She glanced around the yard, as though assuring herself no one was around, and launched into a lively description. "For starters, I'm going to rent the meeting hall in that vacant building downtown, the one that used to be a hotel. It will make a wonderful venue for the party."

"Why can't you just have it here?"

Her musical laugh rang out once again. "Here?" She glanced at the house. "It's much too small."

Warning bells rang. Loudly. "Just how many people do

you plan on inviting? Alex's only close friend is Frankie. Marcie pals around with Norma's eldest daughter, Olivia, and two other schoolgirls, and little Dot plays with Norma's younger daughter, Yvonne. Those children and their families could fit in the parlor."

Lavinia stared at him with the look of a schoolmarm attempting to explain something to an unperceptive pupil. "I thought Pauline told you about our parties."

"She did. They were some of her most treasured memories."

"I can understand that. They're grand events. It would appear she didn't make it clear how many people attend them, though. Our friends come, of course, but Father also invites everyone who works at the Crowne Jewel and their families, as well as our household servants. He hires staff to fill their positions for the evening."

The size of the guest list came as a surprise. That would be at least three-hundred people. And based on hearsay gathered from the employees Henry had met during the construction of Crowne's Philadelphia hotel, the hotelier wasn't known for his generosity. "That's kind of him. You must have a large parlor."

She gave a dismissive wave of her hand. "Oh, we don't use the parlor. Father had a ballroom added to the house, and we hold the party there. That's why I needed to find a place big enough for the one I'm planning."

"Who all will be coming? You still haven't said."

Lavinia fisted her right hand and extended a different finger for each group she named. "All the schoolchildren and their families, the members of the congregation, Norma and her family, Gladys and, of course—" she raised her thumb and sent him a winsome smile "—you."

"That's quite a gathering. I can see why you're planning to rent the hall, but Benedict can be a hard man to track down." He'd tried to locate the owner himself after receiving word of Jack and Pauline's tragic accident— to no avail. If he could buy the building, he could turn it into a hotel, hire a manager and earn the money needed to support the children. And still have plenty of time to spend with them.

"It took some doing, but I found out who's serving as his agent."

"How?"

She patted her curls. "A lady can find out all manner of things if she sets her mind to it."

He chuckled. "You don't strike me as the type of woman who would resort to using feminine wiles to get what she wants."

His jest earned him a saucy smile. "Even though we've only known each other a short time, you presume to know me quite well."

Not as well as he would like. "I know you're deter- mined and won't let anything keep you from getting what you want." She could throw her party, but that wouldn't change anything. "Did Benedict agree to rent you the hall?"

"Mr. Price said he's expecting Mr. Benedict's answer soon. He's considering my offer, but I'm certain he'll take it."

So the well-established lawyer in town was the one serving as his agent. "For your sake, I hope he does." Henry had his doubts. When it came to shrewd busi- nessmen, Benedict's reputation would put him at the top of the list, right up there with Lavinia's father. Come to think of it, since she'd dealt with Paul Crowne all her life, she could have what it took to broker a deal with Benedict after all.

Not that Henry was worried about that. What did concern him was how much he was drawn to the lovely Lavinia Crowne. Nothing could come of it, though, so he would keep his attraction in check.

Or try to.

The rhythmic creaking of Norma's chair as she rocked her baby boy the following Saturday added to the peaceful atmosphere in the cheery bedroom. The muted voices of the five older children seated around the table in the kitchen down the hall assured Lavinia that they were having a good time making miniature wreaths. She'd given them the bits of pine boughs left after the decorating she'd done earlier that day.

Little Dot was relishing the time with Norma's youngest daughter, Yvonne, her favorite playmate. Marcie was captivated by the simple handicraft, as was her friend, Olivia. Alex, cautious boy that he was, had volunteered to cut the twine the girls were using to form their wreaths, or Lavinia wouldn't have left the children unattended. Thanks to his offer, she could enjoy a few minutes with the woman who'd been Pauline's dearest friend.

Norma glanced out the window, which faced the west side of Jack and Pauline's house. "I like the way you've wound the pine boughs around the front porch railing. The bright red bows you added are a nice touch. I'm curious why you've started decorating so soon, though. It's only the eighth of December. Even Pauline, whose love of Christmas surpassed that of anyone I've ever known, gave way to convention to a degree and waited until the week before. We don't do our decorating until Christmas Eve."

Gladys had asked the same question, so Lavinia had a ready answer. "Pauline said that an event as special as the birth of our Savior deserves more than a brief celebration. I think others feel the same. The merchants already have Christmas wares in their windows, and people love to stop and admire them. Since the children are grieving, I decided not to wait this year. They seem happy about that, and their happiness is my primary concern."

"They're having a wonderful time making their own decorations. I'm just used to the way things have always been done. Pauline used to tease me about my unwillingness to break with tradition. She didn't let others' expectations stop her from doing what she wanted, though. That independent streak was one of the many things I admired about her."

"I did, too." Pauline's willingness to take a stand had served her sister well, especially when it came to dealing with their father. She hadn't been afraid to stand up to him. The row she'd had with their father after she announced that she was marrying Jack Hawthorn and would be heading to California had been heated and loud.

Although her sister could endure their father's tirades without flinching—and had on numerous occasions—Lavinia dreaded such confrontations and avoided them whenever possible. The losses she suffered from those arguments tended to outweigh any gains. Paul Crowne wasn't a man one cared to cross. She preferred to appease him to keep the peace.

To do that, she must contest Jack's will, be instated as the new guardian and take the children to Philadelphia with her as her father expected. Many times, his wishes ran contrary to hers, but in this case, she and her father were in agreement.

She should be hearing from Mr. Benedict's lawyer regarding the building rental soon. When she did, she'd ask Mr. Price if he would take her case.

Norma rubbed her droopy-eyed baby's back. "It's nice that you take after Pauline that way."

"Me? Really?" As much as Lavinia wished she had some of Pauline's fortitude, she was lacking in that regard.

"You do what you think is right, no matter what others might say. Take your clothing for instance. You're not in mourning garb because you know wearing the dark, dreary colors makes Dot sad. Standing up for what you believe is right takes courage, and I admire your willingness to do so."

Words eluded Lavinia. She didn't regard herself as brave. She was just doing what was best for the children.

Norma didn't seem to expect a response. Instead, she smiled at the precious infant in her arms, who was having a hard time keeping his eyes open. "Bobby will be nodding off soon. Would you like to rock him to sleep?"

"Certainly." Lavinia took the precious boy, cradled him to her chest and crooned the French lullaby her mother had sung to her when she was young, "Au Clair de la Lune." She breathed in the baby's sweet scent as she sang.

By the time she finished the memory-laden tune, Bobby had succumbed to sleep. Norma motioned for Lavinia to lay the little fellow in his cradle. She managed to get him into it without waking him. A series of S-shaped curlicues formed the sides of the wrought iron creation. She admired the handiwork for a moment and then tiptoed across the room.

Norma followed her out and stood in the doorway, gazing at her sleeping son.

"The cradle is lovely," Lavinia whispered. "Did Henry make it?"

"Yes, not long after he got to California, right after Alex was born. Pauline and I passed it back and forth, as needed."

"He's quite talented, and in so many areas." He'd volunteered to help in numerous ways the past week. She should have declined his offers, but when he accompanied one with his engaging smile, she had a hard time refusing. "I can't help but be impressed."

Norma raised an eyebrow. "Even smitten, perhaps?"

"Oh, no!" Lavinia nearly shouted and then lowered her voice to a whisper once more. "Forgive me for my outburst, but you're mistaken. There's nothing between Henry and me—other than wanting to do what's best for the children, of course."

Norma chuckled. "Perhaps, but I sense more to it than that." Thankfully, she let the matter drop and continued at a normal volume. "And don't worry about the noise. A third baby must get used to sleeping through a certain amount of it. Bobby's sisters see to it that it's rarely quiet around here. Olivia especially. That girl has plenty to say. She gives Marcie some serious competition."

"Marcie takes after Pauline. My sister could talk the bark off a tree, as our grandfather used to say."

Norma's voice took on a wistful tone. "That was another thing I loved about her. An ordinary day became fun-filled when she was around, adding her spark to it. No one could embellish a story the way she could, and her ready laugh was contagious. Life won't be the same without her." She heaved an audible sigh, left the door to Bobby's room ajar and headed toward the kitchen. "Let's see what the other children have been up to, shall we?"

Lavinia could empathize. The thought of never seeing her beloved sister again was almost too much to bear. The ten years they'd been apart was hard enough. During that time, she'd been holding out hope that the rumors her father had heard about "Crazy Judah" were true. The well-educated engineer, Theodore Judah, was a visionary with a plan to build a railroad that would connect the East with the West. When it was built, a person would be able to travel across the country in a week's time. She'd envisioned making a quick trip to California to visit her sister while her father was off touring his other hotels and dealing with his anger after the fact. But Pauline had gone to her heavenly home before that could happen.

The moment Norma and Lavinia entered the kitchen, the girls held up their creations and began talking at once.

Norma sent them a good-natured smile. "It appears you're all having fun, but I can only listen to one of you at a time. Alex, why don't you start?"

Marcie was quick to protest. "How come he gets to go first? He's not even making a wreath."

Lavinia was ready to respond, but Norma beat her to it. "Because he's the oldest and offered to help the rest of you. So how did things go, Alex?"

"Good, but the girls want to know if you have some ribbon. They want to tie bows on their wreaths the way Aunt Livy did on the porch railings."

"Hmm. Let me think." Norma tapped her chin, stared at the ceiling for a moment and snapped her fingers. "I just remembered where it is. I'll go get it."

Marcie tugged on Lavinia's sleeve. "Look at my wreath, Aunt Livy. Isn't it pretty?"

"It's very nice. You did a fine job." Marcie must have kept Alex busy cutting pieces of string to keep the many lengthy boughs in a circle.

"Mine's the biggest." Marcie flicked her curls out of her face and beamed.

Dot turned toward her sister, her pretty face pinched. "That's 'cause you took all the long pieces."

"It's a nice size, Marcie, and will be just the thing to hang on the front door." Lavinia picked up Dot's creation and examined it. "I like yours, too. It will look lovely in that little window beside the door. Alex is right, though. Some ribbon would add a nice bit of color to your wreaths." She walked around the table to where Norma's three- and five-year-old girls sat and admired their work.

A knock at the front door sent Norma scurrying from the back room to the entryway. She returned moments later with Henry. "Look who wants to join the fun."

"Uncle Henry!" Dot ran into his open arms. He picked her up. "Look at the reefs we made."

Marcie scoffed. "They aren't *reefs*. They're *wreaths*."

"That they are, and pretty ones, too." Henry set Dot down and went around the table, admiring each girl's handiwork in turn, coming to a stop by Lavinia. "I have a hunch it was your aunt's idea to make them. Seems she's eager for Christmas. The house—" he inclined his head toward it "—looks quite festive."

Olivia, Norma's outgoing daughter, joined the conversation. "You're right. It was Miss Livy. She brung over all the extra pieces from the branches, but she run out of ribbon. Mama went to get us some."

"I found a few pieces in my scrap bag." Norma held

out a handful of ribbon, most of it white with a few pastel shades. "None are very long, but you're welcome to them."

Olivia raised herself up on her knees, rested a hand on the table and rifled through the pile. "These are boring. I want red like Miss Livy used." She turned to Lavinia. "Can you give us some?"

She shook her head. "I'm afraid there isn't any left." Pauline's sewing basket had yielded a nice supply, but Lavinia had used everything she'd found. She'd asked Gladys to pick up some more while she was doing the shopping.

"Perhaps this will help." Henry reached into his jacket pocket and produced three spools of ribbon—red, green and a red-and-green plaid.

Lavinia stared at the selection and shook her head. "How did you know what we needed?"

He sent her one of his charming smiles that she was fast finding irresistible. "I have my ways."

She picked up the spools and handed them to Alex. "Would you please cut off pieces for the girls? And Norma, could I ask you to help them tie their bows?"

Her new friend nodded. "Certainly."

Taking Henry by the arm, Lavinia tugged him to the side and spoke in hushed tones. "So tell me. How did you know we could use some ribbon?"

His lips twitched, as though he was keeping laughter at bay. "You're a curious one, aren't you?"

"And you—" she gave him a playful poke in the chest "—are an exasperating one. You will tell me, won't you?"

The room had grown quiet. She turned to find six pairs of eyes fixed on her and Henry. Norma's telling smile brought back her comment from earlier, but it was the eagerness in Alex's eyes that drew Lavinia up short. Did the dear boy think she and Henry…? She dropped her hand to her side with haste. "Everything's fine. You can get back to work."

The four girls returned to their wreath-making, but Alex leaned close to Marcie, who was seated beside him.

Henry cleared his throat, drawing Lavinia's attention back to him. "If you must know, I ran into Gladys at the grocer's. The subject of your decorations came up, and she mentioned you'd used all the ribbon you had. I figured you could use more."

"That was thoughtful of you. You surprised us all."

He rubbed his strong jaw. "I have two more surprises. The first is that Mr. Price asked me to tell you that he'd like to see you Monday afternoon about the rental of the building."

She smiled. "Wonderful. He must have heard from Mr. Benedict. And the second?"

"You mentioned that Gladys takes her time on the shopping trips. I don't think it's due to her rheumatism as much as it is a certain grocer. I caught the two of them talking and got the feeling there was more to the conversation than what was on her shopping list."

Lavinia shook her head. "I doubt that. Gladys is a practical person. She was probably just asking his opinion or something like—"

A squeal from Marcie turned Lavinia's head. The expressive girl was grinning at Alex. "Yes! Do it."

"Do what?" Henry asked.

Marcie spun around wearing a gleeful grin. "Alex is tired of helping us. He wants to go play in our backyard, but he wasn't sure you'd let him. Please say he can. We don't need a boy around anymore since you and Aunt Livy are here to help us."

Henry chuckled. "I understand that, Buddy. A fellow can only take so much time with a gaggle of giggly girls. Go have yourself some fun."

Dot looked up, a frown on her pink-cheeked face. "We aren't giggling, Uncle Henry. We're making re— re—" she glanced at her sister "—these." She held up her wreath.

"And those *wreaths* are looking mighty nice, Dimples. I like all the ribbons on yours."

Dot beamed. Alex jumped up, grabbed his jacket from a peg in the entryway and flew out of the house.

Lavinia looked at the back door he'd closed with a bang. "How odd. He's usually happy to help. Oh, well." She smiled at the circle of girls around the table. "There are plenty of grown-ups to help you."

The next twenty minutes flew by as Lavinia snipped ribbon, tied bows and complimented the girls on their creations. Everything went smoothly until the end, when they were cleaning up and she reached for the scissors at the same time Henry did. His hand ended up on top of hers. She pulled hers away quickly, but the girls had witnessed the collision. Marcie laughed, which set the other girls off. Before long, they really were giggling.

The instant the table was cleared, Lavinia, cheeks still warm, urged her nieces to gather their wreaths, thank Norma for her hospitality and don their coats as quickly as possible. A chorus of goodbyes followed.

Lavinia and Henry followed Marcie and Dot out the door, down the street and through the gate in the wrought iron fence. Marcie bounded up the walkway to the porch where Alex sat on the top step and whispered in his ear.

Although she'd been eager to send her brother away earlier, she seemed happy to see him again.

Marcie straightened. "Aunt Livy, can we hang my
wreath now?"

"Mine, too!" Dot hollered.

Their pride and excitement warmed Lavinia's heart.
Even though she'd intended to create an elegant wreath
to grace the front door, the girls' desire to see their work
displayed was more important. There would be lovely
decorations to enjoy in Philadelphia in the years to come,
but this Christmas was about them. She could make a
concession here and there, couldn't she? "That's a wonderful idea."

Marcie held out her wreath to Lavinia. "Will you hold
it up so I can see how it will look?"

"Of course." She stood in front of the door and centered the wreath at eye level. With its many colorful
bows, it was sure to elicit smiles from everyone who
entered the house. The refreshing pine scent from the
boughs surrounding the doorway added to the festive
atmosphere. She inhaled deeply, relishing the fragrance
that would always bring with it memories of her sister.
"Do you think it looks good here?"

Marcie stood back and tilted her head to and fro. "I
think it should be a bit higher."

Lavinia raised the wreath a few inches and looked
over her shoulder. "How about that?"

"Yes!" Marcie smiled. "I like it there. Can we put it
up right now?"

"We can," Henry said. "I'll get a hammer and nail
from the shed."

"I already have them." Alex pulled his hands from
behind his back, revealing the items.

Henry took them. "You certainly planned ahead, Buddy."

Alex shrugged. "I knew Marcie wouldn't want to wait."

Lavinia laughed. Alex knew his sister well.

Henry joined Lavinia at the door, used the nail to mark the spot where it would go and asked her to remove the wreath. She lowered it and moved aside.

In no time, he'd pounded in the nail. She cast a glance at the children, who had their heads together and were whispering among themselves. They jumped apart when they saw her, guilty looks on their faces, almost as if they'd been caught doing something wrong.

"We're ready if you want to watch me hang it."

They nodded in unison. Clearly, they were up to something. No doubt, she'd find out soon enough. She stepped up to the door where Henry stood, hammer in hand, and hung the wreath.

"Uncle Henry, Aunt Livy, look up!" Marcie hollered.

Lavinia lifted her head at the same time Henry did, spied a sprig of mistletoe tucked between the boughs overhead and froze.

"It's mistletoe," Dot announced.

"Yes," Henry said, his voice thick. He cleared his throat. "I see that."

"You're supposed to kiss."

Lavinia didn't need Alex's reminder. What she did need to do was breathe. She gulped in some air, slowly lowered her head and looked at Henry, who appeared as dazed as she was.

His gaze dropped to her mouth, causing her heart to slam against her corset. She'd never allowed a man to kiss her before, although several had wanted to. Even so, she half hoped Henry would dip his head and touch his lips to hers.

All sounds faded except for his whisper-soft exhale. Her gaze traveled over the smooth planes of his cheeks to his strong jawline. If she leaned toward him ever so slightly...

No! Although the idea of kissing Henry appealed to her far more than it should, she couldn't give in to her wayward feelings. She'd vowed to wait until she met a man she loved for her first kiss.

She produced a shaky smile, took two steps back and worked to regain her composure. Hopefully, Henry would attribute the color in her flaming cheeks to the chill in the air.

"Stop!" Marcie wailed. "It's mistletoe. You *have* to kiss him."

Disappointment was etched in the faces of her nieces and nephew. "I know that's the way it works, but a kiss is something special, and your uncle and I haven't known each other that long."

Dot frowned. "Uncle Henry's nice. Don't you like him?"

"I do, but..." How could she explain her tangle of emotions to a four-year-old when she didn't understand them herself?

"If you want some kissing, Dimples, I can make that happen. Here." Henry handed the hammer to Alex, picked up Dot and gave her a loud smack on her cheek. "How's that?"

Dot smiled. So did Lavinia. Once again, Henry had saved the day. She'd have to make sure there were no more encounters like this one because the longer she knew him, the more she liked him. But they weren't destined to be friends. Even if they weren't at odds over the children, her father would never approve of his remaining daughter harboring romantic feelings for a Hawthorn.

Not that she did, of course. Henry was a friend. Nothing more.

Chapter Five

The scent of lemon wax greeted Lavinia as she entered the attorney's well-appointed offices Monday afternoon. She also welcomed the warmth, which was a nice change from the chill outside.

She spoke with Mr. Price's clerk and took a seat on the plush sofa in the waiting area. An ornate vase on a claw-legged table held a small branch, from which several exquisitely crafted German-made ornaments hung. They reminded her of the tall tree that would be set up in her father's ballroom back home soon.

Memories of Christmases past flooded her mind, with Pauline at the center of them. Her sister's enthusiasm for the holiday and its celebrations had known no bounds. She would have eagerly endorsed Lavinia's plan to throw the biggest party Sutter Creek had ever seen.

Surely, Pauline would have supported Lavinia in challenging Henry for guardianship, too. After all, her sister had made it clear years ago she wanted Lavinia to care for the children should the need arise, well before Jack had written his will. Perhaps Jack hadn't even talked with

Pauline before naming Henry. Not all men felt a need to apprise their wives of such matters.

The door to the right of the clerk's desk opened, and a portly gentleman with a neatly trimmed beard appeared. Mr. Price crossed the waiting area and stood before Lavinia. "Miss Crowne, what a pleasure to see you again. Thank you for coming. If you'll head on back, we can conduct our business." He held out a hand toward the open door.

She followed him to his office and took the proffered seat in front of his gleaming desk. The surface was free of all but an elegant rosewood inkstand, a blotter and a key. If things went well, the key was the one she'd walk away with.

Mr. Price sank into the large leather chair behind his desk. "I've heard from my client."

The lawyer's serious tone put Lavinia on alert. She summoned her most businesslike manner. "Did Mr. Benedict agree to rent me the meeting room?"

"He did, but due to a change in his circumstances, he's been forced to increase the rental fee." The lawyer named a figure that made her breath catch. Other than batting her lashes a few times, she contained her surprise. Or so she hoped.

Although she'd wanted to keep her expenses down, she had no choice but to pay the outrageous sum. There was no other place available in town that could accommodate both the children's congregation and the families of their schoolmates. "You may tell Mr. Benedict I will accept his terms, but I want the amount we've agreed on in writing."

"Very well." Mr. Price pulled a sheet of paper from a

drawer, dipped his pen and dashed off a note to that effect, which he handed to Lavinia.

"Is that—" she nodded at the key "—for the building? If so, I'd like to take a closer look at the meeting room."

"Certainly."

She took the key he offered but remained seated. Niggling doubts clawed at her, but she brushed them aside. "I have another matter I'd like to discuss with you. A legal matter. Shall I make an appointment with your clerk, or do you have time now?"

"I do. Go ahead."

"You might be aware that Henry Hawthorn was granted guardianship of our nieces and nephew in his brother's will."

"I didn't know, but it makes sense. He's the children's closest relative and has been doing a wonderful job of caring for them from what I hear."

Mr. Price's quick defense of Henry didn't bode well. "He has, but I believe I could do as well. What's more, that's what my sister wanted."

The lawyer raised a salt-and-pepper eyebrow. "She had a will? Women don't generally prepare one."

"No, but Pauline wrote to me long before Jack made his and said that if anything happened to them, she knew I'd take good care of their children. I have the letter." She pulled it from her reticule and placed it in front of him.

He scanned the portion she pointed out and looked up, his eyes filled with compassion. "Miss Crowne, I know you love the children, but a letter, even one that predates the will, doesn't invalidate it. Perhaps she and her husband changed their minds in the ensuing years."

Lavinia drew in a deep breath, detecting a faint scent of cigar smoke. She lifted her chin and assumed an authoritative tone. "Or maybe she didn't know Jack had named his brother. What I want to know is how to go about changing the designation."

"That's not possible. It's legally binding."

"Wills can be broken, can't they?"

Mr. Price slid the letter across his desk to her, leaned back and folded his arms. "Are you planning to contest it?"

"If that's what it takes. The children belong with me and my father. In Philadelphia. He can provide for them in ways Henry can't. They'll live in a fine home, wear nice clothes and receive a quality education."

The kindly lawyer clasped his hands and tapped his thumbs together. "All of which are available to them here, correct?"

How could she explain without coming across as proud or boastful? "My father is a man of means. He intends to see that they have every advantage."

"You can't take the children away. They're Henry's responsibility. Unless he refuses to serve or is declared incompetent, nothing can change that."

She could see why her father grew impatient with naysayers. As he often said, there was always a way around things if you looked hard enough. "Wills are successfully contested sometimes, are they not?"

"They are, but from what I've heard, you don't have a case. Not one I'd take, anyway."

"Then I'll make one." She scanned the leather-bound volumes on the bookshelf behind Mr. Price. "Those contain the laws, don't they? If you would be so kind as to point me to the portion that relates to estates and guardianship, I'd be grateful."

The lawyer chuckled. "You want to read the statutes for yourself?"

His patronization grated on her. "I do. It's possible I might find something that could help."

"What you'll find is that the law is on Henry's side. Even if you were to dig up a charge and find a lawyer willing to take your case, it would be tried in Amador County by a jury of Henry's peers. He's known here. You're not."

Even more reason for her to make a good impression on the residents of Sutter Creek. "Be that as it may, I'd like to read the pertinent sections. I'll gladly pay for the privilege."

Mr. Price shook his head. "If you're that set on it, you may sit in my conference room and wade through the statutes—free of charge. I'll even provide a pen, paper and ink so you can take notes."

Why had she thought the man kindly? He was as quick to dismiss her as her father. How many times had she eagerly listened to him talk about his hotels only to have her suggestions dismissed? She might be a woman, but her ideas were as valid as any man's. If given the opportunity, she could help run his hotels. Not that he'd considered her. Like so many men, he didn't think her capable.

Well, she would show them. She would pore over the volume Mr. Price had handed her. If there was a way to defeat Henry, she would find it.

The sooner Henry could leave the smithy, the better. The lingering scent of charcoal in the air caused his eyes to sting and his chest to grow heavy. Everywhere he looked, he could see Jack. If it weren't for his appointment with a prospective buyer, he wouldn't be here now. At least the man hadn't wanted to fire up the forge.

Mr. Weitemeyer scanned the shop. His gaze came to rest on Henry. "I appreciate you taking the time to show me the place, Mr. Hawthorn, but I had something else in mind. The blacksmith shop I worked at up in Placerville is larger, as is the town itself. I want to build a business like that, so I don't reckon Sutter Creek is the spot for me."

"I understand. Thanks for coming down. I wish you well on your search."

Mr. Weitemeyer strode in the direction of his horse, which he'd left tied up nearby. Henry locked the doors of the smithy, blew into his hands to warm them and heaved a sigh of relief. Although little remained in Jack's bank account, Henry wasn't ready to let go of this tie to his brother yet. He had no interest in returning to the profession, but this shop had been Jack's dream. Perhaps if a young man came along who loved it as much as Jack had, Henry could part with it. He prayed the Lord would lead the right buyer his way.

Lavinia closed the door of the lawyer's office three doors down, stepped onto the plank walkway and headed toward Henry, although she had yet to see him. She appeared to be focused on something in her hand. Her meeting with Mr. Price must have been successful because she looked happy.

Her smile drew his attention to her lovely lips. He'd thought of them far too often the past couple of days. When he'd looked up and discovered the mistletoe above them, he'd had the strongest urge to give the children what they'd wanted and kiss their beautiful aunt. Yes, beautiful. He'd tried his best not to notice, but with that mass of dark curls piled on her head, her expressive cocoa-colored eyes and her heart-shaped face, she was striking.

What he'd found most interesting about Lavinia's reaction to the children's surprise was the way she'd blushed. For a moment, he'd gotten the impression she was considering welcoming his kiss, but she'd stepped back before he could be sure.

He might have been disappointed if it hadn't been for the girls' probing questions. When Marcie had asked why Lavinia didn't kiss him, she hadn't laughed at the idea. Instead, she'd said, *a kiss is something special, and your uncle and I haven't known each other that long.* That answer held exciting possibilities. Her response to Dot's question had made him wonder if Lavinia was as attracted to him as he was to her. She'd said without hesitation that she liked him, Henry Hawthorn, former blacksmith. A man beneath her station. He'd been more than willing to spare her further embarrassment after that and had given Dot a kiss instead.

Lavinia drew near, saw him and held up the key.

"You got it?"

She nodded enthusiastically, setting the loose curls at her temples bobbing. "I did."

"Good. I was afraid Benedict would let you down."

"He didn't do that, but he raised the price." She named a figure that caused him to let loose with a low whistle. "I'm just thankful he let me rent the place."

If Henry had any doubts how much Lavinia had invested in holding her party, she'd just dispelled them. She was willing to pay an amount for one night's use of the hall equal to what he would take in if guests booked all fifteen rooms in his hotel. Even if he had that kind of ready cash, which he didn't, he would have turned Benedict down cold. But not Lavinia. It appeared she was determined to host an event unlike anything the children had ever seen. "You seem to be taking it well."

"I'm disappointed, of course, but the important thing is that I can proceed with my plans. Right now, I need to pick up the children at school. After that, I can take a closer look at the meeting hall. Would you like to join me?"

Very much. "Sure."

His response earned him another of Lavinia's sunny smiles. He strolled along Main Street with her by his side, occasionally steadying her. Due to the rain yesterday, followed by a dip in the temperature today, the wooden walkways were slippery.

If anyone would have told him ten years ago that she would be at his side with her hands firmly wrapped around the crook of his arm, he wouldn't have believed it. He certainly wouldn't have believed how much he enjoyed having her there. Then again, what man wouldn't welcome the opportunity to escort a beautiful woman?

There was more to Lavinia than he'd first thought. She might be hosting a party the likes of which Sutter Creek had never seen to prove to him how capable she was of caring for the children—which was entirely unnecessary, since she wouldn't be taking them with her— but he'd watched her push herself in other ways. She was learning how to cook. He wouldn't forget her childlike glee when she mastered the art of flipping a fried egg or her satisfied smile when her attempts to tame Marcie's mass of curls into a braid finally earned the finicky girl's approval.

Walking into Norma's kitchen Saturday morning and

finding Lavinia bent over the table as she helped the girls with their handicraft had filled him with hope. If she could enjoy the simple pleasures of the season, perhaps she'd see their value and realize the children didn't expect her to go to great lengths to make their Christmas special. Just having her here would help them through this first celebration without Jack and Pauline and make it memorable.

A stab of guilt stopped him. How could he have forgotten that this Christmas would also be Lavinia's first without her sister? Perhaps she needed to do all she could to recreate the happy times when Pauline had been part of her life. If that was the case, he ought to be more supportive.

Lavinia stopped and peered up at him, her breath coming in a white puff. "Is something wrong?"

"I was thinking about your party. It sounds like it's going to be quite the event. Tell me more about it."

Her eyebrows drew together. "Why the sudden interest?"

"I wasn't sure it was happening, but since it is…"

She studied him for a moment, and they started up the street again. "I never had any doubts. Of course, I'm not happy about the increase in the rent, but I'm used to dealing with shrewd businessmen. At least I can proceed with my plans. There will be desserts—plenty of them—and presents for all the children. I'm working on entertainment. Norma told me about a visiting concert pianist who could play carols. When I was at the mercantile, I heard that there's a highly regarded puppet troupe performing in Sacramento City right now. Perhaps they could be persuaded to come to Sutter Creek."

Gifts for all, a concert pianist and a puppet show? Lavinia's event was going to have her guests' mouths gaping. "We have some fine musicians here in town, and I know a miner who used to perform his ventriloquist act at children's parties. I could ask him if he'd be interested in helping you out."

"I play passably myself, but I would never think of performing for such a large gathering. And while I appreciate your offer to contact your friend, I'm sure the children would enjoy seeing a professional show."

Now was probably not the time to tell her that the entertainer-turned-miner had been invited into the homes of some of Boston's most influential families. Lavinia clearly had a vision for her party, and she intended to see it realized.

Sadly, he feared her extravagance—and expense—might not yield the results she was after. One evening of fun couldn't compete with years of tradition and treasured memories. But just to be sure, he had a plan of his own that would delight the children and, if all went well, convince a certain woman there was joy to be found in the simple things her sister had come to value. Why that mattered so much to him, he didn't know, but it did.

Lavinia halted in front of the grocer's plate glass window. "What is Gladys doing in there? I sent her to the store over an hour ago."

"It appears she's talking with Mr. Staples."

"I can see that, but she should have been back at the house starting supper by now. I need to have a word with her." She shoved open the door, setting the bell to ringing, and strode over to the counter where her housekeeper was hanging on every word coming out of the shop owner's mouth.

It didn't take much to see that the older woman was

smitten. The grocer seemed sweet on Gladys, too. Henry followed, eager to see how Lavinia would handle the situation.

Mr. Staples was the first to notice her. "What can I do for you, Miss Crowne?"

Gladys spun around, her eyes the size of cracker barrels. "Miss Lavinia. What are you doing here? I thought you had a meeting with that lawyer fellow."

"I've concluded my business and think it's time you do the same. Where's Dot?"

"Over yonder." Gladys waved a hand toward the back corner where Dot sat in one of two chairs flanking a pot-bellied stove.

Dot pulled a peppermint stick out of her mouth, hopped up and dashed over to them. "Aunt Livy! Did you come to get me?"

"You may join us, yes. I'm sorry you've had to wait so long."

"It's all right. Mr. Staples gave me candy, and his cat was sitting with me."

A gray tabby sidled up to Henry and wove between his ankles. "She's a pretty one, isn't she, but not as pretty as you, Dimples." He hefted Dot into his arms, careful to avoid her sticky fingers.

Lavinia frowned. "How much candy have you had?"

"This many." She held up three fingers.

Mr. Staples gave Lavinia an apologetic smile. "Sorry 'bout that, miss. I guess I lost count."

"It appears my housekeeper has lost track of the time, too. School will be letting out soon."

Gladys clapped a hand to her chest. "Oh my! I had no idea. Emery and I—" she winced "—that is, Mr. Staples and I got to talking, and before I knew it, there you were.

I'll be getting on home now." She took the brown paper package the grocer handed her, cast him a lingering look and turned to leave.

"We'll talk later, Gladys." Although Lavinia's tone was level, it had an edge to it.

"Yes, Miss Lavinia." The older woman rushed out of the shop and pulled the door closed with such force that the glass center vibrated.

"Now, sweetie, let's get you cleaned up." Lavinia turned from Dot to the grocer. "Do you have a wash basin we could use, Mr. Staples?"

He held out a hand toward a doorway at the back of the shop. "Behind that curtain. You can't miss it."

She took Dot and marched away, leaving Henry alone with the grocer.

Mr. Staples speared a hand through his wiry gray hair and blew out a breath. "I didn't mean to get Gladys in trouble. It's my fault. We get to talking, and afore you know it, an hour's gone by. I don't have to tell you, though, do I? I'm guessing you and Miss Lavinia lose track of time ever' now and then, too." The older man chuckled.

Henry didn't appreciate the insinuation. "Miss Crowne and I have a good deal to discuss, but our conversations are centered on the children."

"If you say so, but I saw the way you were looking at her. I can understand. That young lady is as purty as she is strong-minded."

He couldn't argue with that. Time to steer the conversation in a new direction. "I heard you got a shipment of spices. I hope there was some nutmeg extract. I'm sure the children would enjoy a batch of Bethlehem Stars." The small star-shaped cakes had been a favorite of his when he was a boy. He'd have fun showing Alex and the girls how to make them.

A discussion of Christmas confections followed, setting Henry's mouth to watering. Lavinia and Dot returned and listened with interest until he checked his pocket watch and brought things to a close. "Alex and Marcie will be waiting for us, so we'll bid you good day, Mr. Staples. We'll have to talk treats again some time."

"That we will, Mr. Hawthorn."

Once outside, Henry took charge. "I'll carry you, Dot, since it's slippery out." He hefted her onto his left hip and offered Lavinia his right arm. "If you'll hold on to me, we can be off."

She adjusted her scarf and wrapped her hands around his elbow. "Brr. That wind is brisk."

"Sure is." Not that he minded. It had been a long time since he'd had a woman at his side, but Lavinia wasn't just any woman. Bright, beautiful and a mite bull-headed at times, she kept life interesting and him on his toes, figuring out ways to show her that the children weren't lacking, as she seemed to think they were, while granting her due respect at the same time. Not an easy task, but he relished a challenge.

He left Main and headed west down Spanish Street toward the white clapboard schoolhouse. He shortened his stride to accommodate Lavinia's. With the high-heeled emerald green boots she wore today, the trek would be challenging. "Are you doing all right?"

"I'm fine. For the most part."

What was that supposed to mean? "Do we need to slow down?"

"No. It's not that. It's the surprise I was just dealt at Mr. Staple's shop. I didn't want to believe what you told me, but I saw for myself what I'm up against. I'll handle it, though."

He pitied Gladys. The older woman had finally found some happiness, but judging by the set of Lavinia's lovely features, it appeared Gladys's budding romance would be cut short.

They made it to the schoolhouse without mishap, picked up Alex and Marcie and were back on Main Street a few minutes later. Lavinia led the way toward Benedict's building.

Marcie squeezed between him and Lavinia. "Where are we going, Aunt Livy?"

"To see the hall where I'll be hosting a party."

"A party?" Marcie peppered her aunt with questions. "When? Where? Do we get to come?"

"Friday after next, that building with the bench out front, and of course, you may come. You, Alex and Dot are the reason for it."

"We are? Why?"

Henry's gut clenched. If Marcie was this excited about the party without even knowing what Lavinia had planned, how would the outgoing girl react when she learned more about the lavish event her aunt had in mind? Would she be tempted by the luxurious lifestyle Lavinia could provide and feel like she'd be missing out?

"I thought you might like to see what Christmas was like when your mother was your age." They'd reached the door to the building. Lavinia pulled the key out of her handbag and slipped it in the lock.

Marcie stood at one of the windows, cupped her hands and peered into the vacant building. "Why will the party be here? This place hasn't been open in ages."

"The meeting hall inside will hold all the guests I'll be

inviting. Wait until you see it. There are beautiful chandeliers, lovely brocade draperies and a floor that's been polished until it gleams in the lamplight, which would make it good for dancing."

"Dancing?" Alex scoffed. "Who wants to do that? Not me."

Henry stifled a laugh. His prediction of Alex's reaction had been on the mark. "Don't worry, Buddy. Your aunt assured me there won't be any dancing."

"Good. I don't want to get that close to a *girl*." He gave an exaggerated shudder.

"Believe it or not, you won't always feel that way." Lavinia stepped into the lobby and held the door open. "Come along now."

Marcie and Alex clomped inside. Henry followed, ducking to make sure his top hat cleared the head jamb.

"Follow me." Lavinia crossed the lobby, passed through another door and traveled down a dusty corridor.

Dot sneezed. "This place tickles my nose."

"I'm sorry about that. Here you go." Lavinia handed Dot a lace-edged handkerchief and continued until she reached a door with a plaque bearing the words *Meeting Hall*. She opened it, revealing a large room cast in shadows. "It's dark, so I'll open the drapes. Wait here."

No sooner had Lavinia left than three pairs of eyes locked on Henry. Alex looked doubtful, Marcie curious and Dot irritated.

Marcie peered up at Henry. "Aunt Livy said she's having her party here to show us what Mama did when she was a girl, but Mama didn't have parties in big ol' places like this, did she?"

He debated how much to say. He might as well be forthcoming since Lavinia would tell them herself. "She did, actually. Her father has a big house with a ballroom, and he holds a Christmas party in it every year."

Alex's jaw dropped. "Mama's house had a room this big?"

"Yes." From what Lavinia had said, it was twice as large, but he'd leave it to her to share that detail.

Marcie's mouth gaped. "That sounds like a palace. Was she a princess?"

Henry smiled. "No, Muffin. Her father just has a big house."

"Don't you remember, Marcie?" Alex chided. "Mama told us about him once. He owns lots of hotels, so he's got piles of money."

"She didn't say that!"

"She did, too." Alex scuffed a boot over the carpet runner. "Well, not the money part, but if he has all those hotels and a great big house, he must be rich."

Footfalls signaled Lavinia's approach. "Who are you talking about?"

Henry chose his words carefully. "They were asking about the parties you and your mother enjoyed as girls, and one thing led to another."

Marcie gazed at Lavinia. "Uncle Henry said you don't live in a palace, but Alex said if your house has a room this big, your papa must be rich. Is he?"

"My father has worked very hard and has done well for himself, but it wasn't always that way. When he was a boy, he had to put newspaper in his shoes because he'd worn holes through the soles."

"He was poor?" Alex asked.

Lavinia nodded. "That's why he's worked so hard." She gazed into the room now filled with light. "He wanted your mama and me to have nice things."

"You do." Marcie glanced at her aunt's outfit and dropped her gaze to the floor, where the toes of Lavinia's boots peeked out from beneath the hem of her gown. "I only have one pair of boots, but you have five."

Lavinia opened her mouth but closed it without speaking. She reached back to massage her neck.

Dot shifted in Henry's arms. "Are you mad, Aunt Livy?"

"No, sweetie. I was just remembering a time when your mother and I took off our boots in the ballroom and went skating."

"Skating?" Alex asked. "What do you mean?"

"In Philadelphia, the rivers and lakes freeze over in the winter. We wear skates with sharp blades on the bottoms and glide over the ice, like so." She modeled the basic forward movement. Due to the recent waxing she'd requested when she first offered to rent the place and her smooth leather soles, she could move with relative ease.

"When your mama and I were young, our friends invited us to join them. We wanted to go, but our mother thought ice skating would be too dangerous. We took off our boots and skated over the ballroom floor in our stocking feet instead. Your mama got going so fast that she took a tumble and did three somersaults before coming to a stop."

"Did she get hurt?" Leave it to cautious Alex to think of that.

Lavinia shook her head. "I think she got a couple of bumps, but she didn't care. She started laughing, and I joined in. We laughed so hard that we stopped making any noise."

"I'm going skating!" Marcie plopped down on the

floor and removed a boot. She dropped it with a thud and started on the second.

"I wanna skate, too. Put me down, Uncle Henry. Please."

He deposited Dot on the floor, knelt and helped her take off her shoes. He glanced over his shoulder at Alex. "How about you, Buddy? We can't let the girls have all the fun, can we?"

A slow smile spread across his nephew's face. "No, Uncle Henry, we can't. Are you going to skate, too, Aunt Livy?"

Henry paused. He wasn't above applying some pressure if it would help Lavinia relax and enjoy herself. She might even release her musical laugh and favor him with another smile or two. "Yes, Lavinia. You need to join us. After all, this was your idea."

He'd issued the challenge. How would she respond?

Chapter Six

The meeting-room-turned-skating rink faded as images from the past swirled through Lavinia's mind with dizzying speed. Pauline sprawled across the ballroom floor laughing until tears streamed down her cheeks. Sneaking into her sister's bedroom in the middle of the night during a thunderstorm and listening to stories that Pauline dreamed up to chase away their fears. Waving to Pauline, a newly married woman, as Jack's wagon lumbered down the road, leaving Philadelphia—and a grieving younger sister—behind.

Oh, Pauline. I miss you so much.

Marcie slid over to Lavinia, her skirts swishing as she skated. "You have to play, too, Aunt Livy. It's fun. See?" Her niece raised her arms over her head and spun in a tight circle.

With Marcie's head thrown back and laughter bubbling out of her, she looked so much like Pauline that Lavinia couldn't keep from smiling. "You're definitely your mother's daughter."

Marcie came to a stop and held out her hands to steady

herself. "Of course I am. She liked to have fun, and so do I. Are you gonna have some, too?"

"I'm having fun watching you."

"That's not fun. That's boring. I'm going to skate." Marcie darted off toward her siblings.

Henry's sweeping strides brought him to Lavinia's side quickly. "I'd imagine seeing Marcie like this brings back memories."

Lavinia nodded.

"You've succeeded in your mission then."

"What do you mean?"

Henry held out a hand toward the children. "You wanted them to see what their mother's life was like, and they are."

"That's not what I meant. I want them to see how we celebrated Christmas."

"And they will, but isn't this just as important?"

Before she could answer, Dot barreled toward her. Lavinia braced herself for the impact.

"Why aren't you skating, Aunt Livy?"

"It's not la—" She caught herself just in time. How many times had her mother kept her daughters from enjoying themselves by exerting pressure on them to behave in a ladylike manner? Too many. Pauline hadn't let their mother's gentle rebukes keep her from having fun. Her sister had embraced life with gusto as her children were doing now.

"It's not what?" Dot asked.

"It's not…something I've done in a long time."

Alex drew up alongside her. "If you're scared of falling, you could hold on to Uncle Henry."

She glanced at Henry and had to fight to keep her composure. A challenge, along with something that looked a lot like attraction, dwelled in his clear blue eyes. The combination was irresistible—and disturbing. "I can manage on my own."

Alex smiled. "Then you're going to do it?"

Marcie rushed over, and the three children lifted expectant faces. "I will."

"Goody!" Dot clapped.

Lavinia couldn't bring herself to look at Henry. Instead, she headed for the nearest window and closed the gap between the lacy curtains that had been hidden beneath the brocade drapes. The thin fabric let in the light, but it would keep those outside from witnessing her breach of etiquette. She took a seat on a nearby bench, removed her boots and wiggled her toes. Such freedom. She hadn't walked around in her stocking feet since she was a girl, and yet here she was prepared to slide across the meeting room floor.

She stood and slid a foot forward slowly, tentatively. Nice and slippery. No wonder the children could zip about with such ease. She'd have to be careful or she could take a tumble just as Pauline had that December day so long ago. She removed her coat and hat, leaving them, her gloves and her reticule filled with the notes she'd taken at Mr. Price's office on the bench, and set off across the floor with a gentle swaying motion.

The years melted away, and she was back in the ballroom with Pauline. Lavinia could almost smell the invigorating scent of the fir tree that the servants had set up in anticipation of her father's first Christmas party, although they had yet to do the decorating. It was '42, the year she'd turned ten. When he'd heard about Queen Victoria and Prince Albert setting up a tree for their family the year before, her father had planned to embrace the new custom, which he'd done in his usual grand style, importing ornaments from Germany for the occasion.

Lavinia and Pauline had slipped away from their governess, eager to see the tree. No sooner were they in the ballroom than Pauline peeled off her boots and began skating. At her sister's urging, Lavinia had enjoyed a gleeful few minutes slipping and sliding and spinning over the floor.

Shoving her memories aside, she turned, began sliding backward and prepared for a jump. She lifted off, arms flung wide and hit something solid. Henry. He managed to remain standing, but she ended up seated on the floor, her stocking feet clearly visible beneath her splayed skirts, a most unladylike pose.

Henry was on his knees beside her in an instant. "Are you all right?"

She was mortified but uninjured. "I'm fine."

"I'm glad to hear it." He straightened, offered her a hand and helped her to her feet, sending a rush of warmth surging through her. "I didn't expect you to fall all over yourself in your attempt to best me."

She stood there, staring up at him. When he smiled like that, with merriment dancing in his bright blue eyes, she had a hard time forming coherent thoughts. She pulled her hand free and said the first thing that came to her mind. "I didn't expect you to be there."

The irritating man grinned. "I have a knack of showing up when you least expect it, don't I?"

Indeed. "I think I'll focus on going forward." And avoiding any more confusing collisions with Henry that caused her traitorous heart to race.

Not that she was smitten. He was just being nice. There was nothing between them—and never could be.

* * *

Nine years had passed since Henry had bent over a forge and made his living as a blacksmith. Standing at Jack's the following day with hammer in hand while awaiting another possible buyer sent a flood of memories rushing though Henry's mind.

He'd spent his first months in Sutter Creek working on the railings and fence for Jack and Pauline's house, receiving room and board in exchange. Since Jack had used the forge by day, Henry had worked at night. He'd learned to sleep during the daylight hours, despite the many noises that came with having a baby in the house. Thankfully, Alex hadn't cried as much as Marcie. She'd made her presence known from the start.

How quickly the children had grown up. Dot would be heading off to school before he knew it. Until then, he could use the money from the sale of the smithy to cover the household expenses. The loss of Jack and Pauline had driven home the fact that life was fleeting. He intended to spend as much time as possible with the children. Once they were all in school, he could figure out what his next venture would be.

As hard as it would be to part with the business Jack had poured ten years of his life into, the last thing Henry wanted was to take up the trade again. He was a good smith, but he'd spent more than enough time dealing with the stifling heat, sore muscles and deeply embedded grime. He set down the hammer, held out his hands and flipped them over. They were no longer stained, and he wanted to keep them that way.

He'd offered a hand to help Lavinia get back on her feet after she'd taken that tumble during their skating adventure, and she hadn't hesitated to take it. She'd kept hers in his for several seconds while she gazed at him with admiration. At least, that's what he liked to think. It was more likely that she'd just been embarrassed or flustered.

The possibility of Lavinia Crowne being attracted to him was laughable. He wasn't in her social class. She'd probably end up choosing one of the *suitable* men her father picked out for her, like that Stuart Worthington fellow, and be content with a companionable marriage, but she deserved so much more. She deserved a man who saw her for the loving, caring, generous woman she was, not one who was eager to increase his bank account by becoming the heir to the Crowne hotel empire. A man who would respect her, cherish her and challenge her to be the woman God made her to be, free of constraints.

For the first time in his life, Henry wished he had more to offer.

Lord, help me be content with what I have and not pine after what is out of reach.

He pulled out his pocket watch and checked the time. Five after nine. The potential buyer should have been there by now. What was keeping him?

Ten more minutes passed before the door creaked open. *Finally.* He'd begun to wonder if Mr. Dealy had changed his mind.

"I'm sorry I'm late, Mr. Hawthorn. Old Gus over at the barbershop was moving his jaw faster than his scissors."

Henry chuckled. "He does like to talk. Are you ready to look around?"

"Yes, sir."

Because of Dealy's barrage of questions, the tour took the better part of an hour. The muscular young man, who was all of twenty years old, had a good grasp of the trade and all it entailed. Not having owned a shop of his own before, though, he was understandably curious about the business aspects, which Henry appreciated. He took his time explaining all that went into running a successful smithy.

At length, Dealy seemed satisfied. He leaned back against the forge that hadn't been fired up since Jack was alive and folded his arms. "I want the place."

"Good. And we're agreed on the price?"

Dealy drummed the fingers of one hand against his biceps and stared at Henry, unblinking. "It's fine."

"When would you like to complete the transaction?"

The drumming of the young man's fingers grew faster. He was as nervous as a hen on a hot griddle, as Henry's mother used to say. "I'd hoped to take ownership by the end of the year."

"Sounds good to me. We could have a lawyer draw up the papers this afternoon if you'd like."

"We can't." Dealy's frenzied movement ceased. "I wanted to buy the place right away, but... I don't have the money."

"I thought you were going to get half the proceeds from the sale of your claim."

The young man scowled. "So did I, but my partner up and left town. He took my share of the profits with him, the scoundrel. We'd done real good. I would have been able to pay for the smithy and have some left over."

"That's terrible. Do you have any idea where he went?"

"None. He done slunk off in the middle of the night, leaving me with next to nothing." He grabbed the hammer Henry had held earlier and brought it down on the anvil, tapping out a forceful rhythm.

"Mr. Dealy!"

He stopped and looked from the anvil to Henry, his eyes wide. Dealy set down the hammer and tugged at his collar. "Sorry. I don't know what came over me."

His anger was understandable. "Did you report the crime?"

"Sure did, but the sheriff don't hold out much hope of finding the two-faced fraud, so I won't be able to buy the smithy after all. Unless..." Dealy rubbed the back of his neck.

"Yes?"

"I *could* buy the shop if you was willing to hold the note yourself and let me give you a percentage of the profits each month. I'm a real hard worker. If I bunked in the back room to keep my expenses low, I reckon I could own the shop free and clear in a few years' time."

Earnestness shone from the young man's eyes, reminding Henry of the day eight years ago when he'd stood in front of a seasoned carpenter and asked if he'd be willing to take on a partner. To Henry's surprise, the man had accepted his offer, enabling him to boost his savings and buy his hotel three years later.

"Here's what I propose, Mr. Dealy. Fire up the forge and show me what you can do. If I'm satisfied with your work, you'll be the new blacksmith in town."

The young man grinned. "Thank you, sir. I won't let you down."

That remained to be seen, but Henry had a hunch the young fellow would prove himself worthy.

An hour and a set of expertly crafted horseshoes later, Henry had his answer.

"You've proven yourself, Mr. Dealy. The shop will be

yours as soon as we can get the sale recorded." He extended his hand, which the young man shook with vigor.

"Thank you, Mr. Hawthorn. You won't be sorry."

He hoped that proved to be the case.

Chapter Seven

"Angels from the realms of glory, wing your flight o'er all the earth." Dot walked around the settee, clutching the rag doll Pauline had made her and singing the words over and over. Loudly.

Henry leaned against his brother's rolltop desk in the corner of the parlor where Lavinia had been camped out ever since supper, making plans for her party. She seemed oblivious to Dot's ear-splitting rendition of the carol, which their youngest niece had heard her siblings practicing for their upcoming school concert. Unfortunately, she'd only learned the first two lines.

Alex and Marcie had escaped upstairs, where they were rehearsing their parts for the play the children would be performing at the Christmas Eve service. Alex, a shepherd, had three lines. Marcie, an angel, had one, but no line in the entire play would be as well-rehearsed, Henry was sure of it.

He stooped and spoke into Lavinia's ear. "How can you concentrate?"

She looked up, putting her so close to him that he could see gold flecks in the dark brown of her eyes. "I've heard her sing those words so many times the past couple of days that I don't really notice them anymore."

He'd been busy finalizing the sale of the smithy with Dealy and helping him get settled in. Because of that, he'd only been around at mealtimes, so he'd been spared the constant barrage. "Why haven't you asked her to stop?"

"I did, but she has a good reason for singing. Once I heard it, I didn't have the heart to silence her." Lavinia tapped the end of the pen against her lower lip. "I'd like to get these lists finished, but perhaps you could distract her by asking her why she's singing that particular song. Would you do that, please?"

"Very well." If he wanted to hear himself think, he had no choice.

He stepped into Dot's path. "Dimples!"

She swerved to miss him and kept marching and singing.

"So, you think you can avoid me, do you?" He laughed. "Well, you'd better watch out because I have long legs."

She increased her speed. He slowed his, waited for the right moment and spun around and scooped her up. "I got you!"

Instead of giggling as she normally would have, she glared at him. "Put me down, Uncle Henry. I have to sing."

He sat in Jack's favorite armchair with Dot in his lap. "Why is that?"

"Because." She clutched her doll to her chest and jutted out her chin.

"Because why?"

A tear trickled down Dot's cheek. "Because Mama and Papa are up in heaven where the angels are, and I'm down here. I have to sing loud so they can hear."

He thumbed away the tear. "They do hear singing."

"They do?"

"Let me show you." Henry reached for his brother's well-worn leather Bible on the side table and flipped through Isaiah. He located the verse in chapter forty-nine that he'd read many times since receiving the news about the tragic accident. "It says here, 'Sing, O heavens; and be joyful, O earth; and break forth into singing, O mountains; for the LORD hath comforted His people, and will have mercy upon His afflicted.'"

"What does that mean?"

"That there is singing in heaven and here on earth. It also tells us that God will comfort and care for those who are sad."

Two more tears spilled over. "I'm sad. Are you sad, too, Uncle Henry?"

His chest tightened as it did whenever he thought about their loss. "I am."

She caressed his cheeks with her tiny hands. "I miss Mama and Papa, but God gave you to us. That makes my heart happy."

He returned the Bible to the table and pulled her to his chest, his throat too thick to attempt a response, and placed a kiss on top of her head. They sat there a good minute before he trusted himself to speak.

"God brought your aunt all the way from Philadelphia, too. If you ask her nicely, she might help me teach you the rest of the words to that song." Lavinia could use a break from her party planning, even if she couldn't see that. Besides, he'd missed her company.

Dot perked up. "Will you help, Aunt Livy?"

"I will, but could you wait a few minutes, please? I'm almost done here."

Dot's shoulders drooped. "You're always working." She turned to Henry. "Can you teach me?"

He could, and he would. Perhaps when Lavinia saw the fun they were having, she'd be enticed to join them. "Sure. Why don't you run upstairs and see if Alex and Marcie want to join us? Tell them we'll be singing some of the carols from their concert."

"Goody! This will be just like when Mama was here. She played the piano for us all the time." Dot hopped out of his lap and dashed from the room.

With her gone, it was so quiet in the parlor that Henry could hear the scratch of Lavinia's pen as she worked on her lists. He rose, stood behind her at the desk and rested a hand on her shoulder. "How are things coming?"

She tensed, not relaxing until he removed his hand. Was it his friendly gesture or the interruption that had stiffened her shoulders? "I'm having a hard time concentrating, so everything's taking longer than I expected."

Definitely the interruption and not his touch. Good. "Pauline used to say that becoming a mother had taught her the meaning of the word *flexibility*."

Lavinia placed her pen on its stand and looked up. "My sister balked at rules and conventions. She didn't make plans because she didn't want to be bound by them."

"You said her adventurous nature was one of the things you admired most about her."

"I did. She broke free, but I was left behind to—never mind. It doesn't matter." Lavinia exhaled an audible breath and picked up the pen.

Clearly, it mattered a great deal. "What was it like after she was gone?"

"Different." She dipped the pen in the ink bottle and proceeded to add another item to her list.

If she didn't want to talk about it, he wouldn't force her. But perhaps he could show her how much fun she could have if she embraced life's unexpected pleasures.

He sat at the piano, lifted the fallboard to reveal the keys and launched into one of his favorite carols, "God Rest Ye Merry, Gentlemen." The words and music chased away the melancholy of the past few days. Disposing of Jack's business had dredged up memories of good times spent there with his brother and intensified the pain of Henry's loss.

Lavinia's chair scraped on the floorboards. She headed his way, stood beside the piano and watched him. Her blank expression gave no indication what she was thinking, but her folded arms told him she wasn't happy.

He finished the stanza and stopped. "Are you taking a break after all?"

"You didn't tell me you play." Her clipped words sounded like an accusation.

"It didn't come up."

"We talked about music. For the party. Don't you remember?"

Of course he did.

"You could have told me then."

"I saw no reason to. It's not like you'd want me to play at your party. I'm not that good."

She gave a dry laugh. "How can you say that? I just heard you play. You're as accomplished as I am, or more so."

Really? He found that hard to believe. She'd probably received lessons from some of the finest instructors in Philadelphia. "You're too kind."

"When did you learn to play?"

"One of the miners who took a room in my hotel was

an accomplished musician back east before he contracted Gold Fever and headed west. I offered to discount his rent if he could make a pianist out of me. He was a patient fellow and didn't give up on me and these clumsy workman's fingers." He wiggled them.

"How resourceful. I'd never think of bartering like that, but you did it to get those cooking lessons, too."

She wouldn't have had to resort to bartering, not with all the money at her disposal. To better himself, he'd done whatever he could to acquire new skills, including granting a few favors or exchanging labor for lessons. "I've found most people are more than willing to help me out."

"That must be nice." She heaved a wistful sigh. "I've had numerous people attempt to take advantage of me just as Mr. Benedict's done."

So she was bothered by the greedy building owner's tactics after all. "I'm sorry he did that."

"I'm used to it. It's one of the disadvantages of being Paul Crowne's daughter—and a woman. I should have asked you to negotiate for me." She picked up a porcelain bird from the top of the piano and studied it.

"Why didn't you? I'd have been happy to help."

She set the figurine down and pinned him with a steely gaze. "Has it occurred to you I might not want your help? This party is my undertaking, my opportunity to show you that—" She clamped her lips together and turned away.

"To show me what? That you're determined to win the children's affection? I know that. I just don't think you're going about it the right way." *Ugh!* How tactless could he be? "What I mean is—"

"I know what you mean." She whirled around, her dark eyes flashing. "You think you can do a better job caring for them than I can, that because I've led a sheltered life I don't have the necessary skills. You think you're going to show me that they belong here with you. But you're mistaken. I'm more capable than you give me credit for."

"I think you're more capable than *you* give yourself credit for. You traveled all the way to California, even though you had to challenge your father to do it."

To his surprise, she didn't correct his assumption, which told him his suspicion was correct. Knowing she'd stood up to her domineering father for the sake of the children ran counter to Henry's earlier view of her. Lavinia was more like her spirited sister than he'd thought.

Since she made no move to speak, he continued. "You arrived to find that life here isn't what you're accustomed to, but you don't complain or put on airs. You just roll up your sleeves and tackle whatever tasks need doing."

She sank into the nearest chair and stared at the rug for several seconds before looking at him. Determination shone from her dark eyes. "I appreciate your kind words, but if you think plying me with compliments will make me see things your way, you're mistaken. My father and I could offer the children a life beyond their wildest dreams. This party is just the beginning."

Even if that was true, he was the children's guardian. They wouldn't be going anywhere, especially not to live under Paul Crowne's roof—and his thumb.

"I'm sure the party will be spectacular, but life is made up of everyday pleasures mixed with plenty of love and a sprinkling of laughter. Like your idea of skating in the hall. The children will remember that for years to come."

"That was fun, but a few minutes spent sliding over a polished floor can hardly compare with a party like the one I'm planning." She rocked onto the balls of her feet, her eyes aglow. "I can hardly wait to see their faces when they walk into the meeting hall and experience the excitement in the air."

Most likely they would be overwhelmed. Well, maybe not Marcie. She embraced new experiences, but Alex and Dot were more reserved.

"Come on, slowpokes!" A clatter of feet followed as Dot raced down the stairs.

Henry chuckled. "I think we're in for some excitement now."

Dot burst into the room, jammed her hands against her hips and shook her head. "I went up to tell Alex and Marcie we're gonna sing Christmas songs, but they said they was too busy practicing for their play. Will you still play for me, Uncle Henry?"

"Of course, but I don't think it will be long before your brother and sister show up, especially if we're all singing. You will join us, won't you, Lavinia?"

She twirled a loose curl around her finger and looked deep into his eyes, her own lit with mischief. "That depends."

He raised an eyebrow. "On…?"

Her lips twitched for a moment, as though she was holding a smile back. It burst forth suddenly, warm and radiant. "On whether or not I know the song you're playing."

"How about 'I Saw Three Ships'? Even if you or this eager singer—" he inclined his head toward Dot "—don't know the words, they're easy to pick up."

"Good thinking. We'll do such a fine job together that we're sure to draw Alex and Marcie in."

Dot tugged on his jacket. "What are the words, Uncle Henry?"

"Some of them change, but just remember 'on Christmas Day.' We'll sing them a lot. Can you do that?"

She nodded.

He launched into the carol, one he'd played many times for the miners up in Marysville. Lavinia sang along, her voice a bright silvery mezzo soprano that harmonized well with his baritone. Dot chimed in on her lines with gusto.

They'd just started the second verse when Alex and Marcie rushed into the room, breathless, having thundered down the stairs. The two caught on to the song's repetitive pattern in no time and joined in.

Their little group reached the end of the nine verses, and Dot clapped with glee. "More, Uncle Henry. Play some more, please."

"What would you like to hear?"

Alex was quick to answer. "Can you play the songs we'll be singing in the school choir?"

"Could you remind me what they are?"

"Yes, Alex. He needs to know that." Marcie pulled a face at her brother.

Lavinia gave Marcie a pointed look and tilted her head toward Alex.

Marcie held out her hands and feigned innocence. "What? I was just trying to help."

"Apologize to him, please." Lavinia waited a moment, but Marcie said nothing. "Now."

"Fine. I'm sorry."

Although Marcie's apology lacked sincerity, Lavinia didn't press the matter. Her patience with the children was admirable. "What carols are you singing, Alex, other than 'Angels From the Realms of Glory,' that is? Thanks to Dot, I know about that one." He tugged on her braid, earning him a smile.

"'O Come, O Come, Emmanuel,' 'O Come All Ye Faithful' and 'It Came Upon the Midnight Clear.'"

"I know all of them except the last one."

Lavinia began singing that carol, her voice strong and sure. The joy radiating from her was palpable. Henry watched, enthralled, as did the children. She completed the first verse, stopped and looked from face to face, surprise reflected on hers. "What is it?"

Dot was the first to speak. "You're the bestest singer I ever heard, Aunt Livy."

"Thank you, sweetie. I didn't mean to get carried away, but 'It Came Upon a Midnight Clear' is my favorite carol."

"It's a beautiful song." Henry swept a hand over the keyboard. "Could you play it for us?"

"Certainly. If you'll let me have the bench…"

He scooted to the left. "If you don't mind, I'd like to watch and see if I can pick it up."

"All right." She cast him a quizzical glance but took her place and began playing and singing. Alex and Marcie sang along.

Lavinia had been having trouble concentrating earlier. Now Henry fought to remain focused. She was so near that he got a good whiff of the delicate rose scent she favored. He'd asked Gladys about it. The housekeeper had said it was Otto of Roses, the most expensive perfume available, made from the blossoms of rose trees near the Sea of Galilee. She'd confided with obvious pride that, thanks to Lavinia's generosity, she'd been granted permission to dab it on herself a few times.

Henry dragged his gaze from Lavinia's lovely face and forced himself to watch her hands move over the keys, her slender fingers graceful and sure, like the woman herself. He managed to keep his attention on the notes she was playing…until she glanced at him. The movement of her petal-pink lips as she sang made all thoughts of music slip from his mind. All he could think about was that moment under the mistletoe when the children had urged him to kiss her.

Dot sidled up next to him and whispered. "I can't sing, Uncle Henry. I don't know all them words."

He leaned close and spoke in her ear. "I don't either. We can hum instead."

Satisfied with his response, Dot did just that. He hummed along with her while forcing himself to keep his gaze on Lavinia's hands and not on her mouth.

She completed the second verse and started the third. He played along with her, note for note, matching her tempo. When she began the fourth verse, he added a few embellishments, mindful of her role as primo, supporting and showcasing her in his as secondo.

They finished, their final notes fading simultaneously, leaving him feeling more festive, more free than he had since receiving the news about the tragic loss of Jack and Pauline.

Lavinia's idea of wholeheartedly embracing the joys of the season was a good one, even if the way she'd chosen to go about doing so wasn't in line with what Henry envisioned. If he was patient, he could help her see how much fun informal family activities such as this could be. She'd certainly immersed herself in this one.

She leaned toward the children, her tone bright. "What shall we do next?"

"'Angels From the Realms of Glory,'" Marcie stated firmly. "I like it best since I get to be an angel in the church play." She flipped a hand at her dark curls.

"Very well." Lavinia faced Henry. "Since you know this one, would you like to play it on your own?"

"We can play together. Which position would you like to take?"

She graced him with a shy, almost apologetic smile. "Since you're the stronger player, why don't you stay there?"

Smiles and compliments? This was a worthwhile activity, indeed.

The next hour, filled with music, song, laughter and even more smiles, came to an end far too soon. He could spend several more seated next to Lavinia, enjoying the occasional brush of her arm against his and the unexpected sense of camaraderie.

Gladys entered the room. "I'm sorry the concert's over. I enjoyed listening to those beautiful tunes while putting the kitchen to rights, but—" she rested a hand on Dot's back "—it's time for a young lady to go to bed. Give your aunt and uncle a hug, and I'll take you up."

Dot climbed onto the piano bench, wedged herself between Lavinia and Henry, wrapped an arm around each of their necks and planted noisy kisses on their cheeks. "I'm glad we singed together. Now I know all the words to 'Angels From the Realms of Glory.' I'm so happy."

So was Henry. He wouldn't have to endure her endless repetition of the first line.

Gladys beckoned with a crooked finger. "Come, our little singer. Your pillow is calling."

Dot trooped after the housekeeper, she and Gladys both singing the carol together on the way upstairs.

Lavinia stared at the open door, slack-jawed. "That's the first time I've ever heard Gladys sing. I don't know what's gotten into her, but she's downright cheery these days. Interesting."

Marcie produced a smug smile. "I know why. She's in love."

Lavinia leaned back, startled. "What do you know about such things?"

"I know what love looks like. I saw how Mama and Papa looked at each other. It's the same way Uncle Henry was looking at you while you were playing the piano." She mimicked an adoring gaze.

Henry inhaled sharply and coughed. Repeatedly. Marcie was full of surprises, but she'd never said anything so shocking—or so ludicrous.

Lavinia cast a glance at him, concern creasing her brow. "Are you all right?"

He held up a hand and nodded to indicate he would be—provided the subject of his supposed attraction to her was dropped quickly. He might have looked at her, might even have admired her a time or two, but he most certainly had not gaped at her as though love-struck. She was attractive, talented and resourceful, but he didn't have feelings for her. He couldn't. Lavinia Crowne was, well, a Crowne, and he was a Hawthorn. Their values were as far apart as Christmas and the Fourth of July.

She turned to their niece. "Your mother and father loved each other very much, but I'm afraid you're mistaken about your uncle. We were having fun together, but he and I are just friends. And as for Gladys, maybe she's just happy about Christmas."

"We did have fun, didn't we, Aunt Livy?" Marcie smiled. "Christmas is going to be good, isn't it?"

"I'm doing all I can to see that it is."

"Does that mean we're going to get presents?"

Alex scowled at his sister. "Marcie, it's not polite to ask about that."

Lavinia laughed, an airy sound free of reproach. "It's all right, Alex. Since things are different this year, her question makes sense." She took Marcie's hands in hers. "Of course you'll have presents. I'll see to that."

"I want a pair of pretty red boots like you have." Marcie pulled her hands free and pointed at the toes of the boots peeking out from under Lavinia's skirt. "Red's my favorite color."

"I'll be sure to remember that. Now, how about you and Alex head upstairs and get your nightclothes on? I'll be there shortly to tuck you in."

The children trooped up the stairs. Henry jumped to his feet. He must put distance between himself and Lavinia now that they were alone. No telling what she was thinking after Marcie's startling declaration.

Lavinia covered the keys with the fallboard and ran a hand over it. "I can't recall a time I had as much fun playing as I did tonight. We'll have to do it again."

"That's a great idea. We could teach the children enough songs so we could go caroling. I'm sure they'd enjoy a simple activity like that. Would you?"

She spun around, and he forced himself to look casual, as though that awkward question of Marcie's hadn't happened. She studied him for the longest time before speaking, which suggested she was thinking about it, too. He fought the urge to fidget.

"I know what you're trying to do."

Did she? He silently urged her to continue.

"You want me to see what a wonderful job Jack and

Pauline did raising the children despite their limited means. Well, I have. But I could do even more good if given the opportunity."

She wholeheartedly believed she could. That much he knew, but what she couldn't see was that her idea of *good* wasn't what was best for the children. Their past, present and future were in Sutter Creek. With him. "You could offer them things they can't get here, but how do you know they want them?"

"They do. Look." She lifted her hem just enough for him to see her cherry-red boots and stamped her foot to draw attention to it. "Marcie wants boots like these." She released her skirts, and they swished around her ankles. "She could have them, along with clothes made by the finest dress designers on the eastern seaboard. Think of how much it would mean to her to wear such lovely creations."

If Lavinia thought she was going to win him over with an argument like that, she was misguided. Marcie had been content with her black boots until Lavinia had come along, boasting an abundance of footwear. Having boots to match each outfit might be important to her, but in his world that was a luxury. He'd ensure that the children had the clothes and shoes they needed just as Jack and Pauline had. He wouldn't allow anyone, not even their well-meaning aunt, to cause the children to question the decisions their parents had made or see themselves as lacking.

Pauline had walked away from her lavish lifestyle, and she hadn't regretted her decision. She once said that what she'd gained by marrying the man she loved more than made up for what she'd lost. Her only regret, she'd confided in him one day soon after he'd arrived in California, was having left Lavinia behind. If Pauline could have figured out a way to take her younger sister with her, she would have. She'd told Henry that she'd suggested the idea to Lavinia, who'd stared at Pauline like she was addlepated before flatly refusing to leave their father. If only Lavinia didn't hold Paul Crowne in such high regard.

"I'm sure Marcie would welcome a new pair of boots or a fancy dress, but she's happy with what she has." At least, she had been, and he intended to keep it that way. "Do you know what she'd really like?"

Lavinia eyed him warily. "What?"

"She wants the things money can't buy—love, kindness, understanding. You've given her those and more ever since you arrived."

"I've done my best, but I want to give her and the others more than that. Children like presents. You heard her. Christmas won't be the same without them. The trouble is, I haven't been able to find what I'm after. The shops here have a limited selection."

For someone used to shopping in Philadelphia, with excursions to New York when it suited her, that would be true. She was accustomed to finding wares from Europe and beyond, but getting items like those to California was a slow, costly process. The shop owners in the small Gold Rush towns couldn't afford to carry much aside from the basics.

"Do you know of someplace else I could go? I'm not familiar with the other towns yet."

"Jackson's just five miles down the road. I could take you there if you'd like." What had possessed him to make that offer? He didn't even like shopping.

Lavinia beamed. "Oh, would you? I'd like that. How

about tomorrow? I could leave Dot with Gladys so there wouldn't be any prying eyes."

The only eyes he was thinking about were Lavinia's. They held such childlike delight that he couldn't resist granting her request. "Sure. Tomorrow would be fine."

"That's wonderful. I'm looking forward to it."

So was he. More than he should.

Chapter Eight

The front door closed with a bang, and Gladys rushed into the kitchen with a wicker basket full of groceries slung over her arm. "Sorry I'm late, Miss Lavinia. I lost track of the time."

Again? Talking with Mr. Staples, no doubt. Lavinia bit back the reprimand fighting for release. Gladys had been faithful to the family for years. She deserved respect, but the situation had to be addressed.

"I'm glad you're here now, but I'm disappointed. You knew Henry would be coming soon and that I need you to watch Dot and be here to pick up Marcie and Alex from school if I'm not back in time."

Gladys pulled a bag of sugar from the basket, reached for the large tin in which it was stored and plunked it on the counter. "Henry's not here yet, but he will be soon. I saw him at the livery renting the prettiest little buggy." She tossed a grin over her shoulder. "Looks like he wants to impress you."

"Perhaps he just wants a comfortable ride." She'd certainly appreciate one. Bouncing around on a wagon seat could get tiresome.

"In my experience, a feller doesn't usually think of such things unless he's sweet on a gal. I should know. Emery's brother's in town for a couple of weeks and can watch the shop for him, so he intends to take me for a ride as soon as my half day begins this coming Saturday. He said I'll be traveling in style."

It was a good thing Gladys wasn't facing Lavinia because she couldn't keep her mouth from gaping. She closed it and processed the startling news. "Is Mr. Staples...courting you?"

Gladys shook out the last of the sugar, turned around and giggled. Like a smitten schoolgirl. "I do hope so."

"I see. I didn't realize things had gotten so serious. You know I'm counting on you to bake the desserts for the party. I can trust you, can't I?"

Gladys dropped her hands to her sides, the empty sugar sack dangling from one hand. "Have I ever let you down?"

Not back east, no, but she'd done so several times since they'd arrived in Sutter Creek. "To be honest, I haven't been able to rely on you like I used to. I don't begrudge you your happiness, but I expect you to do your job."

The housekeeper's shoulders slumped, making her appear older than she was. She hung her head. A few seconds passed before she lifted her chin, her gaze slowly following.

"You're right to be upset with me, Miss Lavinia. I guess I didn't want to own up to having let you down, but I know I have. I don't have a good excuse. The truth is, no man has ever paid me any mind, not since I lost my beau in the explosion at the gunpowder factory where he worked, so when Emery took a liking to me, my head was turned. If you want me to send word and tell him I can't accept his offer, I will."

"Oh, Gladys, I'm sorry you lost your young love. I didn't know that. I can understand why you want to encourage Mr. Staples, and I won't stop you. I just want your assurance that you'll see him on your own time. I need your help—with the children and the party."

"Yes, miss. I know. I'll tell Emery so when we go driving Saturday afternoon."

"I appreciate that." Without Gladys's help, she wouldn't have anything to serve her guests—unless she asked Henry to help, which she wasn't about to do. He'd agreed to take her shopping, but he wasn't excited about her plans to throw the party, although just why that was, she couldn't be sure. Perhaps she'd be able to find out during their outing. "I'll get my things, say goodbye to Dot and be off."

"I hope you have a fine time. And don't worry about things here. I'll take good care of the children."

"I know you will."

Lavinia found her niece in the parlor, crooning carols to her rag doll in hushed tones. "I'm going to be leaving soon, Dot, so I—"

"Shh!" Dot pointed at her doll, which was wrapped in a blanket and nestled in a corner of the settee beside the darling girl. "Zoe is almost asleep. It's her nap time."

Lowering her voice to a whisper, Lavinia bid Dot farewell and tiptoed out of the room just as Henry stepped into the entryway.

He gave a hearty laugh, accompanied by one of his endearing smiles that made her want to smile right back. "I didn't expect you to be waiting for me."

"I wasn't." Not really, although she was glad to see

him. "I wanted to warn you to be quiet," she said in a stage whisper. "Dot's baby is about to nod off."

Henry lowered his voice. "I'll be as quiet as a mouse, but I have to give my girl a kiss before we go." He tiptoed into the parlor, stooped to buss Dot's cheek, wished her a lovely day and returned. "Are you ready to go?"

"I am. I've been looking forward to the trip ever since you suggested it." She mentally kicked herself. She hadn't meant to sound quite so eager.

"Have you, now? Then let's get underway, shall we?" He opened the door and swept an arm toward the waiting buggy, a beautiful model with shiny black wheels and a black leather top that had been folded behind the single seat.

He helped her inside, climbed up and grabbed the reins. She ran a hand over the plush green seat cushion, reveling in the velvet's softness. "This is lovely, but where will we put the parcels?"

"The livery owner modified the seat so it lifts. We can put them inside."

"How clever." That still didn't leave much room. She couldn't help but wonder if Henry had planned on that to curtail her shopping. Not that she'd let the limited storage space stop her. If she found what she was after, she'd have the items shipped to her.

A gentle breeze blew, the air crisp but not too chilly. Brilliant blue skies stretched for miles, a sharp contrast to the grass-covered hillsides. "It's so green."

"Enjoy it while it lasts," he said, turning to look at her. "Come May, when the rains stop, everything turns brown."

"How depressing that must be."

"You get used to it. There are those who say it's fitting. After all, this is the Golden State." He grinned but sobered quickly. "Not that you'll be here to see it then, of course."

"True." She and the children would be back in Philadelphia strolling through Rittenhouse Square and taking walks along the Schuylkill River—provided she could come up with grounds to have the will overturned or Henry removed from his position as guardian.

She'd spent a good two hours taking notes on the statutes listed in Mr. Price's book that day. All she had to do was figure out a way to use one of them to her benefit, which she would. She wasn't about to leave Sutter Creek without Alex, Marcie and Dot.

The drive flew by as Lavinia and Henry talked about the children's antics, Christmases of their pasts and more, avoiding the topic of guardianship as though by mutual consent. Before she knew it, they neared the outskirts of Jackson.

He directed her attention to men working in the distance, the ringing of their picks against the rock creating a unique beat. "That mine off to the left is the Kennedy. The one on the right is the Pioneer."

"I'd heard mining was backbreaking work, but it looks even harder than I'd imagined. Did you ever do any?"

"I tried my hand at it during my first year here, but it didn't take me long to realize I'd rather do other things." He glanced at her. A lock of his wavy hair had fallen across his forehead. She reached up to brush it into place, just as she would have done for Alex, but stopped herself. Lowering her wayward hand, she lapsed into silence. It stretched for a good minute, growing more awkward by the second before Henry broke it.

"We're only a mile from town, so we'll be there soon."

"I hope the shops have what I'm after."

"What are you looking for?"

"I wrote a list." She opened her reticule, pulled out the sheet of paper and unfolded it. "To begin with, I'll find some toys. Each of the children could use some clothes and a nice warm coat, too."

"What's wrong with the clothes they have?"

Their wardrobes were suited for their lives here in Sutter Creek, but their functional outfits weren't something a child in her father's house would wear. How could she respond without coming across as prideful or disparaging? "They're fine, but I thought they might appreciate something new."

"I see." His reply, coupled with a raised eyebrow, told her he knew perfectly well why she planned to buy the children some clothes. So be it. Surely, he could understand that Paul Crowne's grandchildren couldn't show up in corduroy and calico.

They lapsed into silence once again, giving her an opportunity to study Henry. He was an incredibly handsome man, but appearances weren't as important to him as they were to those in her social circle. Other than his coat, hat and cravat, items intentionally purchased to convey a certain image, his clothing was unremarkable, although the man himself was anything but.

The longer she knew him, the more she found herself drawn to him. He had many admirable traits—kindness, helpfulness and an easygoing nature. And he was quite talented. His creativity was evident in his cooking, his music and his metal working, among other things. He was wonderful with the children, and he treated her with respect. If only things were different. He was a man she could believe in, the kind of man who stirred feelings in her no other man ever had.

She mustn't let herself think about Henry in that way, though. Even if they weren't at odds over guardianship of the children, they were from different worlds. Nothing but heartache could come of giving way to her growing attraction.

Lavinia pulled herself from her bittersweet musings when Henry drove into town a short time later. The wide main street with shops lining either side reminded her of the one in Sutter Creek, although it was shorter, ending with a row of two-story buildings facing them. "Jackson's not any bigger than Sutter Creek, is it?"

"You can't see it all from here. The road turns down at Water Street, where the Louisiana House sits, and turns again on to Broadway, which continues up the hill on the other side of Jackson Creek. Businesses line all three streets."

He parked in front of the Union Livery Stable, hopped out and came around to help her down. She took his hand, exited the buggy with his assistance and prepared to pull away, but he continued to hold on. His grip was firm but not uncomfortably so. She looked up to find him staring at her.

"I know we disagree on things, Lavinia, but can we declare a truce today? You've been looking forward to this outing, and I want you to have a good time."

Henry was full of surprises. She hardly knew what to think, but she had to say something. It would be nice to enjoy a day spent in the company of an attractive ma— another adult. "Fine. A truce, but that doesn't mean our disagreements have been—"

"Resolved? I understand, but it does mean we've set

them aside for the time being and will act more like friends than foes."

Henry, a friend? Lavinia smiled. "Or perhaps friendly foes?"

He chuckled, a warm, rich sound that seemed to rumble in his chest. "Friendly foes it is." He gave her hand a squeeze before releasing it, accompanied by a smile that lit his beautiful blue eyes.

Beautiful? What had come over her? She might have agreed to set their differences aside for a day, but she mustn't lower her defenses.

He left her to wait for him on the raised sidewalk, out of danger from passing wagons, and went to converse with the liveryman, returning a short time later. "What would you like to do first? Get your shopping done or eat?"

It was so like a man to think she could complete her shopping quickly. She needed time to see all the wares the various merchants offered, ponder her choices and make her decisions. For all she knew, she might not find what she was after, requiring additional outings to other destinations. "I'd like to peruse the shops first, enjoy a meal next and make my purchases afterward."

"Do you like French food? If so, we could dine at E. Le Jeune's French Restaurant."

"We can get French food here? I had no idea. I would love to have *filet de bœuf aux champignons* with *beignets de pomme* for dessert, if they have those." She hadn't savored either since visiting Delmonico's at her father's request two years before. He liked to know what the competition was serving, but he was too well-known among the staff at New York's hotels and restaurants to conduct scouting missions himself. She was more than willing to perform them in his place.

"Tenderloin with mushrooms and apple fritters?" Henry patted his stomach. "Sounds good. If they have them, I'll order the same."

Not until she heard his translation did she realize she'd used the French words for the items. "Do you speak French, too?" She wasn't as fluent as she would have liked to be, but she'd learned some from her mother, who had emigrated with her family from the village of Saint-Omer in northern France when she was a girl. Lavinia's *grand-père* had turned his knowledge of glass-making into a lucrative business, leaving her mother with a sizable inheritance that had given her father his start.

"I learned some words that relate to cooking, but that's all."

Lavinia tossed a playful smile his way. "And here I thought there wasn't anything you didn't know."

He acknowledged her gentle teasing with a wink, a gesture that set her traitorous heart to tripping. "Since you're ready to go shopping, Mademoiselle Crowne, shall we begin?" He held out an arm, and she slipped her hands around it without hesitation.

They set off down the wooden walkway, their boot heels thudding in unison. She rarely strolled with a gentleman, but Henry wasn't like the potential suitors her father had sent her way, each of whom had hoped she'd take a shine to him. The men had known that her father was eager for her to choose a husband and male heir he could train to take over the running of his hotels. They'd all been well educated, hardworking and ambitious—like her father. The trouble was that they didn't care about her thoughts, her opinions or her dreams any more than he did. She wanted a man who cared about what she had to say and loved her for who she was, not for what he could gain by marrying her.

Henry and Lavinia spent the next hour exploring the shops. It took little time for her to see that the wares available in Jackson weren't much different from those in Sutter Creek. Surely, he was aware of that. If so, had he suggested the trip to make a point? No. That couldn't be it. He was a kind person and had been honest with her from the start about what he wanted and what he thought.

They reached the foot of Broadway, and she inclined her head toward a bench alongside Jackson Creek. "Could we stop for a minute? There's something I'd like to ask you."

"Sure." He led the way, and they sat facing each other. "What's on your mind?"

"Why did you offer to bring me here?"

"You wanted to go shopping somewhere other than Sutter Creek. This was the closest place."

"So there was no hidden motive?"

He shook his head, but whether to indicate a negative answer or in disbelief, she wasn't sure. She said nothing, patiently awaiting his response.

"If you want to know my reasons, I'll tell you. First, I hoped I might be able to help you choose things the children would like."

She worked to keep her tone as calm and as level as his. Not an easy task. "You don't think I could make the selections on my own?"

"Of course you could. I just thought that because I've known the children all their lives, you might welcome my insights."

"I see. And what insights might those be?"

He raised an eyebrow. "Are you sure you want to hear them?"

She nodded.

"Very well. You said you'd like to get a pair of red boots for Marcie. She already has a perfectly fine black pair that isn't but a few months old."

"But she admired my red ones."

"She did, but I think there are things she'd like more."

More than boots in her favorite color? Perhaps he didn't know Marcie as well as he thought. Girls loved fancy footwear. She always had. "Such as?"

"You're right about Marcie liking to look nice, but there are things more important to her than that. Think of what she likes to do most of all."

Lavinia shrugged. "She likes to talk."

Henry smiled. "Exactly. So, what could you give her that would enable her to talk *and* have people eager to listen to her?"

"I don't know, but apparently you do. What do you have in mind?"

"You picked one up in the mercantile and used it to ask me a question."

Understanding dawned, sending a ripple of surprise racing down her spine. "You're talking about that puppet, aren't you? Yes! That would be ideal. If I get her some puppets, she could put on plays for her friends— or even with them. She would love that." When they got back home, Lavinia could have a portion of the nursery turned into a stage, complete with red velvet curtains like those in a real theater.

Perhaps she'd been too quick to doubt Henry's motives. It seemed he did want to be helpful. "What about Alex? I don't have experience with boys."

"I think you know more than you realize. Tell me about him."

"Well, he's bright and inquisitive, but he's cautious, too."

Henry nodded his encouragement. "So, what might he like?"

She thought back through everything they'd seen in the shops, trying to remember what Henry had looked at, anything he'd said. "You asked the hardware store owner about a small block plane. Were you thinking Alex would like one?"

"I was. He spent an entire morning with me on the shed roof, listening and learning. I excused him soon after you and I talked that day, but he stayed and saw the job through, working alongside me the entire time and asking insightful questions. I think he has a knack for woodworking."

"But isn't he a bit young to have tools of his own?"

Henry's lips twitched, as though he was trying not to smile. "I was in the smithy working with Pa and Jack before I could even see over the forge."

"Why, you wouldn't have been much older than Dot. What could a child of four or five possibly do to help?"

"Plenty. I swept the shop floor, hung completed horse-shoes, hinges and other items on hooks and carried in coal from the shed out back. Alex is old enough for me to teach him basic carpentry skills. He'll have fun while learning a valuable skill."

"I can see that, but tools seem so…utilitarian."

Henry laughed, a hearty sound without a trace of censure. "Forgive me. It's just that men and tools go together like a baker and flour."

For rugged men like Henry, perhaps. Her father

wouldn't dream of hefting a hammer and didn't even own one, as far as she knew. He hired workmen for such tasks.

Just as he'd hired Jack and Henry to forge and install the iron work for the Royal Crowne Hotel. And then he'd disparaged Jack when Pauline had fallen in love with him as *a no-account smithy with more brawn than brains*.

How wrong her father had been. If he'd taken the time to get to know Jack and his family, he would have seen how hardworking they were and realized how clever Henry was, designing railings that elicited compliments from many, including her father himself.

She welcomed Henry's insights. He'd suggested gifts sure to please Alex and Marcie. She would get her nephew a nice selection of carpentry tools, and when they got back to Philadelphia, she would have a workshop built for him.

"Tools it is, then. And now for Dot. She's such a loving, nurturing child, doling out her hugs and kisses freely. I know she treasures that rag doll of hers, so I thought I'd get her a lovely porcelain doll like those my sister and I had when we were young."

"She does love that doll. Pauline made it for her. I can still remember Dot's squeal of delight when she saw it the first time."

Henry's faraway look and pensive expression gave Lavinia pause. "You don't think she'd appreciate a new doll, do you?"

He returned his attention to her. "She might, but I wonder how such a fragile toy would hold up. As you've seen, the children can be a boisterous bunch. How did the dolls you and Pauline had fare?"

A memory surfaced. She and Pauline hadn't been allowed to play with their dolls for fear they might break them. Their governess had forced Lavinia to sit in a chair whenever she held her doll, issuing a warning to be very careful. It had taken much of the fun away.

"You have a point. I'll get her the cute wicker baby cradle I saw, instead." It was small enough that Dot could keep it with her on board the ship. Gladys could make some dresses for the doll, too. Once they were back home, Lavinia would have a playhouse added to the nursery filled with child-sized furniture and a bed for Dot's beloved doll.

Henry's stomach rumbled. "Forgive me."

"You're hungry." She glanced at the watch pinned to her bodice. "I didn't realize what time it was. Shall we eat?"

He smiled. "I'd like that." He rose, offered her his arm and led the way to the restaurant.

The meal was delicious, even if they had to settle for *gâteau de pommes*, or apple cake, instead of beignets. As good as the food was, the conversation was even better. Henry made a delightful companion. If it weren't for the seemingly insurmountable obstacle between them, she might have been willing to think of him as a friend. When she penned him letters from Philadelphia with updates on the children, she would enjoy writing them and including anecdotes sure to make him smile as he was now.

Why *was* he smiling?

"You didn't hear a word I said, did you?"

She hadn't. She'd been too busy thinking about him. Heat crept into her cheeks. She fanned her face. "Does it feel warm in here to you?"

He grinned. "I've enjoyed the time with you, too."

Had she been that transparent? "I'm glad you suggested this place. Everything was delicious."

"I should see to the bill so you can complete your shopping now that you've made your decisions." He motioned for the waiter.

Henry's generosity meant a great deal to her given that his funds were limited. "Thank you for treating me to such a wonderful meal."

"I'm glad you enjoyed it. I certainly enjoyed the company." He winked at her.

They returned to the various shops, and she made her purchases. Henry carried the wicker cradle by the handles with two colorful puppets, a hammer and a small plane inside. She would see about getting the other items she wanted in Sutter Creek.

The return trip flew by with Henry recounting tales of his life out west. He was a wonderful storyteller and had her laughing many times. No wonder Pauline had spoken so highly of him in her letters.

He stopped the buggy in front of the house. "I'll help you down, hide your gifts at my place and come back to see how Marcie did on her history recitation today. I shouldn't be too long."

Lavinia went inside and was welcomed with a warm hug and smack on her cheek from Dot. The older children arrived a short time later and gathered around Lavinia in the parlor where she sat on one end of the settee, Dot on the other. Marcie regaled them with an animated account of the school day.

When the exuberant girl wound down, Alex, who sat cross-legged on the rug, looked up at Lavinia. "Did you have a nice time with Uncle Henry today?"

"I did." She smiled at the memory of a delightful outing. Although there had been a tense moment at the start when he'd questioned her decision to buy the children some clothes, their truce had enabled her to enjoy herself. He'd been supportive of her plans, which she appreciated. Perhaps he'd seen her willingness to accept his input as a good sign and was beginning to realize she wanted what was best for the children, too.

Marcie, seated beside her brother, did her best to feign disinterest by smoothing her skirts around her, but her sparkling eyes betrayed her. "Did the stores have what you were looking for, Aunt Livy?"

"If you mean, will there be presents for you on Christmas morning, the answer is yes."

Dot squealed. "Goody!"

Alex stood. "I'm going up to my room."

"Don't be gone long," Marcie said. "Uncle Henry will be back soon."

A mischievous look passed between the older children. Lavinia hoped they hadn't concocted a plan to sneak up on Gladys and startle her as they'd done the day before. The poor woman had been so surprised she'd yelped, launching Alex and Marcie into fits of laughter.

No sooner had Alex's footfalls faded than Henry's could be heard on the porch steps.

"He's here!" Marcie called out loudly. She jumped to her feet and rushed into the entryway.

Dot clambered off the settee and followed her sister. Giggling came from the top of the stairs.

Eager to make sure Gladys wasn't about to be ambushed, Lavinia followed, reaching the entryway just as Henry stepped inside.

The children were nowhere to be seen. Odd.

He stood facing her, his gaze on the upper landing. "I saw the girls dash up the stairs. What's going on?"

"I don't know, but I hope they're not plotting mischief."

His eyes, now focused on her, held amusement. "Our darling nieces and nephew plotting mischief? Whatever gave you that idea? It wouldn't be their little stunt yesterday, would it?" He sobered. "I didn't know they had it in them. Alex usually keeps Marcie in line."

"True, but I had the feeling the idea might have been his, as surprising as that seems. He was certainly acting strangely this morning, whispering with Marcie at breakfast, which makes me wonder what's going on."

"I'll have a word with him, man-to-man, and figure it out."

"I'd appreci—"

"Uncle Henry! Aunt Livy!" the children cried in unison. "Look up!"

She did. Alex, Marcie and Dot knelt on the stairway, peering through the bannister, each wearing an ear-to-ear grin. Alex gripped a long stick with a sprig of mistletoe tied to the other end, which he held above her head.

So that's what they'd been up to. She stepped to the left.

Alex moved the mistletoe with her, keeping it in position above her. "You can't get away this time."

She cast an apologetic glance at Henry, expecting to receive one in return. What she saw instead made her breath catch.

Henry was looking at her with unmistakable attraction glittering in his blue eyes. The sight sent a jolt of awareness through her.

"Kiss her," Marcie called out.

Wonder of wonders, Henry wanted to. Or so it appeared.

His gaze remained fixed on her face, moving from her eyes to her mouth, where it lingered for several seconds before he lifted it again.

He stepped closer, causing her heart to pick up its pace, and whispered. "It appears we can't escape this time. Do you trust me?"

The word *trust*, spoken with sincerity and his beautiful rolled *R* overcame her hesitation. She nodded.

He leaned toward her, coming so close his breath fanned her face.

Her eyes slid closed, as though of their own accord.

She waited, scarcely able to breathe, for the feel of his lips on hers.

Chapter Nine

Fully aware of the three pairs of eyes trained on him, Henry hovered a scant two inches from Lavinia's up-turned face. Her lips, soft and inviting, trembled, a movement so slight he might not have seen it if he hadn't been studying her so intently. Did she want this, or had she agreed solely for the sake of the children? She had reached up as if to brush his hair back in place when they were in the buggy. Although she'd stopped herself, her gesture had shown that she was drawn to him.

He couldn't take advantage of her or the situation, though. She deserved respect, and he would give it to her. He placed a kiss on her flushed cheek, lingering just long enough to feel the softness, inhale the rosy scent that would forever remind him of Lavinia and—hopefully—satisfy their eager audience. He drew back, bracing for her reaction.

She opened her eyes, blinked twice and averted her gaze. The corners of her mouth drooped momentarily, quickly replaced by a shy smile. If he didn't know better, he might think she was disappointed.

He looked up at the children, who made no move to hide their disappointment.

Alex withdrew the stick with the mistletoe, his expression glum. "You were supposed to kiss her."

"I did."

"But you kissed her cheek," Marcie countered. "That's not a real kiss."

Lavinia had turned away, as though unwilling to face him after what had transpired. "You've had your fun, children, so head into the kitchen for your snack, please."

As if on cue, Gladys appeared in the dining room doorway. "I've got some soft gingerbread waiting, fresh from the oven. Who would like some?"

"Me!" the children hollered in unison. They raced down the stairs and followed Gladys into the kitchen.

Henry inhaled the spicy scents of ginger, cinnamon and nutmeg that combined with the crisp pine from the evergreen boughs on the console table to create a festive atmosphere. He'd been too preoccupied earlier to notice anything but Lavinia. Although he'd spent the day with her, he'd rushed to get back to the house as quickly as possible after returning the buggy to the livery, eager to enjoy more of her company.

Arriving to discover that the children were up to more mistletoe mischief had come as a surprise. He ought to have been irritated or annoyed with them, but he wasn't. Truth be told, he'd thought about their previous prank several times since, wondering what might have happened if Lavinia had welcomed his kiss instead of stepping out from under the mistletoe. Thanks to his nephew's ingenuity, she hadn't been able to escape this time.

Henry smiled. Although brushing his lips across her

soft cheek wasn't as exciting as a real kiss would have been, he'd enjoyed the experience nonetheless.

There could never be anything between Lavinia and him, but he couldn't deny being attracted to her. After all, she was a beautiful woman. She was somewhat misguided when it came to what was best for the children, though, but she obviously loved them.

Thankfully, she'd welcomed his suggestions for gifts more in keeping with what Jack and Pauline had given the children in years past. Instead of filling a livery wagon with packages, as he'd expected, her purchases hadn't even filled the small storage space beneath the buggy's seat.

Lavinia turned toward him, wearing a shy smile. Pink still tinged her cheeks. "I haven't had a piece of gingerbread in ages. I'm going to have one. Would you care to join me?"

Her question drew him back to the present. "I would, but I have something for you first." As much as he wished he didn't have to make this delivery, he must. He reached in his jacket pocket and withdrew a letter. "Mr. Little was standing in front of the American House hotel as I walked by. He asked if I'd give this to you."

She stared at the envelope he held, her features taut. "I received mail? When?"

"Mr. Little said it arrived this morning while we were down in Jackson."

"I see." Her hand trembled as she reached for the letter. She took it, slowly turned it over and heaved a sigh of relief.

"What is it?"

"I was afraid it had come by Pony Express."

That could only mean one thing. She was afraid her

father had written. But why? "The postmark is from San Francisco."

He'd shoved the letter in his pocket before he could see anything more, but he hadn't needed to read the sender's name. He knew who it was from—Stuart Worthington, the young manager Paul Crowne had chosen to serve as Lavinia's escort on the trip west. The man she planned to have accompany her, Gladys and the children on their way back to Philadelphia.

Well, Worthington had a surprise in store. He would not be traveling with the children. They were staying in Sutter Creek where they belonged, with him—their uncle and legal guardian.

Lavinia wandered over to the staircase and plopped down on the second step. She removed a hairpin, slit the envelope with one of the two tortoise shell prongs and jabbed the pin back into her mass of curls with haste. "I wonder what he wants," she murmured.

"Why don't you open it and find out?"

She started. "Oh. I'm sorry. I forgot you were there."

"Would you like me to leave?"

"No. Please, stay." She shifted to the side and patted the space next to her.

He debated the wisdom of sitting so close, but it appeared she dreaded finding out what Worthington had to say. If she wanted support, Henry would provide it.

He sat on the step, careful to leave as much room between them as possible.

Lavinia glanced his way, her soft, steady gaze conveying her gratitude. She squared her shoulders, pulled out the sheet of paper, unfolded it and began reading. Her mouth gaped at the start, but before long her lips were pursed and her eyes narrowed. Troubling news, no doubt.

He fought the urge to pull her to his side and offer what comfort he could.

As she continued reading, her lovely features relaxed, easing the knot that had formed in his stomach. She clutched the letter to her chest, lifted her gaze to the ceiling and smiled. "Thank you, Stuart."

A burning sensation formed behind Henry's breastbone. He worked to slow his rapid breathing as he struggled to make sense of Lavinia's reaction. What was her relationship to this Worthington fellow anyhow? Was he more than just an escort?

Her smile fled almost as quickly as it had come, releasing the tension in Henry's chest. She set the letter in her lap and turned to him, her eyes filled with so many emotions he couldn't begin to sort through them. "It's going to be all right."

Even though she'd said the words to him, he got the impression she was out to convince herself. "Is there anything I can do to help?"

She shook her head, causing several curls to break free from the hairpin she'd shoved in earlier. It came loose and clattered onto the step at Henry's feet. He picked up the fancy thing and studied it. The silver crown at the top boasted several diamonds, accounting for the sparkle. A single pearl formed the point. He didn't want to think about what a single pin cost, let alone the half dozen she wore.

He held out the hairpin. "Here you go."

She took it, gathered the loose curls with one hand and inserted the pin with the other. Her attempt left several springy locks dangling over her right temple. She extended her lower lip and blew a breath out the corner, causing the curls to dance. "Oh, bother. I can't do this without a looking glass."

"Would you like me to try?" The words had rushed out before he could stop them, but he couldn't very well take them back. He had no right to make such an offer and deserved the laughter sure to come.

But it didn't. Instead, Lavinia pulled out the hairpin and handed it to him. "Please." She glanced at the doorway to the dining room, as though assuring herself no one was privy to their conversation, and spoke in hushed tones. "Don't tell anyone, but even with a looking glass, I have a hard time taming my mane. Gladys has offered to help, but I figure it's high time I learn to do some things for myself. I'm happy to say I've made progress, but I won't turn down your kind offer."

He'd asked Pauline once, shortly after he'd arrived in California, what it was like not to have servants seeing to her every need. She'd admitted she missed the pampering but said the sense of independence she'd gained more than made up for it. It appeared Lavinia was experiencing a similar revelation. "You might regret accepting my help when you see my handiwork. Now, sit nice and still so I don't poke you with this thing."

He'd never helped a woman with her hair before. Why he'd offered to do so now was a mystery he'd unravel later. The task required him to focus.

Although Lavinia's silky curls seemed determined to elude his clumsy fingers, he managed to corral them with one hand long enough to slide the hairpin in place with the other, careful not to graze her scalp.

She patted the spot and nodded. "That's better. Thank you, Henry."

He'd never been overly fond of his name, but he liked

the way she said it, swallowing the *H* slightly and removing the choppiness by flowing the *N* into the *R*. No doubt that was the result of having learned French at an early age. "You're welcome."

She picked up the letter and read it again.

As much as he'd like to know what was in it, he refused to pry. "I think I'll get some of that gingerbread before the children devour it." He stood.

"My father wants me to leave sooner than was originally planned."

"What?" He plopped back down.

"He sent a letter by Pony Express. To Stuart. In this letter he relays Father's wishes. It seems South Carolina is expected to announce its intention to secede very soon, making travel a risk. Stuart checked on the departures. The Sonora is scheduled to leave San Francisco December twenty-first, and Father expects us to be on it."

Dread settled in Henry's stomach like an anvil. "But he agreed to let you stay until Christmas."

"He did, and I will. Stuart knows how important it is to me not to uproot the children before then."

Uproot the children. How could she say the words so calmly? Had she thought about what she intended to do, or was she simply carrying out her father's wishes? Pauline had stood up to the man, but from what Henry had seen, Lavinia rarely did, which concerned him. How would she fare when she returned to Philadelphia without the children? What price would she have to pay? If only there was some way to spare her the punishment Paul Crowne was sure to mete out.

"So you don't plan to leave ahead of schedule?" *Please, Lord, let that be the case. I'd like as much time as possible to show her that the children will be better off here and make the parting a little easier on her.*

"Stuart did some more checking and discovered that the Golden Age won't sail until January first. He took the liberty of telling my father that's the one we'll be taking."

Had he heard correctly? "Mr. Worthington made the decision without consulting you?"

She lifted her head in regal fashion, her chin thrust forward, and assumed the imperious air he hadn't seen since she'd first arrived and had stated her intention to take the children away from him. "Stuart and I have talked over the matter at great length. He's aware of my wishes."

Henry's stomach pitched. "I didn't realize the two of you were so close."

Why it mattered, he didn't know. But it did.

A wave of nausea washed over him as he waited for her response.

Why Henry's observation bothered her, Lavinia didn't know. But it did.

Her relationship with Stuart wasn't something she wanted to explain or defend. She preferred not to think about it at all. Her father had put forth so many potential suitors over the years that she'd grown weary of the process. Stuart might be the latest one foisted on her, but he didn't make her heart beat faster the way Henry did.

No. She mustn't think about Henry in that way.

He sat beside her awaiting a reply. His curiosity was understandable. After all, Stuart would be accompanying Alex and the girls back to Philadelphia, provided she removed the hurdle of Henry's guardianship in time.

She'd been praying, eagerly awaiting the Lord's guidance, but she had yet to discover anything that could serve as grounds for successfully contesting the will. Not that she'd given up. She wouldn't. She *couldn't*. Returning without the children wasn't an option.

There had to be a way to have the will invalidated and Henry's roles as executor and guardian revoked, and she would find it. She reviewed her notes on the statutes regularly, so she was familiar with them. She'd written Stuart, asking for referrals to the best lawyers in San Francisco. She'd find one who would take her case, come to Amador Country for the trial and—despite Mr. Price's doubts that it was possible to do so—win.

"As I told you the day you pulled that limb off me, Stuart works for my father. He traveled with Gladys and me all the way to Sutter Creek, but he returned to San Francisco right away."

"I take it he has business there."

"That's correct." Was it her imagination, or did Henry look relieved? "Father's heard the city is on its way to becoming the cultural center of the West. He asked Stuart to explore the possibility of opening a hotel there—the Golden Crowne."

"So would Mr. Worthington oversee the project?"

"Not that I know of." She could see why Henry might think that, given what she'd said so far. "Stuart believes Father is testing him to see if he has the skills and expertise needed to make an accurate assessment and formulate a plan. He's already proven his ability to manage a hotel, but establishing one isn't a task Father has delegated before. He's always seen to that himself, but he believes the time has come to train a successor."

"And he's considering Mr. Worthington." Henry was

quick to grasp the situation, but he didn't look happy about it. There was a firm set to his mouth.

"He is." She focused on the carpet runner lest Henry see the pain she had a hard time hiding when she thought about her father's insistence that she marry a man of his choosing, an heir to take over his hotel empire. Other than announcing her intention to attend Jack and Pauline's wedding and her plan to travel to California after learning of their deaths, Lavinia had only faced off with her father one other time. Over this very issue.

It had been a dark, dreary day not long after Pauline had moved away. Lavinia could remember it in vivid detail—the ticking of the mantel clock, the scent of her father's pipe tobacco, the jellylike state of her knees. She'd stood before his desk with her backbone as stiff as his ebony walking stick and stated in no uncertain terms that she resented his interference in her romantic relationships. Although she hadn't yet turned seventeen, he'd already begun to introduce her to men he deemed suitable.

"I gather from the heat flashing in those dark eyes of yours that you don't like the idea of Mr. Worthington at the helm."

She hadn't been looking at Henry, but apparently he'd been watching her. With effort, she schooled her features. At least she hoped she had, but remaining calm while discussing one of the most difficult days of her life wasn't easy. Her chest had been so tight that morning in her father's study that she had feared she'd swoon. The only thing that had kept her from doing so was the thought of her father disparaging her for being a *feeble female*. Any show of weakness opened her to his ridicule, and she couldn't abide that.

One day, she would earn her father's favor and no longer fear him speaking ill of her as he had her bright, beautiful sister. Until that day came, Lavinia would choose her battles carefully.

"I think Stuart would do a wonderful job running the business." That was the problem. Of all the men her father had sent her way, Stuart was the only one she believed to be up to the task.

Henry studied her, as though trying to figure out what she dreaded putting into words. "But…?"

"There's more to it than that." A great deal more. She twirled an escaped curl around her finger and was reminded of Henry's clumsy but kind attempt to put her hair to rights. Why she'd accepted his offer to replace her hairpin, she didn't know. Perhaps it was because they'd agreed to set aside their differences down in Jackson. She couldn't remember ever having enjoyed spending time with a gentleman as much as she had with Henry. He was funny and kind and—

He was staring at her, his eyebrows raised, clearly waiting for her to elaborate.

She drew in a fortifying breath and forged ahead. "Before Father will accept a man as his successor, that man must first become his legal heir."

Henry's eyebrows shot even higher and then dived into a *V*—whether from concern or disapproval, she couldn't tell. "Are you saying Mr. Worthington is your intended?"

"Not at the present, but…" She chose her words carefully. Henry harbored enough animosity toward her father as it was. "Father and I made an agreement years ago when he first began thinking about who would take over his company should he become unable to oversee things himself. He can suggest men he'd like me to consider as prospective suitors, but I have the final say on which one of them I will accept."

Henry raked a hand through his hair, leaving his wavy locks disheveled. Instinctively, she reached up and smoothed his tousled hair as she'd wanted to do earlier that day. She pulled her hand back quickly, but he caught it and twined his fingers with hers.

He gazed into her eyes, his own filled with unmistakable concern. "Are you saying your father planned to choose your husband for you?"

She withdrew her hand, hid it beneath the folds of her skirt and rushed to her father's defense. "It's not uncommon. Some of my friends' marriages were arranged by their parents."

"I know it's done, but I'm glad you aren't willing to settle for that."

She wasn't, but earning that right hadn't been easy. Father had fumed before sending her away. Five agonizing days had passed before he'd relented—with stipulations.

Henry lifted her chin with a fingertip, not removing it until she looked at him. "You aren't reconsidering, are you?"

"Not that's it's any business of yours, but when I marry, I fully intend it to be a love match." She hadn't meant for her reply to have an edge to it, but Henry's questions were forcing her to revisit a topic that triggered painful memories.

"What if the man who claims your heart doesn't meet with your father's approval?"

Standing before her father's desk, she'd asked him the same question when he'd called her into his office to give her his answer. He leaned back in his large leather chair, hands behind his head, and told her in no uncertain terms what would happen if she chose to marry a man who wasn't one of those he sent her way. She knew all too well he'd meant what he'd said.

"That won't be a problem since I only spend time with men he considers suitable."

"You might have gained a small measure of freedom, but your evasiveness tells me there's more to the story. What's to keep you from enjoying the company of gentlemen of your own choosing?"

His probing question tapped into the sense of unfairness she'd battled for years and loosened her tongue. "Not that it's any of your business, but I went along with Father's wishes because it's important to me to remain in his good graces. I refuse to suffer the rejection my sister did. He said terrible things about Pauli—"

She clamped her right hand over her mouth, turned away and gripped a baluster with her left. The wrought iron was cool to the touch, a contrast to her heated state. She'd dropped her guard and had told Henry far too much.

The murmur of the children's voices in the kitchen carried, punctuated by Dot's laughter. At least someone was having a good time.

"Lavinia? Please, talk to me."

As much as wanted to ignore Henry, she couldn't. She released the railing and forced herself to look at him.

The compassion in his eyes seemed genuine. "I'm sorry. I didn't mean to upset you. I was just trying to make sense of things."

She focused on the toes of her forest green boots peeking from beneath her skirts. "I'm the one who's sorry. I shouldn't have lashed out like that."

"It's understandable. I pushed you too hard, but I have a better understanding now."

"Father means well." Surely, he did. He just had a strange way of showing it.

Henry cleared his throat, drawing her attention to him and the tightness of his fine features. "I take it Mr. Worthington has met with your father's approval, given that he consented to have him serve as your escort."

"He didn't have to consent. Having Stuart accompany me was his idea, not mine."

No! She'd done it again, speaking too soon and saying too much.

The tension in Henry's face eased, giving her the impression he'd been battling jealousy, which made no sense. The children had given him the opportunity to kiss her, but he hadn't taken it. Not that she'd wanted him to. Well, perhaps the impulsive part of her had, but the sensible part knew better than to encourage him.

She gave herself a mental shake and changed the subject. "Gladys and I have chosen the desserts she'll be preparing for the Christmas party. Would you like to see the list?"

"Sure."

"It's in the parlor. I'll get it and meet you in the kitchen."

Lavinia hopped up, retrieved her notebook from the desk and stepped into the entryway just as someone rapped on the front door. She opened it. "Oh, Mr. Staples. What a surprise. I thought you'd be over at your shop."

"My brother's handling things for me."

"I see. Well, please, come in."

"Thank you." The grocer stepped inside, clutching his hat by the brim and spinning it 'round and 'round.

"What can I do for you?"

"I wondered if I might have a word with Gladys. If it's not too much trouble, that is," he added quickly.

Mr. Staples had never struck her as nervous before. "Is everything all right?"

"It's fine, Miss Crowne. Better than fine. Leastwise, I think it is. I'll know more when I talk with Gladys."

"I hope nothing's come up to change your plans to take her riding Saturday. She's looking forward to it."

The portly man's smile was as broad as it was unexpected. "Oh, I'll be taking her riding, all right, but if she'll have me, I aim to marry her first."

Lavinia's notebook slipped from her hands and hit the floor with a thud.

How could she manage without Gladys?

Chapter Ten

Two days had passed since Mr. Staples had made his startling announcement, and yet Lavinia was still grappling with the news. The kindly grocer had apologized profusely about the timing of the wedding and honeymoon trip, but he was taking advantage of the unexpected visit from his brother, who had agreed to watch the shop in his absence. Having been cheated by a clerk in years past, Mr. Staples wouldn't leave his shop in the care of anyone but a trusted family member. Since his brother would be heading to the new state of Oregon the day after Christmas and wouldn't be back in Sutter Creek for another year, Mr. Staples had seized the opportunity to marry the woman who had him smiling like a schoolboy.

Although Lavinia understood the grocer's situation, it complicated hers. She'd been counting on Gladys to prepare the desserts for the party. But her departure would give Lavinia an opportunity to show the community—and Henry—that she could cope with challenges. That would serve to strengthen her case when it went to court.

She shook off her concerns. This was Gladys's day, and she deserved to be happy.

The first time Lavinia had seen a bride beaming at her groom was the day Pauline had stood at the back of the small church the Hawthorn family attended and gotten her first glimpse of Jack standing beside the minister, waiting for her to walk down the aisle to him. It appeared Gladys was just as smitten with Mr. Staples. The skies might be overcast that Saturday morning, but the grocer's bride-to-be was radiant.

Lavinia adjusted the simple veil she'd fashioned for Gladys the day before and turned her around so she could see herself in the mirror over Lavinia's bureau. "If I'd had more time, I would have seen to it that you had a lovely wedding dress to go with this, but the emerald gown you're wearing draws attention to your striking green eyes."

Gladys gazed at her reflection with wonder, fingering the soft tulle that flowed around her in a cloudlike mist. "I could be wearing a flour sack for all I care. I thank the good Lord for bringing Emery into my life. I'd given up hope of getting married years ago, but that didn't stop me from wanting to find a feller. At my age, I would have been happy with companionship, but God's given me a man who adores me. I can be a mite prickly at times, but Emery said I just needed someone willing to peel back the layers." Her laugh, although rusty, was a welcome sound.

"It's easy to see how much he loves you. His eyes light up when you walk in the room, but we need something that will make his chin drop when he sees you at the top of the stairs. I have just the thing." Lavinia opened her jewelry box and pulled out the strand of pearls Gladys had often admired. "I wasn't able to get you a wedding present, so consider this my gift to you. Let's see how the necklace looks on you."

Gladys shook her head, threatening to dislodge her veil. "I can't accept that. It's far too generous."

Lavinia kept her tone light and playful. "Now, don't go robbing me of my joy. You've been making me look good for years. It's my turn to do something for you." She slipped the string of pearls around Gladys's neck before she could protest further and clasped it. "There. You look lovely."

The giddy bride whirled around and pulled Lavinia into a hug, a display of affection so unlike Gladys and so unexpected that Lavinia had to take a step back to keep from losing her balance. "You're too kind, Miss Lavinia. I'm going to miss you."

She returned the embrace. "I'll miss you, too." Gladys had been more than a servant. She'd become a friend, although her work with the children had been a huge help. Without her, Lavinia would be hard-pressed to care for them. Her fledgling cooking skills would hardly suffice. She'd only helped with the laundry once and had yet to attempt ironing. Henry, with his vast array of knowledge, could probably tackle those tasks and more. She didn't want to think about what that did to her chances of becoming the children's guardian.

Gladys released Lavinia, pulled a handkerchief from her sleeve and swiped at her glistening eyes. "Look at me, getting all weepy."

"You have nothing to worry about. Mr. Staples is a good man."

"I know that, but I feel like I've let you down. I never intended to have my head turned. It all happened so fast."

"Everything will work out." It would, provided Lavinia could locate a new housekeeper right away. "There's one last thing I want to do before we take our places. You ought to smell as good as you look." She reached for the perfume bottle on her dressing table and handed it to Gladys.

She removed the stopper and inhaled deeply. "Otto of Roses. My favorite. Thank you again, Miss Lavinia." She dabbed some of the fragrant perfume behind each ear and on both wrists, replaced the cork and returned the bottle to the dressing table.

The scent of roses filled the air, a reminder of the grounds around Lavinia's home back east. What fun she would have watching the children explore them. They thought their house and yard were large, which they were by Sutter Creek standards, but wait until they saw the gardens around her father's house. She could imagine them playing hide-and-seek in the neatly trimmed hedgerows as she and Pauline had done when they were young.

Sadly, it being December, there were no flowers blooming in the beds around Jack and Pauline's house, so Gladys wouldn't have a bouquet. She'd said it didn't matter, but Lavinia had searched for silk flowers in the shops on Main Street nonetheless. Unfortunately, they weren't in high demand in a town where men made up eighty percent of the population.

A familiar male voice from the entryway below, where the small ceremony would take place, signaled the arrival of the minister. With the help of Norma's husband, Henry had wheeled in the piano from the parlor and was ready to play Mendelssohn's "Wedding March."

Lavinia checked the watch pinned to her bodice. "It's almost time. I'll see to your veil." She lifted the shorter section of tulle over Gladys's head and covered her face. "Are you ready?"

"Oh, yes. I've dreamed of this day for decades."

"I'll go first, and—"

"Aunt Livy!" Marcie's urgent voice on the other side of the door gave Lavinia pause.

Please, Lord. Let everything go as planned for Gladys's sake. She yanked open the door. All three children were there, looking quite pleased with themselves. Marcie's hands were behind her back.

"What is it?"

Alex opened his mouth to answer, but Marcie beat him to it. "Dot told us you couldn't find any flowers for Miss Gladys in the shops, so we made something else. It's green like her dress." Marcie revealed what she'd been hiding—an artfully arranged bouquet comprised of greenery, including cedar boughs, rosemary stems and mistletoe sprigs. A trio of pinecones were interspersed, making the resulting creation delightful.

Lavinia took the bouquet from her niece. "This is beautiful. How did you manage it?"

This time Alex offered the explanation before Marcie could. "We found everything in the yard, and we asked Miss Norma to help us put it together."

If only they hadn't felt the need to include mistletoe. They did seem to have a fondness for it, though. "You climbed the oak tree again, didn't you? Please tell me you were careful."

"I was, Aunt Livy," Alex assured her. "I did everything just the way Uncle Henry showed me and didn't go too high, but that's the only way to get to the mistletoe."

The thought of Alex up a tree made Lavinia queasy, but Henry had assured her everything would be all right, since Alex had agreed not to go all the way to the top. It appeared she had a great deal to learn about raising a boy. "Well, you children did a fine job. This bouquet is lovely. Don't you agree, Gladys?" She handed it to her housekeeper—her *former* housekeeper, she mentally corrected herself.

"Yes, Miss Lavinia. This bouquet is lovely. Thank you all." She smiled at the children. "I'll be right proud to carry it."

"Alex, Marcie, Dot, come here, please!" Henry called from below. "It's time."

They scurried down the stairs with a thundering of boot heels, as though it were an ordinary day and they wore regular clothes instead of their Sunday best.

Gladys sighed. "Those young'uns can be a handful, but they add spice to life. It wouldn't be the same around here if you whisked them away. Folks would miss them something fierce, especially Mr. Henry. Have you thought about that?"

She had. Many times. "I'll write and let him know how they're doing."

"That's not the same, and you know it."

Apparently, Gladys felt free to speak her mind now that she was no longer an employee. "You know my reasons better than anyone. I can offer the children much more than they have here."

"So you've said, but just make sure you're doing the right thing." Gladys patted Lavinia's arm and smiled. "I know I am. It's time for me to marry that wonderful man who's waiting for me. Go on now. I'll be right behind you. Don't dawdle, Miss Lavinia, or I'll be likely to clip your heels in my hurry. I've waited so long for this day and am as giddy as a schoolgirl." Despite being a more mature bride than most, Gladys was every bit as jubilant as any of Lavinia's young friends whose weddings she'd attended.

What would it be like to have a man love her, faults and all, as Mr. Staples did Gladys, and to love him in return? She might be the daughter of a successful hotelier who sent eligible men her way, but in her experience, they were just out to become Paul Crowne's successor and heir. One day, the Lord willing, she'd meet a man who valued her for who she was and not what he could gain by marrying her.

She roused herself from her musings. This was Gladys's day, and although her marriage complicated things, Lavinia couldn't be happier for her friend because, at the heart of it, that's what Gladys was.

"Since you no longer work for me, feel free to call me Lavinia."

Gratitude shone from Gladys's green eyes. "If you're sure, I'd be honored to… Lavinia."

"Quite sure. I'll be on my way now."

Lavinia stood on the upper landing and gazed at the small gathering below. Mr. Staples stood at the front with his brother beside him. The grocer, who'd closed his shop for the occasion, had invited a few friends, and Norma's family was there, as were Henry and the children.

"There's Aunt Livy!" Dot called out. "Doesn't she look pretty? I picked out her dress." The darling girl had chosen a ruby-red silk that was one of Lavinia's favorites. Although not a color a bridesmaid would wear under normal circumstances, Gladys had pronounced it a fitting choice, saying it would go well with her green one and lend the wedding a Christmas feel.

Alex hushed Dot, but Lavinia barely registered the interruption. She was drawn to Henry, who stood beside the piano in hushed conversation with one of the guests. He wore his cutaway coat, as he had at Thanksgiving, and looked more handsome than ever. He turned, saw her and froze, his lips parted. For a fleeting moment, she imagined what it would be like to walk down the aisle to a fine man like him.

A memory of Pauline walking to Jack, her face aglow, flashed through Lavinia's mind. Her father had spurned her sister because of her choice, though. Lavinia couldn't endure that. With her mother and Pauline gone, her father was all she had left. He was counting on her to carry out his wishes. Even though getting guardianship of the children was proving to be more difficult than she'd thought, she wouldn't let him down.

Henry sent her an appreciative smile and took his place at the piano. She waited for the music to begin, realizing too late that she hadn't asked him what he'd be playing as she descended. If anyone could come up with something fitting, however, he could. She'd learned during their caroling practices that he could hear a piece twice and pick it up. As if that wasn't enough, he had a repertoire unlike anyone she'd ever known.

The first notes floated to her, causing her breath to hitch. He'd chosen a familiar tune by a fellow Scotsman, "O, My Love's Like a Red, Red Rose." She could recite every word of Robert Burns's beloved poem. But why had Henry picked that song out of the many he knew? Could it be that he'd seen her in her red dress, been struck by her appearance and—

What was she thinking? He'd obviously chosen the romantic piece in honor of Gladys and Mr. Staples, celebrating their newfound love.

Despite her racing heart, Lavinia descended the stairs with no mishaps and stood by the minister, with Mr. Staples and his brother on the opposite side. Gladys glided down next, her eyes locked on her adoring groom.

The ceremony, although brief, affected Lavinia deeply. If Gladys could find love later in life, there was hope for Lavinia. One day, if it was God's will, she would gaze at her new husband with adoration just as Gladys was gazing at Mr. Staples.

The minister pronounced the couple man and wife. Mr. Staples gave Gladys such an ardent kiss afterward that the dear woman's cheeks turned as red as Lavinia's dress.

Dot giggled. A mysterious look passed between Alex and Marcie. What were those two up to now? Lavinia wasn't sure she wanted to know. She glanced at the doorways off the entryway. Other than the mistletoe in Gladys's bouquet, there was none to be seen.

The men rushed forward to congratulate Mr. Staples while Lavinia hurried over to Gladys and grasped her hand. "I'm thrilled for you, Mrs. Staples."

Dot appeared at Lavinia's left, Alex and Marcie on her right.

"Do we have to call her Mrs. Staples now?" Marcie asked.

Gladys responded before Lavinia could. "I had a talk with your uncle, and he said it would be all right for you to call me Grandma S, if you'd like. Mr. Staples could be Grandpa S."

Dot clapped her hands. "Goody! We've never had a grandma and grandpa before."

The floor under Lavinia's feet seemed to shift. "How did that happen?" Henry's choice would make it even harder on the children when she gained custody and took them away.

"I mentioned to Henry how happy I was to marry but let it slip that I would miss the children when—"

"No!" Lavinia exclaimed. If the children learned about her plans to take them back to Philadelphia with her before she and Henry had come to an agreement, things could get complicated in a hurry.

Gladys smiled sweetly. "It's all right, my dear. I was just going to say that I'll miss them when I get back to town and am living in Mr. Staples's house. That's all. There's no need to say anything else, is there?" Her words were innocent enough, but Lavinia detected an unspoken message. Had Gladys chosen to take Henry's side regarding the guardianship? They had spent a good deal of time together. He'd even figured out how to make her laugh.

"Everything's fine." Lavinia resisted the urge to fan herself with her hand. The room had grown warm all of a sudden. She needed to get out of there. She raised her voice. "Ladies and gentlemen, if I could have your attention!"

The buzz of conversations ceased. "In honor of Mr. and Mrs. Staples's marriage, we have refreshments for you in the parlor. Feel free to help yourselves." Gladys had offered to make the desserts herself, but Henry had overheard her and insisted on doing the baking. He'd spent most of yesterday filling the house with mouth-watering scents.

The guests joined the happy couple around tables laden with tempting treats. Henry had seen to it that there was a nice selection. If he wanted, he could open a bakery and make a success of it. Lavinia sighed. Was there anything he couldn't do?

Henry remained behind, moving the chairs the guests had used during the ceremony back into the dining room. Lavinia followed him and waited until the last of the chairs was in place. "Could we talk?"

"Now? There's a wedding reception taking place across the way." He inclined his head toward the parlor.

"It won't take long. Gladys said you told the children they could call her and her husband, grandma and grandpa."

"I take it you don't like the idea."

She didn't. It would be hard enough for the children to say goodbye to their friends as it was. Having to leave behind a set of honorary grandparents would make the parting even more difficult. "They already have a grand-father."

Henry gripped the back of the chair he'd just set in its place, drew in a breath and released it slowly. His tone was firm but kind. "They do, but he's shown no interest in them before now. I realize he expects you to return with them, but I have to ask myself, why now, after all this time?"

"He wants to get to know them, to give them opportunities they don't have here."

"Perhaps, but he doesn't know what they have here, and he doesn't want to. You do. You've seen how happy they are. Taking them away isn't the answer, Lavinia." He closed the distance between them and looked into her eyes, his gaze tender but probing. "Deep down, you know that. You must."

Thinking clearly grew difficult when he was so close, so caring, so…captivating. She struggled to come up with a strong argument. "I know you believe they're better off here. That making wreaths, singing carols and skating in their stockings is enough. But there's more to life than that. California is in its infancy. There are those who expect great things to happen here someday, but those things are available back east right now. My father can see that the children have access to the best our country has to offer. You want that for them, don't you?"

A burst of childish laughter in the parlor put a smile on Henry's face. Marcie's, if Lavinia wasn't mistaken. Henry glanced at the doorway and back at her. His expression and his voice softened, almost like a caress, even though he hadn't touched her. "I want them to be happy. I want the same for you, but I don't think taking the children back to your father's house is the answer. You've been happy here. It's given you an opportunity to break free, to see what you're capable of."

She wasn't sure about herself, but he was capable of muddling her mind, making her question things she'd taken for granted. She was happy. Wasn't she? She had a good life back home, and she could offer the children the same. She must keep her goal in mind. "California has more to offer than I would have thought, but it's all the children have known. If they could see Philadelphia for themselves, they might appreciate it just as much. There were things you liked about it, weren't there?"

"Since my parents passed on shortly after Jack and Pauline's wedding, I can honestly say that everything I want is right here in Sutter Creek."

His statement, uttered with those softly rolled *R*'s and such sincerity, filled her with hope. Was Henry letting her know that he liked having her here? Or was she just hearing what she wanted to hear? She'd have to give that some thought later, but what she needed now was to steer the conversation in a new direction before he figured out the effect he had on her. "Well, I'm here now, and I intend to see that the children have a good Christmas. My party should go a long way to making that happen."

Henry took a step back, breaking the delightful sense of connection she'd felt with him. "How are things coming with that?"

"Just fine." She wasn't about to tell him that no one had responded to the advertisement she'd tacked up at the mercantile seeking a housekeeper. It had only been two days, though. She planned to talk with the ladies after the church service tomorrow. Surely, they would know if any of the womenfolk in town were seeking employment.

"Have you heard from the puppet company?"

She'd sent two letters but had yet to receive a reply. "I expect an answer Monday."

"Let me know if you don't get one. I mentioned the possibility of performing to my ventriloquist friend, and he said he'd be interested."

"I appreciate the offer, but I don't think that will be necessary." If she was to convince the children that she could offer them a life unlike anything they'd ever imagined, she needed to do this on her own.

The clearing of a throat drew her attention. One of the guests stood in the doorway. Lavinia couldn't recall his name, but she remembered Mr. Staples saying that he was a banker. She'd never met him before, having only dealt with the teller.

Thankfully, Henry took charge. "Was there something you needed, Mr. Nichols?"

"I noticed you two were alone, so I wanted to take this opportunity to speak with you."

"Is something wrong?" The concern in Henry's tone didn't bode well.

"I'd like you to come into my office Monday to talk about the mortgage payment."

"What mortgage?" Henry asked. "Jack owned his shop outright."

"It's not the smithy I'm talking about. It's the house."

Henry threw up his hands in shock. "No! You must be mistaken."

The dread in his voice sent a chill racing through Lavinia. "Are you certain, Mr. Nichols? I don't recall hearing anything about a mortgage."

"I'm sorry." The banker took a step back. "I can see this has come as a surprise. If you'll stop by my office Monday, we can sort things out then."

"We'll be there." She nodded, and Mr. Nichols left.

Henry paced the length of the room three times and came to a stop before her, his breathing rapid and his hands clenched at his sides. "This makes no sense. Jack never said a word about taking out a loan."

"Pauline never mentioned anything in her letters either. Perhaps there's been a misunderstanding. You didn't find anything to that effect in Jack's files, did you?"

Henry shook his head. "I didn't look."

She kept her voice low, her tone free of accusation. Letting him know that she was watching his every move, seeking grounds to challenge him in court, could undermine her efforts. "They've been gone three months, but you haven't looked through his desk?"

He dropped into a chair and raked his fingers through his hair. "I should have. I meant to. I even tried several times, but..." A red flush crept up his neck as he stared at the rug.

Despite her eagerness to find enough material to convince a lawyer to take on her case, her heart went out to Henry. She'd been so focused on helping the children deal with their grief that she hadn't thought about what he was going through. She pulled out a chair and sat facing him. "It's all right. We'll do it together. Tonight, after the children are in bed."

She waited for him to speak, the merriment in the parlor a sharp contrast to the silence in the dining room. Several seconds passed before he responded. When he finally did, his voice was thick. "Thank you for the offer. I appreciate it. And if you need my help with the party, what with Gladys being gone and all, you'll let me know, won't you?"

"Of course." Not that she had any intention of taking him up on his offer. This was her opportunity to make an impression on the children, as well as the townspeople, and earn some goodwill. That could come in handy if she found herself facing a jury comprised of locals, which seemed more likely, thanks to the banker's revelation.

She'd prayed for grounds to have Henry's rights as executor and guardian revoked. If what Mr. Nichols had said was true and there was an outstanding mortgage, she might have found just what she needed to secure representation and build a case.

For some reason, that didn't make her as happy as she'd expected.

Chapter Eleven

"Take all the time you need, Henry." Norma cast a glance at the two girls playing in her parlor and smiled. "Yvonne welcomes any opportunity to spend time with Dot."

"Thanks." He didn't like to take advantage of their neighbor's generosity, but with Gladys married and off on her honeymoon with Mr. Staples, and Lavinia already downtown on an errand of some sort, Henry had no choice. He couldn't take a four-year-old to a business meeting. Not that he wanted to go at all.

The weekend had flown by. Normally, he looked forward to Monday and the start of a new week filled with opportunities and adventures, but he wasn't looking forward to what Mr. Nichols had to say.

Even though a search of Jack's desk hadn't resulted in the discovery of mortgage papers, that didn't mean they didn't exist. The banker had spoken with certainty after Gladys's wedding, his startling message having clenched Henry's stomach.

Lavinia had tackled the hunt for the documents with determination and her usual thoroughness, searching every closet, cupboard and bureau in the house. She must be as eager to disprove Mr. Nichols as he was. A man could do well with an ally like her.

And speaking of Lavinia, she'd be waiting at the bank for him, and she valued punctuality. He'd best hustle.

Henry arrived on Main Street just as Lavinia stepped out of the mercantile. Her shoulders sagged, and she shook her head.

He strode after her, catching up to her as she neared the bank. "Lavinia."

She stopped and turned his way. "Oh, good. You're not there yet. I was afraid I was going to be late."

He stifled a smile. Evidently, she'd been baking. "Looks like you tangled with some flour. I'll take care of it for you." He brushed her cheek, removing the powdery streak. Her skin was soft, her eyes wide. He stared at his hand, which he had yet to remove, and jerked it away.

"Did you get it all?" Her question came out whisper soft.

"I believe so. You look lovely."

Lovely? What had come over him? First, he'd let his big ol' paw linger, and then he'd opened his mouth, spouting words he hadn't meant to utter. She was a beautiful woman, though. He smiled every time he thought about her standing at the top of the stairs in that red gown, waiting to come down before Gladys had. Lavinia had so captivated him that he'd begun playing one of the Scottish tunes his father had taught him when he was a wee lad. She'd looked as surprised by his choice as he'd been.

"Thank you. We should be going." She set off down the plank walkway at a brisk pace, her boot heels tapping out a staccato beat.

He matched his stride to hers. "Is everything all right? You were frowning when you came out of the shop."

"I've had a bit of a setback regarding the party. That's all."

"I'm sorry. Is there anything I can do?"

"I appreciate the offer, but you've already done so much. I'm sure things will work out."

Her independence was an admirable trait, but one that made it difficult for her to accept help. "Let me know if you change your mind."

She nodded but said nothing.

They reached the bank moments later and went inside.

"Welcome. I've been expecting you." Mr. Nichols crossed the lobby, extended his hand and shook Henry's. Lavinia offered hers, and the banker shook it as well. "Let's go to my office, shall we?" He swept an arm toward the doorway beside the teller's cage.

Lavinia perched on the flowery armless chair in front of the banker's expansive desk, looking every bit the elegant lady she was, despite the fleck of flour Henry had missed. He took a seat in the supple leather wingback chair. The well-appointed room smelled of furniture polish, India ink and money.

Mr. Nichols plopped down on his centripetal spring armchair, a clever creation on wheels that had Henry imagining what it would take to forge an intricate design like that. The banker reached into a drawer and pulled out a document and ledger. He flipped open the latter, thumbed through it until he came to the page he was after and set a paperweight on the opposite one to keep the book open to that spot.

Henry's stomach pitched when he read the words *Hawthorn Mortgage* at the top of the page. Despite having found nothing in the house to indicate Jack having taken out a loan, it appeared he'd done so. Henry ventured a glance at Lavinia. She, too, was looking at the name penned in crisp black letters.

Unlike him, she appeared to take the revelation in stride. Her calmness while awaiting the news of what would happen to the home Jack and Pauline had worked hard to provide for their family was admirable.

Mr. Nichols looked from Lavinia to Henry. "I owe you both an apology."

Hope sprang to life. Could the banker have gotten his facts wrong? Had he discovered that Jack had paid off the loan years before?

"It was evident neither of you knew about the mortgage, which I found puzzling."

Lavinia leaned forward. "I'm curious why you hadn't mentioned it to Henry before, after his brother's passing. Surely, with Henry being Jack's executor, you would have wanted him to be aware of your bank's claim on the estate."

Her question echoed one Henry had asked himself.

"I'd assumed he would have found the papers among Jack's things and come to see me if he had any questions. Since he hadn't and the date of the payment was drawing near, I decided to bring up the matter when I saw you two alone at Emery's wedding."

"Lavinia and I searched the house afterward, but we didn't find anything."

Mr. Nichols shook his head. "No. You wouldn't have, and that's my fault. It wasn't until yesterday that I recalled a brief conversation Jack and I had back in the fall of '56. Much of Placerville had been destroyed in a series of fires earlier that year. Because fires are common occurrences with the many wooden buildings in the towns here in the Gold Country, such as this one, our bank had just purchased one of Wilder's fireproof Salamander safes, which I'd mentioned to Jack. He brought in the promissory note and asked me to store it inside. I had my teller go through the safe first thing this morning. He located the note in the back behind some papers we rarely remove." The banker held up the document he'd placed on his desktop. "I'm sorry about the confusion."

Henry's mouth had gone dry, making forming his question difficult, but it had to be asked. "Where do things stand?"

Mr. Nichols smoothed his neatly trimmed mustache and cleared his throat, delaying tactics that heightened Henry's anxiety. "I don't know if Jack told you, but he was having some difficulty making ends meet. His annual mortgage payment was due on the thirtieth of June, but he didn't have the money this past summer. When the other smithy in town opened a few years back, he experienced a drop in business. He asked for an extension on the loan this past May. Since he was a valued customer and had never been late on a payment before, the board granted it."

"An extension?" Lavinia asked. "For how long?"

"Six months. The payment is due the thirty-first."

"That's only two weeks from today." She glanced at Henry, the shock on her face mirroring what he felt.

"How much is it?" He braced himself for the answer.

Mr. Nichols spun the ledger around and pointed to a number. Henry and Lavinia leaned forward. "This is how much is due that day, but this—" the banker moved his finger to another figure "—is the total balance remaining."

Henry chest tightened. The amount was equal to five payments, meaning the house wouldn't be paid off for another four years.

Lavinia's lovely features had relaxed, so much so that she appeared calm and composed when Henry was anything but. "My sister did mention in a letter several years ago that she feared Jack might have been out to impress her by building such a large house. Apparently, he overextended himself. What will happen now?"

"Nothing…" Mr. Nichols let the word hang for several nerve-wracking seconds, "provided the payment is made on time."

"I'll make it, but…" Reality settled on Henry with the weight of an anvil. At present, he couldn't even make the mortgage payment due at the end of the month.

Lavinia sat there silently waiting, as did Mr. Nichols.

A grandfather clock stood in the corner like a sentry. Each tick of its pendulum was a stark reminder of how little time was left before the loan payment would come due.

Henry fought a wave of nausea. If he couldn't come up with the payment, he could lose the house. He refused to let that happen—he'd do whatever it took, even if it meant lowering the asking price for his hotel up in Marysville to facilitate a quick sale. "It could take me a few days to come up with the money."

The banker spun the ledger around, closed it with an ominous thump and rested his clasped hands on top of the leather cover. "My friend, Emery Staples, said you mentioned having found a buyer for Jack's shop."

"I did, but things didn't work out quite like I planned." He explained the terms of the sale. "I gave Dealy my word. I can't go back on it."

"Of course not," Lavinia agreed quickly, easing some of the tension in Henry's shoulders, "but there are other ways out of your situation."

His relief was short-lived. The banker might interpret her statement as supportive and encouraging, but Henry knew exactly what she was suggesting. She wanted him to let her take the children back east, but nothing and no one—not even the curly-haired beauty with eyes as warm as a steaming mug of cocoa—would make him consider giving up his nieces and nephew.

Mr. Nichols nodded. "Miss Crowne has a point." It's possible I could find a buyer for the house who would assume the loan and pay you the difference between that and the price you agreed on."

Lavinia smiled. "That would be kind of you." She turned from the banker to him. "Wouldn't it, Henry?"

"I have no intention of selling the house." He stood, gave her a curt nod of dismissal and held out a hand to the banker. "Thank you for apprising us of the situation, Mr. Nichols. I'll be in contact soon."

But first, he had to figure out a solution to the dilemma that had been dropped in his lap.

Sweat ran down Henry's face. His muscles ached and his lungs burned, but he didn't care. Pounding red-hot iron had eased some of the tension that had him tied in knots.

Why had Jack jeopardized his family's future by taking out a mortgage on his house? And why hadn't his brother said anything about it? Those questions had plagued Henry ever since he'd walked out of Mr. Nichols's office two hours ago.

Henry gripped the wolf jaw tongs firmly and studied

the piece held in them. Despite not having worked with metal in eight years, his decorative twists on the long handle had turned out well, as had the elongated bowl shape below them. Now to put the final details on the leaf he'd made earlier before welding it just below the loop from which the utensil would hang.

Dealy nodded approvingly. "You haven't lost your touch, Mr. Hawthorn."

Henry started. He'd been concentrating so deeply on his work that he'd forgotten the young smithy, who was hard at work in the shop that was now his. He'd invited Henry to try his hand. In his present state, taking his frustrations out on metal had seemed like a good idea. It was better than snapping at the woman who could make him happier than a kitten under a leaky cow one minute and madder than a cat caught in a creek the next. "Smithing is like milking. Once you've done it, you don't forget how."

"Why'd ya give it up?"

That was a good question. He set down the items and stared at his hands, which were coated with charcoal and soot. "I suppose it's because I wanted to experience new things."

"I love the work. I can't imagine doing nothing else."

Henry clapped a hand on Dealy's shoulder. "You do fine work. I'm glad to know you'll be keeping Jack's dream alive. He wanted this shop to be one of the best in the Gold Country."

"Don't know if I can make that happen, but you won't find many who work as hard as me."

"I don't doubt that." The young man's confidence reminded Henry of himself. He'd headed west determined to make something of himself, and he had. He'd left Sutter Creek for Marysville eight years ago with his meager savings. Now he owned a successful hotel, providing housing for others, although he hoped he wouldn't own it much longer.

If only a buyer would come along who was willing to buy the hotel at the reduced price he'd telegraphed to his Marysville lawyer before heading to the smithy. He could then use the money to pay off Jack's mortgage and see to it that the children would be able to remain in their home.

He left the shop, completed the gentle climb up Church Street, entered the house and removed his coat, hat and gloves. Once again, he was struck by his hands. He'd vowed not to do the work of a smithy again, not to bear the stains that marked him as a common laborer. What had come over him? He could have bought that silver-handled shoehorn at the mercantile, but instead he'd made one out of iron. Was it the need to release the tension that had been building for weeks, the urge to stand where Jack had stood and remember the bond they'd forged when they were boys—or something else entirely?

The answer came swiftly. He missed his brother deeply, but the reason he'd felt the need to pound iron was because he'd hoped Lavinia would have admitted defeat and retreated by now. She had no right to take the children, and yet she wasn't about to back down. The exasperating woman was as determined as she was beautiful.

He didn't want to fight with her. He wanted to kiss her. Soundly.

Chapter Twelve

Lavinia stood in the kitchen the following afternoon, gripping the mixing bowl with one hand and the wooden spoon with the other and rehearsed to herself. "You offered to help me with the party, Henry, and I'd welcome your assistance."

No, that wouldn't work. If she approached Henry with a request like that, he might get the impression she wanted him around, which she didn't. After the heated look he'd given her when they'd left Mr. Nichols's office, the last thing she needed was Henry thinking she enjoyed his company.

She stirred the dry ingredients with such vigor that she almost fluffed the flour over the side as she had the day before. Apparently, she'd managed to get some on her face in the process. Warmth rushed into her cheeks at the memory of him brushing away the evidence of her mishap.

He'd been so intent on his task that he'd forgotten where they were, or so it had seemed, since he'd started and jerked his hand away. While that had been surprising, what was even more so was the attraction evident in his eyes. She'd thought she'd seen admiration in them when she'd prepared to descend the stairs during Mr. Staples and Gladys's wedding. Perhaps she'd been right, after all, and Henry was drawn to her. She swiped the back of her hand over the spot where his fingers had rested far longer than was necessary and smiled. A woman did like to be noticed by a man, especially by such a handsome one.

Unfortunately, his obstinacy was proving problematic. He was as set on keeping the children in Sutter Creek as she was on taking them back to Philadelphia. What he didn't know, though, was that the meeting with Mr. Nichols had given her the grounds she needed to build a case against him. Henry might be the executor, but he'd violated at least three statutes.

One article of the law allowed him two months to give notice to the estate's creditors, or the court could revoke the letters of administration that granted him his rights. She'd discovered from perusing back issues of the *Amador Weekly Ledger*, loaned to her by Norma's husband, that Henry hadn't placed such a notice in the newspaper. Through a series of tactfully worded questions while at the mercantile checking on her housekeeper advertisement, Lavinia had also learned from the talkative owner that Henry hadn't posted any notices around town either, thus putting him in violation.

If that was all she had to go on, she might have trouble making a case. Sutter Creek was a small town, after all, and everyone was aware of the tragedy that had befallen Jack and Pauline. Any of her brother-in-law's creditors would surely have come forward as Mr. Nichols had.

But Lavinia had more to go on than that. Reading the applicable statutes as many times as she had helped her remember them. When Henry had told her and Mr. Nichols about the sale of the smithy to Mr. Dealy on credit, she'd known right away she had what she needed to challenge Henry's position as executor.

First, he'd neglected to get permission from the probate judge for the sale of Jack's shop, which was required by law. Second, Henry had agreed to sell the smithy, granting Mr. Dealy a loan with payments extending more than three years into the future, which was more than the length of time a guardian was allowed for the sale of property belonging to minors on credit.

As soon as possible, she would pay Mr. Price a visit. If all went well, the lawyer would be willing to take her case now. They could petition the courts to have Henry removed as executor and challenge his rights as guardian at the same time because he'd failed to carry out all his duties. Since she was the nearest relative, aside from her father, who was back east, surely the judge would grant her the guardianship.

That's enough strategizing, Lavinia. She needed to continue her campaign to win support in the community, which meant she must come up with a better way of asking Henry to help her because no one was interested in the housekeeper job. The owner of the mercantile hadn't received a single inquiry about the advertisement she'd placed on the board at the back of his shop. And she couldn't ask Norma to come to her rescue, although her generous neighbor had invited Dot over to spend the afternoon with her playmate, giving Lavinia some much-needed time to figure out how to deal with her predicament.

As she'd experimented with some desserts, the solution had become clear. Her only remaining option was to ask Henry for help. There was no way she could create the refreshments for the party on her own. Although she'd learned as much as possible from Gladys, her cooking skills were rudimentary and her baking skills even more limited.

Another approach was in order. Lavinia stirred the beginnings of the cake batter slowly and strove for a pleasant tone that didn't convey her desperation. "I could use a hand with some baking, Henry, if your offer still stands."

That didn't work either. It sounded like she doubted his sincerity. He was a man of his word, which he'd proven at their meeting with Mr. Nichols. Even though the banker had stunned Henry with the news of the impending mortgage payment, he hadn't given a thought to altering the verbal agreement he'd made with Mr. Dealy regarding his purchase of the blacksmith shop, a choice that could end up working in her favor. Instead, Henry had stated his decision to honor the agreed-upon terms without hesitation.

Yes. That was it. She would follow his example and make her request without prevaricating. "Will you please help me prepare the desserts for the party, Henry?"

"Perhaps."

The wooden spoon she'd been holding clattered to the floor. She spun around. "I didn't hear you come in."

"I gathered that since you've been talking to yourself." He leaned against the door frame, his arms and feet crossed, looking entirely too appealing, which added to the sudden wave of light-headedness causing her to reel. She clutched the counter behind her for support.

"Oh, that." She waved a hand dismissively and stooped to retrieve the spoon, giving her time to come up with a response. "I was just figuring out which approach would be the most effective. You men respond differently to requests than we women do."

"You missed the obvious."

"And what might that be?"

"Compliments. A man thrives on them." His droll smile and waggling eyebrows took her by surprise. Something must have happened to put him in such good spirits.

"I see. So what should I have said? Something like this, perhaps?" She clasped her hands, tilted her head and batted her eyelashes in fawning-schoolgirl fashion. "Henry, you're such a talented baker. I'd be honored if you'd put your culinary skills to work on my behalf. Would you do that, please?"

He swept low in a deep bow and came up grinning. "My dear lady, it would give me great pleasure to come to your rescue."

Her rescue? Had he figured out her party plans were in jeopardy?

"However, I feel compelled to add a caveat."

She fought the urge to gulp. "Yes?"

"I'll do the baking, provided you work alongside me, allowing me to serve as your instructor."

Although his request was reasonable, spending that much time with him might not be wise, considering how much she enjoyed his company. She ought to be keeping her distance, not agreeing to spend days with him in such close proximity, but what choice did she have? "Very well. I'll be your sous-chef."

"Are these your creations?" His gaze rested on the kitchen table filled with her attempts at creating something edible. Sadly, her efforts hadn't yielded anything remotely resembling the tasty treats Henry and Gladys had made.

"Such as they are, yes."

He picked up a snickerdoodle. The cookie broke into

pieces when he bit into it. His quick movements enabled him to catch them before they hit the floor.

"When I first took them out of the oven, they looked fine, but they flattened and got brittle."

He crunched the bite, swallowed and gave her an encouraging smile. "They're tasty."

It was nice of him to find something to compliment. "I did everything it said in the recipe."

"How long did you stir the batter?"

"It said to mix it thoroughly, so I did."

"That could be it. The recipe books don't tell you, but 'mix thoroughly,' in this case, means just until the ingredients are combined."

She extended her lower lip and blew out a breath, causing the curls that had broken loose to flutter. "Well, they should have said that. If I were writing a recipe, I would."

The front door opened, and the children rushed in, chattering as they removed their coats.

Marcie was the first to appear in the kitchen. "Something smells really good. Oh! You made cookies." She grabbed one and chomped down, repeatedly, until a piece broke off. She spat it onto her palm. "What happened? It's as hard as a rock!"

Alex, who had come into the kitchen, frowned. "That's not a nice thing to say, Marcie."

"Well, it's true. You try one."

Henry rested a hand on each of the children's shoulders. "If you two will have a seat, I've got an idea."

Lavinia looked at the doorway. "Where are Miss Norma, Dot and the others? I thought you were all going to walk home from school together."

Marcie set the remainder of her snickerdoodle on the

table. "They were being slowpokes, so Alex and I decided to race up the hill."

A rap at the front door was followed by Norma's cheery call. "We're back!"

Lavinia left Henry and the older children in the kitchen and went to greet her friend. Norma stood in the entryway with Bobby in her arms and Dot and her two girls surrounding her.

"Thanks for watching Dot this afternoon and for walking Alex and Marcie home."

Norma smiled. "My pleasure. Yvonne was happy to have the company, and I was glad to have a few minutes to call my own while this little fellow napped." She kissed her son's forehead.

"Would you like to come in? I did some baking, and you're welcome to sample my disasters—if you're brave, that is."

Norma smiled. "Come now. It can't be that bad."

Lavinia scoffed. "My snickerdoodles are so hard they could be used as cobblestones. Henry about broke a tooth biting into one."

Dot peered up at Lavinia. "Can I get a cookie?"

"I'm not sure that's such a good idea, sweetie. They didn't turn out the way I'd hoped."

"It's fine." Henry stood in the dining room doorway. "You made tasty treats that are great for dunking in milk. They don't crumble or get soggy. So, if you two ladies don't mind, I'll take the girls with me and give you a few minutes to yourselves."

Norma nodded. "Thank you, Henry." She addressed her daughters. "But you'll have to be quick, girls. I need to get supper started."

He left with his charges, having formed them into a

train with himself as the engine and Dot as the caboose. He led the way to the kitchen, providing a piercing whistle and inviting the girls to join him on the chugging.

Norma smiled at the retreating group and turned to Lavinia. "Were you able to ask Henry if he'll help you with the baking?"

"He's agreed."

"Good. Then you have your location and refreshments taken care of. How are things coming with the entertainment?"

Lavinia inhaled sharply. "I'd forgotten about that. I need to get to the post office and see if the letter from the puppet troupe has arrived. They were supposed to have gotten back to me by now. I'd best be on my way. Would you please let Henry know?"

"Certainly."

"Thank you." Lavinia threw on her coat, grabbed her reticule and dashed out the door.

Minutes later, she entered the American House hotel and walked up to the owner who served as the Sutter Creek postmaster. "Do you have a letter for me, Mr. Little?"

He checked the slots filled with mail but returned to the counter empty handed. "Sorry, Miss Crowne. Maybe there will be something in the mailbag for you tomorrow."

That would be too late. She needed to get the invitations out and had planned to add a mention of the puppet show to them that evening. She produced a smile, albeit a half-hearted one. "Thank you."

She squared her shoulders, left the hotel and headed down Main Street. The ever-present rumble of the stamp mills echoed the throbbing at her temples. She'd come to

Sutter Creek prepared to give the children a Christmas beyond their wildest dreams, and yet she'd dealt with one challenge after another.

At least she had the venue reserved. Henry had agreed to help her with the baking, so she'd have desserts for the guests. If she wanted entertainment beyond accepting the church pianist's offer to play carols as background music, she'd have to ask Henry to arrange a meeting with his ventriloquist friend. She could get gifts for the children in town. They might not be as nice as what she'd hoped to find, but at least she'd have something to give them.

The only thing left to take care of was getting a Christmas tree, but she could hire one of the young men in town to chop one down for her and deliver it. If she bought all the decorations the mercantile had and tied the gifts for the children to the boughs, the tree would look passable.

She drew in a deep breath and exhaled it slowly. Everything would be fine—provided nothing else went wrong.

Now to see if Mr. Price would take her case.

Henry hefted the sack of flour onto his shoulder the following afternoon, thanked the younger Mr. Staples, who was running the grocery store while his older brother was on his honeymoon, and headed up Church Street to the house, where Lavinia was waiting for him to give her another baking lesson. She was an apt student. Between the two of them, they would have ample time to prepare the desserts she'd chosen to serve at her party.

The thought of working with her again quickened his pace. When she was immersed in a project, she ceased to be the prim and proper lady society expected. Instead, she became as animated and as talkative as Marcie, peppering him with questions. Lavinia laughed more easily and more often, too. She might not be aware of the transformation but he was, and he liked it.

He entered the kitchen minutes later and proceeded to refill the flour tin.

Lavinia smiled. "Oh, good. You're back. Just in time, too." She grabbed a folded dish towel, opened the oven door and pulled out a tray of hard gingerbread cut into triangular-shaped pieces. A sunny smile burst forth, adding to her beauty. "They turned out just right."

Her joy was contagious. "They look great. I'm curious why you cut them that way, though."

"They're going to be Christmas trees." She held the tray in one hand, grabbed a spatula and began putting the *trees* on a wire cooling rack. "I made some white frosting the way you showed me. I'll put it in a rolled-up parchment sheet and squeeze it out like garland. I've cut some candied fruit into little pieces that the children can use to decorate the trees. They'll have fun, don't you think?"

"Yes, I do. And speaking of the children, where's Dot?"

"Upstairs taking a nap. I expect her to come down soon."

"She's not getting sick, is she?"

Lavinia paused, the spatula suspended midair. "I don't think so. She'd been playing with her doll in the parlor, but she popped in here for a minute and then headed up to her room. I peeked in soon after and saw her curled up in bed. I figured she was just tired out. Why?"

"She stopped taking naps not long after she turned three."

"You're right. I've never seen her take one before. As soon as I'm done here, I'll check on her and make sure she doesn't have a fever." She lifted the last of the gingerbread triangles from the tray and held it out to him. "Would you like to try one and see if it tastes all right?"

"Would I ever." He sank his teeth into the treat and savored the burst of spicy goodness. "This is delicious. You could serve these at the party."

"These?" She laughed. "They're not fancy. They're—"

"Fun. The children would love decorating them, and aren't they the reason for the shindig, after all?"

Lavinia's smile faded. "Now don't go spoiling things, Henry. I've had a good time working with you, but it seems you haven't grasped my vision for the party. It's going to be a grand affair." She frowned. "At least, it's supposed to be."

Of that he had no doubt. She'd told him that morning about the gifts she was going to buy, one for every child at the party. Although she'd intended to purchase things like toy soldiers or tea sets, the limited selections in the shops had thwarted her plans. Instead, every child at the party would leave with a small item such as a yo-yo, a wooden top, or a cup and ball. Although she was disappointed, he felt sure she'd end up happy with her choices and had shared his thoughts as tactfully as possible.

"Thanks to you, I have entertainment now. I just hope everything works out with your friend." She set the empty tray on the stovetop and picked up a full one.

Lavinia had surprised him by agreeing to hire Quinn to provide the entertainment, even though she had yet to meet the talented ventriloquist. It wasn't like her to relinquish control, but with the party just three days away, she'd run out of options. "You can trust me. I've seen Quinn keep a crowd of miners enthralled, and they can be a tough audience. Your guests, children and parents alike, will enjoy his performance."

"I'm sure they will, but I'm still feeling a bit uneasy. I can't explain it."

"Makes sense. This a big undertaking." She was counting on winning Alex, Marcie and Dot over with this event, so she had a lot invested in it. "Have faith. I'm sure things will work out."

"I hope you're right." She put the tray of gingerbread in the oven, stood and dusted her hands on her apron. "I'll go upstairs and make sure Dot's all right."

"Would you mind if I tag along?"

"You don't trust me to detect a fever on my own, do you?" She chuckled. "Fine. Follow me." She led the way up the stairs with him one step behind.

They were on the second landing when she paused. "Do you hear that?"

He did. Dot was crying.

Lavinia raced up the last steps, but he took them two at a time, passing her by. He rushed to Dot's bedside, pulled the sobbing girl into his arms and then held her back far enough so he could look into her tearstained face. "I'm here, Dimples. What's wrong?"

"It hurts here." She put a hand over her heart.

He glanced at Lavinia, who stood to the side. She held up her hands and shook her head, clearly as mystified as he was. He turned back to Dot. "Are you having trouble breathing?"

"I can…breathe," she said between shuddering breaths, "but, I c-c-can't stop…crying."

Lavinia knelt beside the bed. "Are you sad, sweetie?"

Dot nodded.

"Why?"

"Because Christmas is coming, and it's all wrong." Dot dissolved into tears once more.

Henry whipped out his freshly laundered handkerchief and mopped up some of the moisture on Dot's puffy red face. He could handle most things, but crying females puzzled him. If his niece would just tell them what was bothering her, he could make things right. As it was, he felt helpless.

A gentle pressure on his arm drew his attention. He looked down to find Lavinia's hand resting there. "I think I know what's going on. Perhaps if I hold her…"

"Sure." He was happy to hand over the whimpering girl. Lavinia seemed better equipped to extract something from her than he was.

She perched on the edge of the bed, pulled Dot into her lap and attempted to caress her cheek. Their niece turned away, intentionally thwarting Lavinia's efforts. "Your mama loved Christmas so much. It's not the same without her, is it?"

Dot sniffed several times, slowly lifted her head and gazed at Lavinia with red-rimmed eyes. "Do you know what I mean?"

"I think so. You came into the kitchen, saw me wearing your mama's apron and baking Christmas treats like she did, and it made you sad, didn't it?"

Dot nodded. "She was the bestest mama in the whole wide world, but she went away, and she's never coming back."

How did women do that? Know just what to say? He should have realized Dot was grieving.

Lavinia picked up the handkerchief lying on the quilt and tenderly blotted Dot's tear-streaked cheeks. "She was a wonderful mother and loved you very much."

"How do you know? You never comed here before."

"She told me in her letters."

"Why didn't you come?"

Lavinia blinked several times as though keeping her own tears at bay. "I wanted to, but it's a long trip, and…" She heaved a sigh.

Henry waited, as eager to hear what she would say as Dot was.

"My father wouldn't let me." Although the admission hadn't come easily, she'd been honest with Dot.

"But you're a grown-up. Can't you do whatever you want?"

"I wish I could, but I still live with my father, and he… doesn't always let me do what I want to do."

Dot frowned. "That's not nice." She brightened. "But you're here now, and I'm glad."

"I am, too. Things will be different, but we're going to have a very special Christmas."

"And we'll do all the things mama did, right? That's what will make it special."

Henry couldn't have said it better himself. If only Lavinia felt the same way.

"Yes, sweetie, we will, and we'll have lots of fun together." She'd agreed. Better yet, it sounded like she meant what she'd said. Could it be she was realizing the value of the simple celebration the children were anticipating?

The front door flew open. "Aunt Livy! Uncle Henry! We're home."

Lavinia's lovely face lit up as though the older children's return was the highlight of her day. "Let's go, Dot. I have something fun planned."

They trooped down the stairs to the entryway where

Norma stood with little Bobby balanced on her hip. She smiled. "We're back, as I'm sure you noticed."

"So you are. I'm delighted to see you. I have a surprise for all of the children in the kitchen."

The youngsters peppered her with questions. "A surprise? What sort of surprise? Is it something to eat?"

She laughed. "If you'll take off your coats and hats and head into the kitchen, you'll see what it is."

They shed them in a hurry and gathered around the kitchen table, with Norma watching from a distance. Lavinia showed the children the gingerbread triangles and demonstrated the decorating process, her excitement as evident as theirs.

Each of the girls set to work adding ornaments to a tree. Alex stood off to the side with his mouth and shoulders drooping. Henry felt for the boy. Being surrounded by girls all the time couldn't be easy.

Lavinia rested a hand on their nephew's shoulder. "I need to take care of the gingerbread that's ready to come out of the oven, so I could use a careful person to squeeze the frosting on the trees that have cooled. Would you do that for me?"

Alex's glum expression evaporated. "Yes, Aunt Livy. I'll do a good job. I promise." She might say she didn't understand boys, but she was doing a great job with their nephew.

The kitchen was filled with childish chatter and sprinkled with a hearty portion of laughter as the girls placed colorful bits of candied fruit on the frosting zigzagging across the trees.

A rap on the front door sent Lavinia hurrying into the entryway. She said something to a man, although Henry couldn't make out the words. She closed the door after the brief exchange, but instead of returning to the kitchen, her footfalls headed in the direction of the parlor.

Norma cast a curious glance toward the entryway and shifted her gaze to Henry. "If you'd like, I could supervise here."

"Thanks." He set down the tray of cookies, tossed the dish towel on the sideboard and strode to the parlor.

Lavinia sat hunched over on one end of the settee, her face slack, staring at a sheet of paper in her lap. She saw him, straightened and produced a weak smile. "From the sounds of it, the children are having a good time."

"They are. How are you?"

"I'm fine." She let out a forced laugh that belied her statement. "I got some news that wasn't what I'd hoped for, that's all, but I have other options."

"Options for what?"

"A venue. Mr. Benedict had a change of plans, so I won't be renting the hall after all." She'd said the words as though she was talking about a minor inconvenience rather than a crushing blow.

"I can't believe it." Henry reined in the unexpected surge of anger and took a seat beside her. Her party wasn't necessary, but he still didn't like to see her hurting. "What did he say?"

"Here. You can see for yourself."

He took the note and read the brief message.

December 19, 1860
Miss Crowne,

I regret to inform you that Mr. Benedict received a request from a business associate to rent his building here in Sutter Creek this coming weekend. The

gentleman will be hosting his daughter's wedding
and will require the use of the entire building. Thus,
the meeting hall won't be available on Saturday
after all. My apologies for any inconvenience this
might cause you.

Sincerely,
Augustus Price, Attorney-at-Law

"Three days before your party, and Mr. Benedict does
this?" Henry shook the paper. "That man has nerve. You
told me you had an agreement in writing."

"Only to the price. I neglected to ask for anything else.
But things will work out, even if it means I have to make
do with a smaller venue and hold two parties instead of
one." Determination shone in her eyes, currently as dark
brown as Baker's chocolate. She took the note he held
out, wadded it into a ball and tossed it in the fire, watching wordlessly as the blaze devoured it.

"I'm sure they will."

"I don't want to disappoint the guests."

Interesting. Up until now, she'd said she was holding
the party for the children's benefit. Had Dot's tearful
plea shifted her focus?

She picked up the nearest sofa pillow and twisted the
fringe around her finger so tightly that it turned bright
red.

"Don't hurt yourself." He reached over, unwound the
string and rubbed her finger.

She took his hand in hers, turning it this way and that.
He resisted the urge to pull away. "I noticed the stains
when we were doing the baking. What happened? It looks
like you've been working at a forge."

"I was."

"I didn't think you planned to do that anymore."

He didn't, but… "I was at the smithy with Dealy. An idea struck me, and I set to work." The image had come to him with such clarity. It wasn't until he'd finished the piece that he'd questioned his impulsiveness.

"Ideas can be like that." She let go of his hand and rested hers in her lap. "I'm glad you could pursue yours without hindrance."

The sadness in her voice caused his chest to tighten. Lavinia had such high hopes for her party, but she'd encountered one setback after another. "I wish there was something I could do help."

"You've done so much already—teaching me to bake, arranging for your friend to provide the entertainment." She pinned him with a probing gaze. "Why?"

He looked at Lavinia, staring at him so intently, and the answer came to him with startling clarity. He was helping her because he cared about her and didn't want her to leave. If she stayed in Sutter Creek, she could have what her heart desired.

From what Gladys had said, Lavinia's life was a lonely one, although she'd never admit that. All she had was a distant, controlling father and a group of friends who accepted her, provided she followed the rules they lived by. No wonder she'd blossomed over the past few weeks. He knew just how to answer her question.

"I want your party to succeed because I want to see you happy."

She stiffened. "I am happy."

"Are you? Then why does taking the children to Philadelphia matter so much to you? You say it's to give them advantages, but there's little you can offer them there that they can't get here."

"What about an education? We have wonderful colleges."

"We have them too, in Stockton, Santa Clara, San Jose, San Francisco and Benicia. That last one is even a girls' school, so there will be opportunities for Marcie and Dot, too. The children could help shape this great state."

"Perhaps, but it's still rough and wild here."

"Not for long. There's been a rapid influx of culture. Your own father recognizes that. Why else would he have sent Mr. Worthington to scout out a location in San Francisco?"

She bristled. "Leave my father out of it!"

Things with her father must not be as great as she'd led him to believe. "I didn't mean to upset you. I was just making an observation."

Her hand flew to her chest, and she curled her upper body away from him. "I'm s-sorry."

He shifted, wrapped an arm around her and pulled her to his side. "It's all right."

She leaned her head against his shoulder, and a surge of protectiveness flowed through him—along with the realization of how much she'd come to mean to him. Her soft curls tickled his chin. He fought the urge to bury his face in the silky mass and breathe in the rosy scent he would forever associate with her.

The clomp of boots in the entryway caused her to jump aside, out of his embrace. She smoothed the collar of her dress.

Alex appeared in the doorway, looked from Lavinia to Henry and raised an eyebrow.

How much had the young fellow seen? "What do you need, Buddy?"

"We got all the cookies from the first batch decorated. Can we start on the other ones?"

"If they're cool to the touch, yes," Henry said.

"Good." Alex gave them a lingering look, smiled and left.

An awkward silence filled the room, broken only by the ticking of the mantel clock and the popping and crackling of the fire on the grate.

Lavinia spoke first, her voice soft. "I had no right to snap at you. I know you mean well, but you don't know what I'm dealing with."

He had a pretty good idea. "I would if you told me."

She looked at the ceiling as though she was praying, gave a nod and fixed her gaze on a spot near the top button of his shirt, his cravat having been shed when he was helping the children with the cookies. "In order to make the trip out here, I had to promise my father I'd return with the children. I can't—I *won't* let him down."

Her slip was telling. Evidently, Lavinia feared what her father would do if she showed up without them. Given Paul Crowne's history of disowning his eldest daughter, Lavinia's fierce determination not to disappoint him made sense.

If only she wasn't being forced to choose between satisfying her father and remaining true to herself. It was high time the domineering man realized his daughter was no longer a child. She was a bright, capable, kindhearted woman of twenty-six who deserved to live her own life, make her own choices. Sadly, it seemed the only way for her to do that was to walk away as Pauline had done.

Lavinia was strong, but was she strong enough to

break free? That would mean putting the children's needs and her desires ahead of her father's demands. Could she do it?

Lord, I care for Lavinia and don't want to see her hurt, but I'm afraid that's inevitable since the children are staying here with me.

Unless there is another way. If so, please show me.

Chapter Thirteen

The woman Lavinia saw in the looking glass boasted cheeks almost as red as her dress, causing her to laugh at her reflection. She couldn't be sure, but she might even be more excited about this party for the children's classmates and their families than they were. And the youngsters had been talking about it all day, aside from the hour she and Henry had spent helping Alex and Marcie rehearse their carols one last time.

When Lavinia had received that note from Mr. Price three days ago, the floor had shifted beneath her feet—or so it had seemed. She'd feared he was also subtly letting her know that he wouldn't take her case. Although learning that Mr. Benedict wouldn't rent her his meeting room was a setback, it was one she could overcome. Not being able to challenge Henry for guardianship of the children wasn't.

Norma had offered her a solution for her venue dilemma. The levelheaded woman had suggested using the schoolhouse. Although the smaller building with its space limitations wasn't an ideal solution, since it meant hosting separate parties for their school and church friends on different dates than originally planned, things had worked out thanks to the children's understanding and generous teacher. Miss Reed had welcomed the opportunity to combine the children's choral performance with a party for the students' families afterward, agreeing with everything Lavinia had planned—with one exception.

The capable young schoolmistress insisted on using a five-foot Christmas tree set on a table and trimmed with the children's handiwork instead of the twelve-foot one trimmed with store-bought ornaments Lavinia had envisioned. She'd accepted the stipulation graciously while vowing to herself that the children would have a tall tree at home. She could picture a beautiful one in the entryway, reaching all the way to the top of the staircase.

A visit to Mr. Price's office to discuss her need for his services the day after his note about the meeting hall had arrived had given her reason to hope. The lawyer had listened intently as she outlined the ways in which she believed Henry had neglected his duties as executor. Mr. Price had agreed that the probate court might take issue with the way Henry had gone about the sale of the smithy, considering the mortgage on the house and his need for ready cash.

When Mr. Price had agreed, albeit reluctantly, to take her case, she'd managed to school her features. When he'd said he would do everything in his power to get the probate judge to set a court date in the upcoming week due to her urgent need to return east before the fighting broke out, her composure had failed her. She'd given the lawyer such a vigorous handshake that he'd chuckled.

The thought of returning to Philadelphia with Alex, Marcie and Dot lifted her spirits. Her father would be pleased that she'd carried out his wishes. Once he got to know the children and saw how wonderful they were, he would fall in love with them as she had. They would miss their lives here, but once they saw what awaited them, they would adjust.

Leaving Henry would be hard on them, though. She could understand. He was a wonderful man—bright, talented, hardworking and full of love for the children.

She wandered to her bedroom window and gazed at the oak tree where he'd come to her rescue. She'd developed feelings for him. If she didn't guard her heart, she could fall in love with him, making leaving that much harder.

But what if Henry cared for her, too? He didn't, of course, but the possibility put a smile on her face.

"Aunt Livy." Marcie stood in the doorway to Lavinia's room. "Are you ready? Everybody else is."

"I am."

Marcie twirled in a circle. "The party will be fun."

"I'm glad you think so." She had yet to meet Henry's friend Quinn and was doing her best not to worry. Henry had assured her the ventriloquist would be there, and he had yet to let her down. He'd spent the past two days helping her with the baking, the gift wrapping and other tasks. She couldn't have asked for a more supportive friend, even if the fanciful part of her wished they could be more.

"I can't wait for you to see my ornaments," Marcie said.

"I'm looking forward to that."

Her niece darted down the stairs. Lavinia paused at the upper landing as she had the day of Gladys and Mr. Staples's wedding. Just as he had that morning, Henry looked up and saw her, sending her a smile so warm it melted her heart.

If only things were different. He'd come to mean more to her than she would have thought possible, considering their differences. She'd miss him greatly when it came time to leave, just as he would miss the children. Would he ever forgive her for taking them away from him?

She mustn't think about that now. The families would be getting to the school soon, and she was eager to greet them.

After a brisk walk in the chilly night air, they arrived at the school to find things in order. Lavinia was relieved to finally meet Quinn. The ventriloquist had an engaging manner that put her fears to rest. A final check of the desks-turned-dessert-tables that had been shoved against the wall further calmed her nerves. The tempting treats remained hidden beneath dish towels for the time being. A large pot of hot cider sat on the stove, filling the air with the scents of cinnamon and cloves.

In a matter of minutes, the schoolhouse was full of excited children and their parents. Miss Reed helped her pupils find their places. Once the young singers were in position, their kindly teacher stepped to the front, facing rows of benches filled with parents and siblings too young to attend school. Henry sat on one side of Dot, Lavinia on the other. As she looked at other couples with children nestled between them, it struck her how much their trio resembled a family.

A longing she'd been keeping buried surfaced, bringing with it sadness. She dreamed of having a family, and yet she was already twenty-six, an age when an unmarried woman heard the word *spinster* whispered about her behind the fans of pitying matrons. What they didn't know was that there had been several gentlemen interested in her, men her father had sent her way—after they'd received his approval, of course.

The potential suitors were bright and ambitious, although more interested in forming an alliance with her father than in getting to know her. A few of them, such as Stuart Worthington, were personable enough and would make good husbands for other women, but they hadn't made her heart beat faster. Only one man had done that, and he was sharing the bench with her.

Lord, I've fallen for a man I can't have. Even if Henry was interested in me, my father would never approve. What am I to do?

Miss Reed waited until the room grew quiet before speaking. "Welcome to the Christmas concert. If you're not in a festive mood already, you soon will be." She held out a hand toward Lavinia. "Following the children's performance, you're invited to stay for a party hosted by Miss Crowne, who is Alex and Marcie Hawthorn's aunt from Philadelphia. Due to circumstances beyond Miss Crowne's control, her event this fine Friday evening is taking the place of the one she'd originally planned for tomorrow night. And now, prepare to enjoy some beloved carols sung by my talented students."

The pianist, Mrs. Keyes, began the prelude. The kindly woman, who also played for their church services, had accepted Lavinia's invitation to provide the background music later.

Miss Reed faced the children, went up on her toes and raised her hands. She brought them down on the children's opening note. They started singing, their youthful voices filling the room. Not surprisingly, Marcie's stood out.

Lavinia glanced at Henry, who looked as handsome

and as charming as ever, and shared a smile with him. The moment didn't last long, but the sense of connection she experienced left her light-headed. She couldn't remember the last time she'd enjoyed a man's company as much as she did his. The past two days when they'd been holed up in the kitchen baking the sweets for tonight's party had been delightful. As though by mutual consent, they'd made no mention of the barriers between them and had embraced the time together. She was drawn to him, so much so that, at times, she wondered what it would be like if she were free to make her own choices.

The trouble was, their situation hadn't changed. He was determined to prevent her from taking the children to Philadelphia. Even if the children's future wasn't driving a wedge between Henry and her, there was the fact that they came from opposite backgrounds. He'd made it clear he valued a different way of life. Worse yet, he harbored ill will toward her father, blaming him for the breach with Pauline. Their father had been hardhearted, but he'd wanted what was best for her sister. Or so Lavinia had thought. Having experienced Pauline's life firsthand had raised questions. But now was no time to think about that.

Lavinia shoved aside the doubts that had crept in over the past few weeks and focused on the choir. Watching Alex and Marcie perform warmed her heart. From the moment she'd met the children, she was struck with a profound sense of pride and a love unlike anything she'd imagined possible. Pauline had tried to describe that immediate connection in her letters, but until Lavinia experienced it herself, she hadn't understood. She did now, which was why she couldn't leave without the children. They were a part of her heart. So was Henry.

The thought had come as such a shock that she didn't realize the final carol was over until Henry and Dot began clapping. Lavinia roused herself from her musings and joined the hearty applause.

Miss Reed spun around, waved a hand toward her students and beamed. She had to wait several moments for the room to quiet. "Thank you for sharing your children with me. I'm blessed to be able to work with them. They'll be joining you now as we await a visit from a special guest, or I should say special *guests*. Miss Crowne, please come here and tell us what fun awaits us."

Lavinia made her way to the front of the room. "Thank you, Miss Reed, for all you've done to make tonight's choral performance and what's yet to come possible. We'll begin the remainder of this evening's festivities with a visit from a renowned ventriloquist. After that, you'll have an opportunity to partake of hot cider and an array of sweets as you visit with one another while Mrs. Keyes plays some more carols for your listening pleasure. And now, please welcome Mr. Quinn and his friends."

She took her seat, grateful for the enthusiastic applause that greeted the elegantly dressed gentleman. With his swallowtail coat, bib-front white shirt and cravat, he would fit right in with those who attended her father's Christmas parties.

Mr. Quinn made a sweeping bow, straightened and smiled. "Thank you for the warm welcome, everyone, but I know you didn't come to see me. I'm just an ordinary man, but I have some delightful friends. Would you like to meet them?"

His question was met with rousing cheers from the children—and a few parents. Things were off to a good start.

Mr. Quinn wheeled out a cart, sat on the stool behind it and whisked off the first of three brightly colored cloths with his free hand. "Meet Goldie, the sweetest little lady in the entire Mother Lode. Why don't you say hello to the boys and girls, Goldie?"

His blonde sidekick spun to face him. "Because I don't wanna. I want to eat some of those treats the nice lady was talking about instead. They smell really good. Mmm."

The room exploded with laughter, easing the tension in Lavinia's shoulders. Mr. Quinn had grabbed the children's attention from the start. They sat enraptured the entire forty-five minutes as Goldie and her pals, Frank N. Sense and Murray, carried on a lively conversation that included a recounting of their visit to the manger when they'd delivered gifts to the baby Jesus. The talented entertainer invited different children to the front to assist him throughout his performance, including Marcie, who enjoyed being in the limelight, and Alex, who looked like he wanted to slip between the floorboards.

All too soon, Mr. Quinn brought his portion of the evening's festivities to a close. Lavinia thanked him and invited the guests to enjoy the refreshments. As Henry had predicted, the table set up with gingerbread trees, frosting and candied fruit bits was a huge hit. Two of the older students had volunteered to help the younger children decorate their trees, leaving Lavinia free to mingle.

Alex and Marcie were huddled in a corner with some friends. Her nephew's animated gestures came as a surprise. He usually let others take the lead. It was nice to see him overcoming his reticence. He glanced her way and waved. Lavinia waved back.

"Aunt Livy!"

She spun around to find Dot sitting on Henry's shoulders. "Oh, my! I didn't expect to see you up there."

"There's so many people. I asked Uncle Henry to put me up here so I can see everything."

"What a good idea. Your uncle's tall, so you have a great view now, don't you?"

Dot nodded. "I'm so high up that I can see a feather coming out of your hat. I'll stick it back in, but you gotta be still."

Henry smiled at Lavinia. "Everything's going well. You must be pleased."

"Very much so. Mr. Quinn was wonderful. I laughed so hard at times that my sides ached. Forgive me for doubting you."

He spoke with sincerity. "I was happy to help."

"You've gone above and beyond. I'm in your debt."

"You don't owe me a thing. Friends help each other."

He'd said the word *friends*, but the attraction in his arresting blue eyes gave her the impression he meant more than that. Or was she imagining things? That must be it. She averted her gaze, not an easy task when she couldn't move her head. "Are you done, Dot?"

"Yep. Would you put me down, Uncle Henry? I wanna get something to eat."

"Certainly." He lifted her over his head and set her down.

Dot joined her siblings, who welcomed her into their group without protest. How odd. They usually didn't want their little sister tagging along when they were with their school chums.

Lavinia cast a sidelong glance at Henry, but he was looking at the children. "It's nice to see them having fun."

He turned to her. "I didn't support your plan at first, but this party was a good idea."

She smiled. "We still have the one with the congregation to look forward to on Christmas Eve, too." Along with more baking—and more of his delightful company.

"Aunt Livy!" The voice was Marcie's this time. She stood with Alex on one side of her and Dot on the other, all three of them looking up at her and grinning mischievously.

Something was afoot. "What is it?"

Alex answered, his tone gleeful. "There's some mistletoe on your hat. And we're at a Christmas party, so you know what that means, don't you? Uncle Henry *has* to give you a kiss."

Lavinia's hand flew to her hat brim. Sure enough, there was a sprig of the felt-like foliage tucked among the plumage. So that's what Dot had been up to.

The children's friends rushed over. "Kiss her!" they cried in unison.

"What are you waiting for, Mr. Henry? Give her a kiss!" a familiar voiced called above the hubbub.

Lavinia scanned the crowd, looking for Gladys. She found her former housekeeper on the arm of her new husband, sporting a smirk. When had they returned?

The children gathered around Henry and Lavinia and set up a chant. "Kiss her! Kiss her! Kiss her!"

A couple of the older boys added some rhythmic stomping and were soon joined by the rest of the children.

There was no escaping this time. Lavinia lifted her head, looked in Henry's eyes and was lost in the deep blue depths. The admiration she'd seen earlier was back. There was no mistaking it. He wanted to kiss her.

The voices faded, leaving the rush of blood in her ears the only sound she could hear.

Henry's gaze locked with hers, filled with a silent question.

She gave him the barest of nods, but it was enough.

He tilted his head and leaned toward her.

She closed her eyes and waited, curiosity and excitement leaving her light-headed.

Henry's lips met hers, a soft brush filled with promise. The sensation was so beautiful, so overwhelming that she swayed.

He reached out, gripped her by the upper arms and pressed his mouth to hers firmly and completely, giving her a kiss. A real kiss. Her very first.

She'd dreamed of this moment for years, and it had finally arrived. She responded as best as she knew how, savoring the experience. Oh, that this moment could last forever.

All too soon, Henry pulled back and grinned. Lavinia gazed at him. She couldn't speak. She could scarcely breathe.

The whoops, hollers and cheers from the children brought her back to the present. She'd just kissed Henry Hawthorn in front of a crowd of witnesses. And she'd liked it. They had to have seen that.

Lavinia quickly schooled her features. She smiled and replied in what she hoped was a lighthearted tone, although to her ears it sounded a bit breathy. "All right, my darling nieces and nephew, you've succeeded in having your fun. Now, go enjoy this time with your friends." She waved the children away.

Thankfully, the guests returned to their conversations

and the dessert tables, which left her alone with Henry. How was she to act after that kiss?

He reached toward her hat. "Since this has served its purpose, let me take care of it." He slipped the sprig of mistletoe in the breast pocket of his frock coat.

"I'm sorry about that," she said in her normal voice. "I had a hunch they were plotting something, but I had no idea they would put us on the spot the way they did."

The engaging smile of his that she loved appeared in full force. "I'm not sorry. What man wouldn't welcome an opportunity to kiss the loveliest lady in the room?"

His comment, although delightful, took her aback. She had no idea how to respond. Thankfully, Gladys chose that moment to approach them.

"I'm so glad Emery and I got back to town in time for the party. We were expecting it to take place tomorrow at the meeting hall. I gather things changed."

Lavinia quickly filled Gladys in.

"I'm sorry about the setbacks, but things worked out quite nicely from what I see. The choir did a fine job, and the ventriloquist was wonderful, but—" Gladys smiled "—my favorite part was seeing the children's latest matchmaking attempt work out so well. I told them not to give up."

"You encouraged them?" Lavinia hadn't meant for her question to have such an edge, but Gladys had no business interfering.

"Of course I did. I see the way you two look at each other."

"It's not like that. We were just…" How could she explain what had happened when she wasn't even sure herself?

Gladys raised an eyebrow. "Just what? Enjoying yourselves? That's what it looked like from where I stood."

She had, but that was beside the point. "Henry and I couldn't very well make a fuss in front of so many people. We satisfied everyone, and now we can put the matter behind us."

"And you agree with this, Mr. Henry?" Gladys stood with her hand on her hips, awaiting his reply.

The light had left his eyes, and he looked...disappointed? Or was it hurt? "I don't wish to discuss the matter now. We're here to enjoy the evening, are we not? If you'll excuse me, ladies." He performed a crisp bow and left.

Gladys clucked her tongue. "I've known you since you were a girl in short skirts, Lavinia. You've never let a man kiss you before, but speaking as one smitten woman to another, it was clear you welcomed Henry's. I've watched you two fall for each other, and I couldn't be happier."

"It's not like that." She liked him. She was probably even smitten, but he'd said nothing to indicate that he returned her feelings. "Besides, even if we were interested in each other—and I'm not saying we are—there could never be anything between us. Henry and I don't share the same values. Father would never forgive me if I chose a man who lacked his approval."

Gladys took Lavinia's hands in hers. "My dear girl, it's high time you start thinking for yourself. Your sister did that, and look at what she gained."

"Look at what she lost. I won't disappoint Father the way Pauline did."

"I've said my peace, but I'll leave you with this. Think about your Heavenly Father and what He wants for you."

Gladys gave Lavinia's hands a squeeze and headed over to the children.

Her maid-turned-housekeeper-turned-friend meant well, but Gladys hadn't been privy to the scathing comments about Pauline that Lavinia had heard her father make over the years. She couldn't bear to think of him saying such things about her. Pauline had let him down, but Lavinia refused to do so.

She'd enjoyed Henry's kiss. There was no denying it. He'd said he enjoyed kissing her, too, but his curt comments and abrupt departure made her wonder if she'd imagined the attraction she'd seen in his eyes. Perhaps the kiss had meant nothing to him, after all.

Henry might be a wonderful man who caused her to feel things no man before him ever had, but she couldn't entertain fanciful thoughts about him. Her father had made it clear Henry was no different in his eyes than Jack. The sooner she won her case, was granted guardianship of the children, left Sutter Creek behind and returned to the life that awaited her back home, the better. Memories of her time here would fade. One day she would meet a man who would make her as light-headed as she'd been when Henry's lips—

Stop that, Lavinia. You must get a hold of yourself.

She summoned her best parlor smile and spent the next hour making the rounds. Despite the party not working out the way she'd planned, her guests had enjoyed themselves. Several had even gone so far as to say it was the best party they'd ever attended. She'd succeeded in achieving her goal of gaining the community's support, despite the changes she'd been forced to make, and yet her victory felt hollow.

The first family left the schoolhouse just as a gentleman wearing an overcoat as fine as Henry's entered. She would have recognized the man's raven hair and green eyes anywhere.

Stuart Worthington.

He spotted her and strode her way. Although he was as good-looking as ever, he was the last person she wanted to see when her emotions were running amok. What would Henry think?

"Lavinia, what a pleasure." He lifted her hand and planted a kiss on the back of it.

"I, um, wasn't expecting you so soon. Has something come up?"

"Nothing's amiss. I just thought it would be more pleasant to spend Christmas here in Sutter Creek with you than alone in San Francisco."

How was she to deal with Henry and Stuart in the same town at the same time, especially after what had just taken place? Thankfully manners dictated her response. "Of course. I'm sure you're eager to meet the children."

His warm smile came as a surprise. "By all means. I understand I just missed their performance. I'm sorry about that. I would have liked to have seen it."

"Really? I didn't know you had an interest in children." Despite the many conversations they'd had, the topic hadn't come up.

"Very much so. I look forward to having a family one day. Now that my career is getting established, I can think about making that happen."

Stuart had been the consummate gentleman on the trip west, keeping things between them cordial. His statement, coupled with the quick raising of his eyebrows, caused a warning gong to sound in her head. Was he hoping to woo her, after all?

"How did things go in San Francisco? Do you have a favorable report for Father?"

He blinked twice, and his professional manner reasserted itself, much to her relief. "I do. The city is well on its way to becoming one of the largest and most influential in California. By establishing a hotel now, we could secure a piece of property in the area between Market and Montgomery. I've scouted out several prime locations."

"He'll be happy to hear that."

"I hope so. Now, would you be so kind as to introduce me to your nieces and nephew?"

"Certainly." He seemed genuinely interested in meeting them, and yet she couldn't help but wonder about his motives. She'd had no such qualms in the past, but he hadn't made his intentions quite so obvious before. "I must ask you not to mention my plans to take them to Philadelphia. I've encountered some hurdles." She updated him on her pending court case.

"I'm sorry things have been so challenging, Lavinia. You can trust me not to say a word."

"Thank you." She spotted Alex by himself, surveying what was left on the dessert tables, and headed over to him. He picked up a molasses fritter.

"Alex."

He spun around, a guilty look on his face. "Aunt Livy, I've only had three things so far."

"It's fine. You may have another. I just came over to introduce you to my…my friend, Mr. Worthington. Stuart this is my nephew, Alex."

"I'm pleased to meet you, young man." Stuart held out a hand.

Alex looked up at Stuart with narrowed eyes and made

no move to accept his offer of a handshake. "You're the man who brought Aunt Livy here, aren't you?"

Stuart returned his attention to Alex. "You're right. I'm the one who was privileged to serve as her escort on the trip here, and what a journey it was. We traveled on two ships and a train."

Alex eyed Stuart suspiciously. "You're not her sweetheart, are you?"

To his credit, Stuart didn't appear surprised. "I work for her father, but she and I are friends."

"It's a good thing you're only friends because my uncle Henry just gave her a great big kiss in front of everybody."

Of all the things Alex could have said, that had to be the most cringe-worthy. Mindful of her nephew's feelings and Stuart's stunned silence, Lavinia chose her words carefully. "You and your sisters took your uncle and me by surprise with that bit of mistletoe mischief. We went along with it because we knew it was all in fun."

"But you like him. I know you do."

"Of course I like him. Your uncle is a fine man, and he's very good to you and your sisters, but he and I are just friends." And despite her surprising reaction to Henry's kiss, that's all they could ever be.

"Speaking of your sisters," Stuart said, bringing the awkward conversation to a close, "I'd like to meet them, too, so your aunt and I will leave you to enjoy that dessert. I look forward to seeing you again, Alex."

Lavinia took the arm Stuart offered, grateful to escape her nephew's probing questions. The last thing she wanted to do right now was examine her feelings for Henry. Or his lack of feelings for her. She scanned the room, spotted Marcie and Dot by the Christmas tree and led the way to them.

Marcie saw them first, and her eyes widened. She looked from Stuart to Lavinia. "Who is he?"

She introduced him. "And these are my nieces, Marcie and Dot."

Stuart held his closed hand to his waist and leaned toward the girls in gallant fashion. "Your aunt didn't tell me what lovely ladies you are."

Marcie smiled and passed a hand over her dark curls. "Do you want to see the decorations I made? Aunt Livy's been too busy to see them."

The way Marcie shrugged off Lavinia's apparent lack of interest brought her up short. She'd been so focused on the party that she'd forgotten to look at her niece's ornaments.

Henry appeared at Lavinia's side. "Your aunt's here now, Muffin, and I'm sure she'd love to see your creations."

Lavinia welcomed the opportunity to concentrate on something other than the men standing on either side of her, giving her time to compose herself after the series of surprises she'd faced in the past few minutes. "Yes, sweetie, I would. Please, show us all."

Marcie ate up the attention, eagerly pointing out her handiwork while directing her comments to Stuart. "I made angels since I'm going to be an angel in the Christmas play. I even have a line to say. Will you be there, Mr. Worthy, um, Worthing?" She frowned. "I forgot what it is."

"It's Worthington, but since that's such a long name, you can call me Mr. W. And yes, I will be there. I look forward to hearing you deliver your line. I'm sure you'll do a wonderful job."

"My niece is quite talented." Henry smiled at Marcie, but the icy look he shot Stuart could freeze the water flowing in Sutter Creek.

Lavinia could avoid the inevitable no longer. "Stuart, allow me to introduce Henry Hawthorn, the children's uncle. Henry, this is—"

"Mr. Worthington. Yes, I know. Welcome." Henry extended a hand, still stained from his day spent working in the smithy. His eyes held a challenge.

Stuart returned Henry's piercing gaze with an unflinching one and shook his hand without hesitation. "I'm pleased to meet you, Mr. Hawthorn. Lavinia has told me a great deal about you."

The tension between the two men put Lavinia on edge. "You must be tired after your travels, Stuart. Have you secured lodging yet?"

"I booked a room at the American House hotel. I'll be heading there shortly, but first I'd like to sample some of those desserts and have a cup of that delicious smelling cider, if I may?"

Lavinia nodded. "By all means."

"Aunt Livy, can Mr. W. go with us to get our Christmas tree tomorrow?"

Stuart had obviously made an impression on Marcie. "It's nice of you to ask, sweetie, but I'm not sure he'd want to do that."

"It's going to be quite an adventure. This little lady—" Henry swung Dot into his arms "—has never seen snow. Her brother and sister did once, but they were too young to remember. I thought it would be fun to head up the mountain and find a tree above the snowline. That will require traveling in a wagon over two hours each way."

Henry's announcement was unexpected. Several days before, Lavinia had suggested granting the children's wish to see snow, but he'd said the trip could end up being more trouble than it was worth and that they could find a tree much closer. Something had obviously changed his mind. It was clear he was out to dissuade Stuart from joining them.

Dot stared at Henry, openmouthed. "We get to see snow? Goody!"

"Please say you'll come, Mr. W. You could help Uncle Henry cut down the tree and carry it to the wagon." Marcie leaned toward Stuart and spoke in a stage whisper. "Alex thinks he's old enough to do it, but he's not. He's still a boy, but you're a big, tall man."

Stuart smiled. "It sounds like fun. I'd be happy to join all of you, provided, of course—" he turned to Henry "—that I wouldn't be in the way."

"There's plenty of room on the wagon."

Lavinia stifled a sigh. Henry hadn't exactly come across as welcoming, but he could use the help. It would take two men to carry the tree she wanted.

"Good," Stuart said. "I'll be ready when you show up at the hotel."

A steely-eyed look passed between the men. She got the impression they were facing off. Were they out to show her that they cared about impressing the children? Or could it be that they were trying to impress her?

She would be delighted if Henry made his attraction clear. If he did, that could change everything.

Chapter Fourteen

"Are we there yet?" Dot asked for the tenth time since leaving Sutter Creek.

"We'll be there soon, sweetie." Lavinia was as eager to arrive at their destination as her niece.

Bouncing on the plank seat the past two hours between Stuart and Henry had been challenging. Stuart had carried on a lively conversation with the children, whereas Henry had said little beyond responding to direct questions. If she didn't know better, she'd think he was jealous. Although he'd said nothing to indicate that he'd fallen for her, she took his brooding silence as an encouraging sign. A lady could hope, couldn't she?

"Look at all that beautiful snow." Marcie's excitement had intensified with each additional inch of white on the ground. "Can't we stop now, Uncle Henry? We've been riding for ever so long."

"There are only four or five inches, but I suppose that's enough to build a snowman." He brought the wagon to a halt at last and hopped down.

The children scrambled out of the wagon bed. Alex scuffed around in the snow. Dot tossed a handful of the powdery stuff into the air. Marcie hit Henry with a snow-ball and burst out laughing when he jumped.

He came to life, scooping up some snow and forming it into a ball. "Look out, Muffin. I'm going to get you back."

The other children joined in the snowball fight. Their gleeful shouts rang out, a sharp contrast to the hush of the forest.

Stuart climbed down and helped Lavinia to the ground. She took a step, but he stopped her.

"I'd like to spend a few minutes with you. Alone." His request, delivered in that serious tone, sent a shiver racing up her spine.

"Is everything all right?"

"I received a second letter from your father not long after the first arrived. He's fine, but he's made some plans that won't sit well with you."

That wasn't surprising. She didn't agree with many of his decisions. "I see. We could slip away for a few min-utes after our picnic lunch." She was in no hurry to find out what her father wanted. If it had Stuart concerned, it must be quite distasteful.

Lavinia and Stuart joined in the fun. Although she hadn't participated in a snowball fight since she and Pau-line were young, her aim was as good as ever. The snow-ball she sent sailing Henry's way struck him in the middle of his back as planned.

He wheeled around, realized who'd pelted him and took off after her, holding a huge snowball in his hands. She should have waited until he'd lobbed it at someone else. He ran fast, but she zigzagged through the trees.

"Go, Aunt Livy!" Marcie and Dot called.

"Get her, Uncle Henry!" Alex hollered.

She turned to see how close Henry was and ran into

Stuart. Henry sent the snowball sailing. She ducked, and it smacked Stuart in the face.

He brushed himself off and laughed. "Look out, Hawthorn. I'm coming after you."

A fierce battle ensued. The men fired snowballs back and forth with surprising speed.

Alex and Dot cheered for their uncle. Marcie shouted encouragement to both Henry and Stuart. Lavinia watched in amazement as the men pommeled each other relentlessly. Although it was a game, the determination on their faces spoke of a deeper reason for their rivalry.

The futility of their efforts had her shaking her head. She cared about Henry deeply, but despite this unexpected show of jealousy, he seemed to be holding back, much to her dismay. Stuart appeared to be interested in her, but she wouldn't encourage a man for whom she felt nothing more than friendship.

She waved her arms over her head and stood between the men. "I'm declaring a ceasefire. We have a snowman to build."

"That we do." Henry took charge. "Alex and I will make the base. Stuart, you and Marcie can take the middle, and Dot and Lavinia can form the head. Is everyone in agreement?"

They nodded.

"All right then. Ready. Set. Go!"

Before long, the snowman took shape. The children added twigs for arms, rocks for the face and moss for buttons down the snowy fellow's front.

Dot admired their creation. "He's the bestest snowman in the whole wide world, isn't he?"

"That he is," Stuart agreed, "but he's missing something." He dashed to the wagon and returned with a well-worn derby and scarf he'd rescued from the hotel's lost-and-found barrel. "If you'll allow me to hold you up, you may have the honor of putting these on our new friend."

She glanced at Henry, as though seeking his permission. To Lavinia's relief, he nodded.

"There." Dot put the hat and scarf in place and smiled at Stuart for the first time. "He looks just right now."

He returned the smile. "That he does, Miss Dorothea."

Her mouth fell open. "You know my long name."

"Of course I do. Your aunt told me."

She narrowed her eyes. "What about Alex and Marcie? Do you know theirs, too?"

Stuart nodded. "Alexander and Marcella. Each of you was named after a grandparent."

His way with the children eased Lavinia's concerns about his ability to help her look after them on the trip back to Philadelphia. Hopefully, Henry's had been put to rest as well. She looked his way and caught him watching her, his fine features pinched in a frown.

He turned toward the children. "Are you ready to find a tree?"

His question was met with joyful exclamations.

"All right then. We're looking for one this high." He held an arm over his head and bent his fingers.

Lavinia clomped over to him. "I was hoping to get a tree twice as tall."

"Why? The parlor has a ten-foot ceiling."

"I thought we'd set it up in the entryway. It would look wonderful there."

Alex joined them. "We can't do that, Aunt Livy. Mama and Papa always put the tree in the parlor."

His drawn eyebrows and downturned mouth tugged

at her heart. "I'm sorry, Alex. I didn't think about that." She'd been so focused on her vision for the celebration that she hadn't thought to ask the children what they wanted. "We'll put the tree in the parlor like your mama and papa did. And we'll decorate it just the way you want."

Alex's features relaxed. "Really? We can make popcorn and cranberry strings and hang the ornaments Mama made?"

Lavinia nodded. "We'll make the garlands as soon as we get back. I promise."

"Can we decorate the tree tonight, too?" Alex asked.

"Is that what they did?"

He shook his head. "They made us wait until Christmas Eve, but that's two days away. I like seeing the tree. It makes it feel more like Christmas."

"You're right. We'll get it decorated tonight, provided your uncle agrees." Hopefully, he would. She couldn't haul the tree inside and set it up herself.

"Wholeheartedly." Henry sent her a smile so warm it could melt an entire snowman in no time, setting her heart beating double time. "Your aunt's a wise woman. Christmas is special and deserves to be celebrated for more than just a day or two. That's why she's worked so hard to spread Christmas cheer at the parties she's planned."

His compliments drew her up short. If he knew that the real reason was to gain support from the community, his opinion of her would change. At least she wouldn't have to tell him about her pending case against him until after Christmas since Mr. Price hadn't been able to secure a court date before then.

"Come, Alex." She beckoned. "Let's get your sisters.

I've never gotten to pick out a Christmas tree before, so I need the three of you to help me find the very best one. And we must remember that it can't be much taller than your uncle Henry when he's wearing that lovely top hat of his."

The next two hours flew by as they cut a tree, loaded it in the back of the wagon and enjoyed their picnic while seated on a quilt-covered tarpaulin spread beneath the clear blue sky. A gentle breeze whispered through snow-laden branches, sending glittering flakes floating to the ground. The sun overhead transformed the landscape into a blanket of glistening diamonds.

Lavinia gathered the remains of their lunch and carried the wicker basket to the wagon.

Stuart followed her. "Would you care to take a short walk with me before we get underway?"

She had no interest in hearing her father's plan, especially when it was sure to put a damper on this delightful day. "Certainly. Just let me tell Henry so he knows to keep an eye on the children."

"There's no need. I've already let him know."

"Oh. And what did he say?"

Stuart chuckled. "Very little. I get the impression he's not too happy that I showed up."

"I can understand since he knows I intend to have you help me take the children away from him."

They set off. Although the ray of sun she'd sat in had warmed her, Lavinia tucked her hands in her muff before Stuart could offer his arm. She'd caught him studying her several times with the unmistakable look of a man who'd taken an interest in her. His lingering gazes had lacked the level of attraction she'd seen in Henry's eyes before he'd kissed her, but even so, she had no intention of giving Stuart the wrong impression. If only looking into his eyes made her breath hitch the way it did when she lost herself in the clear blue of Henry's.

She spotted a granite boulder alongside the creek. Henry and the children were visible in the distance, giving her a sense of security. She trusted Stuart, but he'd been acting differently. "We could sit here."

"Fine. Allow me." He made a cushion using the blanket he'd slung over his arm. "There you go."

"Thank you." She took a seat as far to one side as she could on the small surface, clasped her hands tightly inside the muff and braced herself for what was to come, whatever that might be.

Stuart sat, shifting to one side so he was facing her. He pulled a letter out of his pocket. "I received this some time ago, and ever since I've been debating how much to tell you about what it contains. I realized I have no right to withhold anything from you, even if the news is… somewhat troubling."

His careful choice of words concerned her. "You said Father's all right."

"He is. It's not about him. It's about the children, Alex in particular."

"Alex? Why?"

"Perhaps it would be best if you read the letter yourself."

She removed her muff, took the envelope and pulled out the small sheet of paper filled with words penned in tiny print to allow for as many on the page as possible. Her frugal father had kept the weight under a quarter of an ounce to get the Pony Express's lowest rate.

The first half of the letter dealt with hotel business. The Golden Crowne hotel was not only going to be built, but her father stated clearly that Stuart would be given the task of overseeing its construction.

"Oh, Stuart, you must be thrilled. This is the first time Father has relinquished so much control. I can see why. You've proven you can do the job. I'm curious, though. Will you still be able to escort the children and me back to Philadelphia?"

"It depends. Keep reading."

The next paragraph started with news that seemed too good to be true. Her skin tingled and turned to gooseflesh. "I can't believe it! Father is eager to meet the children. He's never said such a thing before. Pauline would be so happy."

Stuart slid his hands in the pockets of his overcoat and gazed into the distance. Although he said nothing, the firm set of his jaw spoke volumes. The bad news was yet to come. Lavinia drew in a breath of the crisp mountain air and willed herself to keep reading.

At long last, I will have my heir. Lavinia has mentioned what a bright boy Alexander is, but I know remediation will be required after his experience out west. I've engaged a private tutor for him in Boston—far from the hostilities predicted to visit our besieged country soon—where I'll send him shortly after he arrives. As soon as he's of age, I'll see that he's admitted to one of the finest boarding schools.

She held the paper in hands that were shaking so badly she couldn't focus on the remaining lines. "I can't believe it. Why would Father have me bring Alex back only to send him away?"

"He has his reasons."

"I see that, but tearing the children apart would break their hearts." It would rend hers to watch it happen. She blinked several times to clear her watery vision and forced herself to finish the letter, the ache in her chest intensifying as she read.

I'll have a governess ready to take charge of the children when your ship docks in New York. They will require a firm hand after the leniency they've been granted by my daughters. Pauline possessed a free spirit, and although Lavinia is more level-headed than her sister was, she's prone to senti-mentality. I allowed my late wife to pamper our girls when they were young, resulting in outright rebellion when they were older, but I won't make that mistake with my grandchildren. They will be taught to respect my authority, not flout it.

I wish you a pleasant journey, Stuart, and look forward to finalizing our plans for the Golden Crowne prior to your return to San Francisco.

Sincerely,
Paul Crowne

She shoved the paper at Stuart. "You'd best take this before I tear it to shreds." She jumped up and paced, her breath coming in noisy puffs. "He's maligned my sis-ter for years. I kept quiet, but I can't do that anymore. Pauline was a wonderful mother. She loved the children deeply and taught them the value of family. They might squabble every now and then, but they're good and kind and respectful. They don't need a *firm hand*. They need love and kindness and understanding."

Stuart nodded. "And that's what you've given them."

"You're right. I have. I'm going to see that the children get the loving care they deserve." She stopped in front of Stuart and jabbed her fists into her hips. "And if that's too sentimental for Father's liking, well then, he'll just have to deal with it."

"What are you going to do?"

"I'm not sure, but I can't take them back to Philadelphia. I know what it's like to live life under his roof and his rule." She plopped down on the rock, rested her elbows on her knees and held her chin in her hands. Lifting her head required more energy than she had.

Everything in her revolted at what she'd read. She'd spent years overlooking her father's autocratic manner, even making excuses for it, but he'd gone too far this time. He might be expecting her to carry out his marching orders, but she refused to subject those precious children to his sharp tongue and barked commands.

"He can be demanding at times," Stuart said, "but that drives those of us under him to achieve more than we might otherwise. I'm a case in point. I never imagined I'd be chosen to open a hotel for him."

"Pushing his employees is one thing, but putting unrealistic demands on innocent children is simply unfair. I won't be a party to it. If I have to, I'll stay here in California, win my case and gain guardianship myself. That way Father would have no right to send Alex away."

"What will you tell your father?"

"I have no idea. It won't matter anyway. If he's decided to claim Alex as his heir, he won't tolerate me going against him." Nothing she could say would change his mind. In all likelihood, he would disown her as he had Pauline.

Stuart rubbed a hand over his square jaw. "When I read the letter, I anticipated your reaction. I know how much the children mean to you. I also know what it's like to stand up to your father, having watched others do so. That's why I've come up with a possible solution."

She straightened. "Really? What's that?"

"You could stay here in California and marry me."

Had she heard him correctly? "Did you say what I think you said?"

He nodded. "I've given it a lot of thought. If we were to wed, that would give you a stronger case. A judge or jury would look more favorably on a couple than a single woman."

"That's probably true, but if you join me in defying Father, you would be passing up the opportunity to oversee the construction of the Golden Crowne. How could you give that up?" And why would he?

"Not to sound boastful, but my experience working for your father has served me well. Others would like to gain from it. I've had two different groups of investors in San Francisco invite me to open hotels for them. The possibility of working for men who value my expertise is appealing."

She could understand that. Even if her father respected Stuart, he wasn't one to dole out appreciation or accolades. "But why marry me?"

"The group of investors whose offer I'm most interested in have had bad experiences with the single men out here. They're apt to move on as soon as a better opportunity comes their way. The gentlemen want a family man and have given me until the end of the year to find a wife. If I must marry, I can't think of anyone more suited. I realize you don't have romantic feelings for me. Since I don't have them for you either, this would be, to put it bluntly, a marriage of convenience. It's not an ideal solution, but it could benefit us both."

He looked so serious, so sincere. "You're a fine man, Stuart, and you deserve a woman who loves you."

"We might not be in love, but we get on well. It wouldn't be so bad, would it?" He reached out as though to take her hand but pulled his back before making contact. His gaze locked with hers, his green eyes conveying both hope and uncertainty. "I hold you in high regard, Lavinia, and would do my best to be a good and faithful husband."

She grabbed her muff and stuffed her hands inside. "I have no doubt of that, but…" How could she consider Stuart's offer when she felt the way she did about Henry? If only he cared as much about her as she did him.

"If you refuse to honor your father's wishes, I would imagine you'd lose his support. I could provide a good living for you and the children."

The reality of her situation set Lavinia's stomach to swirling. She intended to win the court case. When she did, she would need money to pay for food, lodging and everything else. Her funds wouldn't last long, and then where would she be?

Perhaps she'd been hasty in declaring her intention to stand up to her father and keep him from getting the children. She hadn't had good results when challenging him in the past. What made her think this time would be any different? Stuart was offering a solution to her dilemma, but everything in her balked at the thought of accepting it.

The children's laughter rang out, drawing her attention to where Henry was leading them in a game of Simon Says. They were mimicking his movements, and he wasn't making it easy. He was hopping on one foot and turning in circles while patting the top of his head.

His love of the children knew no bounds. He would make a wonderful father. She could imagine him holding a baby, his tenderness evident in every look and loving touch. What would it be like to see him doting on an infant with his blue eyes and her curly hair?

Where had that thought come from? Henry didn't care for her in that way. He wanted to provide a home for his nieces and nephew, but he'd never said anything about wanting more children. Or a wife.

"Lavinia?" Stuart's voice reminded her of his presence.

"I'm sorry. I was woolgathering. The truth is, I don't know what to say. This is all so sudden." *There must be some other way, Lord. Please, help me find it.*

"You don't need to answer today. Take time to pray about it. You can let me know what you've decided after the Christmas Eve service. If you choose to accept my proposal, we could announce our engagement on Christmas morning."

Christmas? That only left her two days to make one of the most important decisions of her life.

Something significant had taken place between Lavinia and Stuart. Henry was sure of it. He'd forced himself to keep his attention on the game he was playing with the children while they waited to begin the trip back to Sutter Creek, but he hadn't been able to keep from glancing at the couple in the distance every so often.

Lavinia had been pacing at one point, evidently troubled by something. When she and Stuart had returned to the wagon and taken their places on the bench seat, she'd put more distance between herself and Stuart than before and avoided looking his way—a fact that brought Henry a great deal of satisfaction.

As they traveled the rutted road down the mountain, she encouraged the children to tell her about the Christmases they'd spent with their parents, listening intently to their detailed recollections. The shift in her focus from showing them the kind of lavish celebrations they would enjoy back in Philadelphia to learning about the simple, small-town observances they'd experienced and enjoyed was as welcome as the sun on his face after three days of biting cold. He intended to find out what had caused the change.

They reached Sutter Creek two hours later, and Henry pulled up at the American House hotel, only too happy to drop off Stuart. He might be good with the children, but he'd upset Lavinia, which Henry couldn't abide. He had half a mind to hop down and have a word with the interloper, but the thought of facing her afterward kept him in the driver's seat. She'd probably claim he had no right to interfere. The truth was he didn't, which irked him.

Stuart turned to Lavinia, took her hand in his and gazed at her with unmistakable interest. "I look forward to seeing you at the Christmas Eve service and talking with you afterward. I trust you'll have an answer for me."

Her "I will," uttered in a breathy voice, had Henry gripping the reins so tightly his knuckles turned white. He kept his gaze forward, unable to stomach the scene playing out beside him.

"Good. I look forward to hearing it." Stuart bid the

children farewell, gave Henry a cursory nod and entered the hotel.

Henry urged the team forward, saying nothing as they traveled down Main and up Church Street. Lavinia remained quiet and reflective, although the children chatted excitedly about decorating the tree. He pulled in behind the house. Alex, Marcie and Dot clambered out of the wagon, followed by their aunt. He removed the Douglas Fir, grateful it was only seven feet tall instead of sixteen, as Lavinia had originally wanted. He had no idea what caused her to change her mind so quickly, but he was glad she had.

He carried the tree inside, set it in a large tub of sand, added some water and headed to the livery to return the wagon.

The familiar scents of horses, leather and stalls due for their nightly mucking out greeted him—along with the livery owner. "Evening, Henry. How did these lovely ladies do for you today?" The burly fellow patted the two mares in turn.

"Just fine. I'd take them out anytime."

"Glad to hear they earned their oats. I'll unhitch them, and you can settle up with Cyrus."

Henry turned but stopped when he heard his name. "Yes?"

"Almost forgot to tell you. Mr. Little was in this morning. Since he usually takes these girls, your name came up. He asked me to let you know that he has a telegram waiting for you."

"Thanks."

Henry strode up Main to the American House and went inside. Thankfully, Worthington was nowhere to be seen.

The desk clerk looked up and smiled. "Afternoon, Mr. Hawthorn. Come for this, I presume?" He held out an envelope bearing the Alta California Telegraph Company name.

Henry opened it quickly, read the brief message and frowned.

"Bad news, is it?"

"Not terrible, but I'd hoped for better." He'd finally received an offer on his hotel up in Marysville, but the amount the buyer was willing to pay was even less than what Henry had hoped to get, despite having lowered the price.

He returned to the house minutes later to find Lavinia and the children seated on the front porch steps, stringing popcorn and cranberries. "What are you doing out here?"

She looked up and smiled. "Making the garlands."

"I can see that, but why aren't you inside?" Lavinia generally spent most of her time in the house.

"It's been so cold lately that we couldn't be outdoors for very long. I thought it would be nice to enjoy a little more time in the fresh air."

"And here I thought it was because the birds would clean things up for you." He toed some broken bits of popcorn.

She chuckled. "I can't keep anything from you, can I?"

Yes, she could. He had yet to come up with a way to ask her what had happened with Stuart that didn't sound like prying.

"Uncle Henry, look how long my popcorn string is already." Marcie held up a three-foot section.

"You're off to a good start."

"Mine's short." Dot dangled a string with only a few

inches covered. "The popcorn breaks when I put the needle in."

"Would you like some help, Dimples?"

She bobbed her head, her curls bouncing. He plopped down on the step beside Lavinia, pulled Dot onto his lap and gave her a lesson. She soon got the feel for how much pressure to exert and was happily threading popcorn on her string while singing her favorite carol in her adorable little girl voice.

Lavinia and Alex were stringing cranberries and had the red-tipped fingers to prove it. She joined in the singing, as did Alex and Marcie. Henry added his voice to the mix, reveling in the family scene. He'd spent years bouncing from one venture to another, but this was the life he'd dreamed of.

There was only one problem—the beautiful woman next to him was determined to leave and take the children with her. He could prevent the latter, since he was their legal guardian, but he could do nothing to keep Lavinia from walking out of his life. Or could he?

The carol ended, and Dot shivered. "Brr. I'm cold. Can we go in the house?"

Lavinia jerked to attention. "I'm sorry. I didn't realize how chilly it had gotten. We'll move into the parlor and maybe, if you children ask nicely, your uncle will make us some hot chocolate."

"Please, Uncle Henry, will you?" Marcie asked.

Her brother and sister echoed her request.

He grinned. "Of course."

Minutes later, he entered the parlor bearing a tray filled with steaming mugs. The children and their lovely aunt had created garlands aplenty. He set the tray on the table. "Here you are, but be careful. The chocolate's hot.

While we're waiting for it to cool, I have something for you to do. Just a moment." He left and returned with a pasteboard box he'd pulled from the attic.

Alex took it, whipped off the lid and shouted. "Look! These are the ornaments we made with Mama."

The girls peered inside. Dot pulled out a five-sided star made of twigs tied with twine.

Marcie cradled a snowflake fashioned from cinnamon sticks in her hands. She stared at it with trembling lips. Twin tears trailed down her cheeks.

Henry squatted before her and rested his hands on her shoulders. "What's wrong?"

"I remember watching Mama make this. She was artistic, just like me, wasn't she?"

"Yes. You take after her that way."

Marcie wiped away her tears with the back of a hand and sniffed. "I miss Mama and Papa so much."

"We all do, Muffin. I think that ornament deserves a special place on the tree, don't you? I'm sure you can find one."

The grieving girl nodded. She padded over to the tree, hung the snowflake and fingered the cinnamon-scented creation.

Henry joined Lavinia on the settee across the room from the tree, where she sat watching the children eagerly hanging ornaments. He kept his voice low so the children wouldn't hear them. "That box brings back memories. I can almost hear Pauline calling the children to come help her when she'd carry it in each year. Her excitement was contagious."

"She must have been in her element." Lavinia spoke softly. "One of her biggest disappointments when we were girls was that Father refused to let us decorate the tree. He said that was a job for the servants. But it wasn't a job. It would have been fun, and yet he kept us from it like he did so many things."

Lavinia's gaze had grown distant, as though she was no longer there but had traveled back in time. He said nothing, eager to see if she'd continue.

She did, although her voice wavered. "I've told myself he meant well, but I wonder about that now. It seems he does what suits him with little thought of others. I don't understand how he could even think of sending Alex off with a total stranger right after he arrives."

Henry spoke in a heated whisper. "What? He plans to send Alex away?"

Lavinia turned to him and stared deeply into his eyes, as though searching for something. Her probing look continued for several seconds, giving way to sadness. "He wrote to Stuart and said he's hired a tutor up in Boston. I couldn't believe it, but I saw the words myself."

"I won't allow that to happen."

"Neither will I."

He stared at her, although he had a hard time focusing. "What are you saying?"

She picked up a piece of popcorn, pulled off the three fluffy white flakes and placed them on her palm. "Father expects me to deliver the children so he can take charge of them, but I can't do that." She crushed the rounded core in her other hand.

"So you've realized I was right?"

She threw the hard ball into the popcorn bowl and rubbed a finger over each of the flakes. "I have. The children are happy, so I'm going to do everything in my power to keep them here."

He'd waited weeks to hear those words. He could rest

easy knowing the children's future was no longer in question, but Lavinia leaving was something he didn't want to think about. "I'm relieved, of course, but your father won't take kindly to having his plans disregarded."

She held her hand over the bowl, brushed the remaining pieces of popcorn into it and faced him, determination making her brown eyes even darker. "He won't, but I'm not going to let that stop me. The children's needs come first."

"What about you? What will you do?"

"Stuart's made me an offer that would enable me to stay here with the children."

The hairs on the back of Henry's neck stood at attention. "What kind of offer?" He dreaded the answer, but he had to know.

Lavinia took a sudden interest in the bottom button on her bodice. "A marriage proposal."

"What? But I thought—" He clamped his lips together to keep his protest from pouring out and fought to regain control, not an easy task when he felt like punching something.

Her shoulders rose and fell as she drew in a series of deep breaths. "This would be more of a business arrangement, if you will. My father seems to have settled on the idea of accepting Alex as his heir. When he finds out I won't be delivering him, I fully expect my father to retaliate as he did when Pauline defied him."

A business arrangement? She was talking about a marriage of convenience. How could she consider such a thing? A woman as wonderful as Lavinia deserved all the love a man had to give—and then some.

She continued in a halting voice, twisting the button so hard that Henry expected to see it pop off. "If I was to form an alliance with Stuart, I'd be in a better position to provide for them."

"What do you mean? I'm their guardian. I'll take care of them."

"You are now, but I love them, too, Henry. You've touted all California has to offer. I could give them that myself in San Francisco."

The weight that had lifted from his shoulders fell back in place with a jarring heaviness. She wasn't giving up her fight after all, but it appeared she was considering giving up her dreams for the sake of the children. While that was admirable, the possibility of her marrying Stuart sickened him. "You haven't given Mr. Worthington an answer, have you?"

She shook her head. "He's expecting it after the Christmas Eve service."

There was still time for her to change her mind. If only he was in a position to tell her how much she'd come to mean to him. He couldn't stomach the thought of her as another man's wife, but he wasn't free to declare his feelings when he couldn't care for her properly. His finances were precarious. He wasn't even sure how he was going to make the mortgage payment that was due at the end of the year since the prospective buyer for his hotel had made such a low offer. Unless he accepted it, he didn't have enough money.

Worthington could give Lavinia the kind of life she was used to, but what kind of life would that be without love? She wanted it. She deserved it. "What will you tell him?"

"I'm not sure. My options are limited. Stuart's given me one, and I feel compelled to consider it."

"So you're willing to settle for a loveless marriage, after all?"

"I'm willing to make the sacrifice if that's what it takes to get what I want. Can you give me a good reason why I shouldn't?"

"No." Although he desperately wished he could, he was unable to. Not yet, anyhow.

But he could make a sacrifice of his own, too. Would it be enough?

Chapter Fifteen

Lavinia sat at her dressing table, pinned her curls in place and pinched her cheeks to add some color. She reached for her perfume. Perhaps the rich rose scent would lift her spirits.

Caroling had seemed like a great idea when Henry suggested it weeks ago, but that was before Stuart had arrived in town and changed everything. Ever since she'd told Henry about the proposal, she'd been in a state of turmoil.

Despite her hope that he would protest or beg her not to settle for a loveless marriage, he'd said nothing. Even when she'd asked him straight out if there was a good reason why she shouldn't consider Stuart's offer, Henry hadn't said anything to indicate that he had feelings for her.

How could she have misread things so badly? His kindness? His helpfulness? His kiss? She'd relived that incredible experience many times, and every time she'd come to the same conclusion—Henry might have given in to the children's mistletoe ploy at the school party two nights ago, but he'd wanted to kiss her. He'd said as much afterward. Surely, that had to mean something.

Things between them had been strained ever since their talk while the children were decorating the tree the day before. She'd asked him what was troubling him. All he'd said was that the mortgage was weighing on his mind.

The way he'd been watching her when he thought she wasn't looking, his handsome features downcast, said there was more to it than that. He bristled whenever Stuart was mentioned, making it clear he was the cause of Henry's ill humor. Although that gave her hope, his stony silence ate at her.

She corked the bottle, returned the perfume to its place and closed her eyes.

I've fallen in love with Henry, Lord, but he doesn't love me. If only he did, I wouldn't have to keep up this fight. We could raise the children together. Since he doesn't return my feelings, I have no choice but to consider Stuart's proposal. Being married to him would help me win my case and enable me to raise the children myself. I know Henry thinks he can do it on his own, but they'd be better off with me. I could give them many of the things Father planned to.

Father!

Her eyes flew open. She picked up the letter she'd started that morning, her third attempt to write one to him since learning of his plans to send Alex away. The right words wouldn't come. Thankfully, she had a few more days to figure out how best to explain her decision.

Even though she had no intention of taking the children back, knowing what awaited them if she did, she dreaded her father's reaction to the news. The reply he was sure to send her would be scathing. At least she wouldn't have to *hear* the words as she had his criticisms about her sister. She could read the rebuke and retribution and burn the paper they were printed on afterward.

"Aunt Livy!" Marcie called up the stairs. "Are you coming soon?"

"I'm on my way!" She shoved the letter into her dressing table drawer and joined them in the entryway.

Henry, Lavinia and the children donned their coats, hats, scarves and gloves and set out.

"Where will we be singing, Uncle Henry?" Alex asked.

"I thought we'd start on Main, and then we could visit a few homes on Spanish Street."

"Good. Frankie lives there. Can we go to his house?"

"I'd planned on it."

They reached Main Street, stood in the glow of a gaslight and launched into the first of the many carols they'd rehearsed. A crowd formed around them, primarily single miners who cast appreciative glances Lavinia's way, to her dismay.

She stepped closer to Henry, grateful for his reassuring presence. When she was with him, she felt stronger and more capable than she ever had back home. His belief in her meant more than he would ever know. Leaving Sutter Creek would be difficult because, although she'd be taking the children with her once she won her case, she'd be leaving a part of her heart behind. Just for tonight, she could imagine the five of them were a family with Henry as the head.

The time passed quickly. Before Lavinia knew it, they were at the last house, where Frankie lived. They sang two carols. Afterward they were offered shortbread that was still warm from the oven. Alex and the girls were talking with Frankie and his sister, enabling the adults to enjoy a few minutes of conversation.

Lavinia was ready to gather the children and head up the hill when Frankie's father, Cyrus, stopped her cold with a question. "How are things working out with that case of yours?"

Her knees went as soft as whipping cream. She gripped the porch railing to keep from swaying. He couldn't mean her case, could he?

She feigned confusion. "I beg your pardon?"

"I was working in the livery the other day when Mr. Price's clerk came in. He was asking if anyone had asked to have a notice posted about Jack's creditors after yer—" he cleared his throat "—losses. Said his boss needed the information to make a case. I was curious how that was coming along?"

Henry answered before she could, his words clipped. "There must have been a misunderstanding. I haven't hired Mr. Price to check into anything."

Cyrus looked from Henry to Lavinia and produced a weak smile. "I, um, think I've said more than enough. It was right kind of you all to come sing for us. We're looking forward to seeing you at the church service tomorrow and enjoying some more of those fine baked goods of yours at the party afterward."

Lavinia couldn't say their farewells quickly enough. She hustled the children away, putting them between herself and Henry. Their excited chatter would provide a welcome diversion. If all went well, she'd be able to slip inside before Henry had an opportunity to ask questions she'd rather not answer.

When they reached the house, Henry stood on the porch and hugged each of the children good-night in turn.

Marcie lingered. "Can you believe it will be Christmas Eve tomorrow, Uncle Henry? Are you excited?"

"Not as excited as you are, Muffin, but—" he cast a glance at Lavinia before returning his attention to Marcie "—it could prove to be an interesting day."

Lavinia didn't miss his meaning. He'd made his thoughts about her proposal from Stuart clear. Not that Henry's opinion changed anything. Her options were limited. She'd secretly hoped he would present her with another one, but thanks to Cyrus's ill-timed revelation, that possibility had evaporated as quickly as the wispy vapor from their breath in the cold night air.

"And it won't get here if you don't get to bed, sweetie." She managed to get the children inside and a couple of lamps lit without further comment from Marcie. Alex took one of the lamps and headed up the stairs with his sisters behind him.

"Good night, Henry." She held the front door open for him.

He closed it. "I'm not leaving yet, Lavinia. We need to talk."

"I have to see to the children."

"You will. Later. But first, tell me about this case Cyrus mentioned. I assume it's yours and that it's against me."

Facing him wasn't easy, but she must. She looked into a pair of steely blue eyes. "That's correct. I hired Mr. Price to help me find a way to gain guardianship since you refused to relinquish it."

Henry shook his head. "You don't understand, do you, even after all this time? Jack and Pauline wanted me to care for their children. That's why they named me in the will. Not you."

"Your brother named you, yes, but my sister told me in a letter years ago that if anything were to happen to her and Jack, she wanted me to raise them. I have every intention of making that happen."

He scoffed. "Even if that means taking me to court? Do you honestly think that's what Pauline would have wanted? If so, you're mistaken. When she wrote that letter, she was hoping you'd come out here and get to know your nieces and nephew. But you didn't, so she changed her mind."

His air of certainty didn't bode well. "How do you know?"

"She said so when they asked my permission to name me in the will. She was afraid you might take the children back to Philadelphia, and she wanted them to stay here—with me."

Lavinia lifted her chin and responded in a heated tone. "Why haven't you told me that me before?"

"I thought the fact that she and Jack named me as the children's guardian made that clear."

"It didn't, not to me, but—" she heaved a resigned sigh "—I suppose it no longer matters since I'm not going to take them back. I'll be staying here instead."

"Here? I see." He shook his head. "So you're going to accept Worthington's offer after all?"

She hadn't made up her mind, but she wasn't about to tell him that. "I love the children and will do whatever's necessary to be granted guardianship."

"Including having my rights revoked?"

"If you'd relinquish them that wouldn't be necessary."

He stared at her long and hard, his lips pressed into

a firm line. Several tense seconds later, he gave a curt nod. "I admire your determination, but I'd advise you to reconsider. You won't win your case. You'll just make things hard on yourself and those you love."

She loved him, but that didn't seem to matter since he didn't love her. "I'm doing what's best for the children, and as far as winning my case, you might as well know that I have a strong one."

A flicker of doubt crossed his face, followed by a frown. "I'm sorry you think so poorly of me. I thought by now you would have seen what kind of man I am. Good night, Lavinia." Henry marched down the steps, strode down the pathway and left without a backward glance.

The clanging of the wrought iron gate closing behind him shattered what little control she had left. She gripped the doorjamb, drooped her head and drew in a ragged breath. Her struggle to keep the tears at bay failed. A pair of them coursed over her cheeks.

"Aunt Livy!" Dot called. "We're ready for you to tuck us in."

"I'll be right up." She swiped at her cheeks, pasted on a smile and mounted the stairs. The children were expecting a wonderful Christmas, and she would make sure they had it.

"Are my wings on straight?" Marcie looked over one shoulder and then the other.

Lavinia smiled. "Yes, sweetie. You look beautiful."

Her niece shifted her weight from foot to foot so quickly that the flowing white skirt of her angel costume swayed. She rubbed a hand over her stomach. "My belly doesn't feel right. What if I forget the words I'm supposed to say?"

"You won't. You've rehearsed your line many times."

Marcie scanned the curtained-off corner of the schoolhouse-turned-church serving as a staging area for the young thespians. She wasn't the only one with a case of the collywobbles. The nervous energy in the small area was palpable. "Where's Alex?"

"I'm right behind you."

"Oh." Marcie whirled around, her wings fluttering wildly. "Are you ready?"

He nodded. "Are you?"

Marcie shook her head, stopped abruptly and reached up to make sure her halo was still in place. She peeked between a small gap in the curtains. "There's so many people out there."

Alex shrugged. "They're the same people who were at church yesterday. You know all of them. There's nothing to be afraid of."

The reversal of roles came as a surprise. Perhaps Marcie's uneasiness stemmed from the fact that she had more invested in her performance than her brother. He'd only agreed to be a wise man because his friend Frankie was one, too. Notoriety was the furthest thing from Alex's mind.

"You'll both do well. I need to take my seat now, but I'll say a prayer for you."

As she headed to the benches facing the front of the large room where painted backdrops had been hung, Lavinia petitioned the Lord on behalf of all the young performers. She reached the row where Dot sat beside Henry and took the aisle seat on her other side.

"How's Alex holding up?" Henry asked.

"He's doing well, but Marcie is as nervous as a snowman in July." Lavinia could relate. Her stomach was as unsettled as Marcie's. Thankfully, Henry had sent word that he wouldn't be able to join them until now, so she'd had the day to herself. Not that it had been a peaceful one. The children had been so excited that they'd been unusually quarrelsome. If that wasn't enough, the conversation with Henry kept going 'round and 'round in her mind.

"Good evening." The hand on her shoulder that accompanied the greeting caused her to jump. Stuart drew back. "I'm sorry, Lavinia. I didn't mean to startle you."

"It's all right." Her reply had come out breathy, which could give him the wrong impression. He was a good man, but he didn't cause her heart to pound or bring on a bout of light-headedness the way Henry had when he'd kissed her two days ago in that very room. "Dot, would you mind sitting in my lap so Mr. W. can join us? You'll be able to see better."

"I'll hold her." Henry's firm tone broached no argument. He softened it as he addressed Dot. "Up you go, Dimples."

"Thank you." Lavinia smiled, but Henry didn't look her way. She slid next to him, placed a hand on the now-vacant space and looked up at Stuart. "Please, have a seat."

He lowered himself, flipping the tails of his formal tailcoat over the back of the bench. His elegant attire made him stand out. Most of the men wore frock coats that had seen years of service. Some of the miners sported ankle-length dusters that had taken on the reddish color of the soil they worked. Although they differed in appearance from the cultured gentlemen her father entertained, the robust men of Sutter Creek worked hard. They were carving a future out of a rugged land and transforming California into a vibrant place teeming with possibilities.

Stuart leaned close and whispered. "I'm looking forward to the play, the service and our talk afterward. I trust you'll have an answer for me."

"I will." She didn't know yet what it would be. She'd been too preoccupied to come up with it, thinking instead about Henry and wondering what had kept him from spending the day at the house as he usually did.

The minister stepped to the front and the room quieted. "Good evening. It's wonderful to see so many of you here eager to celebrate Christmas Eve. I appreciate the schoolboard granting us the use of this facility again this year, but I look forward to the day we have a home of our own. The good Lord willing, there will be a church at the corner of Church Street before too many more years have passed. He's provided the land, and I trust him to provide the funds needed to erect the building."

Lavinia couldn't help but think of the beautiful church where she worshipped back in Philadelphia. Although the rosewood pews were filled with elegantly dressed men and women sitting in their assigned seats, it lacked the warmth of this makeshift church and the goodhearted people in it.

"Since we have a group of youngsters eager to present the play for us—" the minister inclined his heard toward the curtained corner from which whispers and nervous giggles came "—I'll keep the opening prayer brief and turn things over to their director."

After a short prayer, a young girl walked through the opening in the curtains followed by an older student who served as narrator. A male angel joined them wearing large wings Marcie had admired earlier. The play began with Gabriel informing Mary that she was to bear a child and call him Jesus.

Lavinia watched for Alex and Marcie to appear with eagerness unlike anything she'd experienced before. She mouthed their words along with them and heaved sighs of relief when they didn't miss one. Not even the concerts and plays she'd attended back home had brought her such joy or filled her with such pride.

The children had come to mean more to her than she would have thought possible. If they were sad, she ached along with them. If they laughed, she joined in. If they experienced success, she rejoiced. They'd done a fine job tonight. She couldn't wait to congratulate them, but she'd have to wait until after the service since the performers had reserved seats on benches up front.

When the applause at the end of the play finally subsided, the minister stepped to the front once again. "I'm sure you're eager to enjoy those treats Mr. Hawthorn and Miss Crowne have prepared, which smell so good, and I know the children can't wait to see what's inside those pretty packages on the tree, but I have a short message first that I hope you'll find inspiring."

He launched into the sermon with his usual enthusiasm. His engaging delivery took the story just enacted by the children in a different direction. He talked about examining the birth of Christ from a new perspective, making use of a simple question.

"As we just saw, God spoke to Joseph in a dream, reassuring him that what Mary had said was true, but what if Joseph had been more concerned about the townspeople's approval than he was about following God's plan for his life and had set Mary aside?"

The minister continued talking, but the words sounded like they were coming from the depths of a mine shaft like the one Henry had pointed out to her the day they'd traveled to Jackson. Lavinia stared at the clock above the chalkboard, unaware that her mouth was parted until it grew dry. She closed it and tried to silence the questions bombarding her.

What if she'd been guilty of overriding the Lord's plans for her life? What if taking Henry to court wasn't the right thing to do? She hadn't even prayed about it. Instead, she'd been bent on doing whatever it took to be granted guardianship of the children, even considering marrying a man she didn't love. What if she was about to make a terrible mistake?

Stuart leaned over and whispered in her ear. "Are you all right?"

Unable to speak, she nodded instead.

Despite their differences, Henry sent her an encouraging smile. He'd been supportive of her from the start even though she'd resisted his attempts to help. She would miss him greatly. If only things were different…

What if they could be? What if she surrendered her problems and her plans to her Heavenly Father instead of trying so hard to handle things on her own? What if she trusted Him to do what was best for the children— and for her?

Lord, I should have come to You a long time ago. I'm sorry I didn't. I've made a mess of things, pushing hard to get what I want. In the process, I've even managed to push Henry away. How could he love me when I've been out to discredit him? I'm here now seeking Your guidance. Please help me figure out what to do.

She waited throughout the rest of the message for a sign of some kind. She'd heard of people experiencing a profound sense of peace after they'd given their troubles to the Lord, but nothing happened. She drew in a calming breath, but the sugary sweet scents filling the air made the pitching of her stomach worse.

The minister said the closing prayer, delivered the benediction and turned things over to Lavinia. She rose on legs that felt about as firm as the creamy filling in the éclairs, made her way to the front and faced the congregation.

"As you heard, there's a small gift for each child on the tree. To make things go smoothly, I'll be removing them. I've asked my nieces and nephew to pass them out, so if they will join me—" she nodded at each of them in turn "—we can get started."

Alex, Marcie and Dot delivered the presents. The children made quick work of tearing off the colorful tissue paper Lavinia and Henry had used to wrap them. Gleeful shouts followed.

Lavinia encouraged everyone to visit the dessert tables and help themselves. Mrs. Keyes sat at the piano and played carols as she had at the party for the children's classmates and their families. Many of the adults headed over to partake of the refreshments, but the children were captivated by the simple gifts she'd given them and seemed in no hurry to sample the sweets. Fathers and older brothers showed the younger children how to spin a wooden top, operate a yo-yo or get a ball on a string into a cup.

Lavinia extended Christmas greetings to the people nearest her and moved on to speak with several others after that. Frankie's mother approached her, a plate full of desserts in hand. "The children did a fine job in the play, didn't they? Alex was as well-behaved as ever. I didn't think my mischievous Frankie could be so serious, but he looked like a wise man."

"Indeed. I'm new to all this and didn't know what a joy it is to watch a child you love perform."

"Makes a mother—or an aunt—proud, it does." The rosy-cheeked woman looked around the room. "It was mighty generous of you to give the children presents. When times are hard, like they've been this past year, they don't get many toys. There's some youngsters who'll be happy to find a peppermint stick and an orange waiting for them tomorrow morning. We're doing a bit better than most. Frankie will be getting a set of tin soldiers, and I found an adorable little tea set for his younger sister."

Lavinia managed to finish the conversation on a cheery note, despite the tightness in her chest. If she'd given the children the presents she'd planned to, they could have overshadowed their parents' offerings. Her time in Sutter Creek had taught her a valuable lesson— simple gifts given with love meant more than lavish displays intended to impress. Even though they had very little, the people here were more content than many of those she knew back east, who were always striving for more.

Like her father.

He had so much, and yet he wasn't content. He was intent upon expanding his empire, which took him away from home for months at a time. She'd spent most of her childhood under the watchful eye of a governess.

But her nieces and nephew wouldn't. Once she was granted guardianship, she could take them to San Francisco with her, where she would care for them herself and see that they had the best opportunities possible.

Henry's rich voice reached her with its wealth of rolled *R*'s, as appealing as the man himself. He was talking with Mr. Nichols while balancing Dot on one hip. The darling girl doted on Henry, and it was easy to see why. He showered the children with love just as he'd been doing ever since they'd lost their parents. He'd even said he was going to stay home with Dot until she started school. For a man as active as Henry, that would be quite a sacrifice. But that's who he was. He'd do anything for those he loved.

But she wasn't one of them.

She stepped behind the curtained area and blinked to clear her blurred vision.

A light touch on her arm alerted her to the presence of another. "What's wrong, Lavinia?"

She spun around. "Oh, Gladys, it's you. I thought it was—" She pressed her lips together and placed a hand over her racing heart. She'd come too close to admitting how much she'd hoped Henry had come looking for her.

Gladys folded her arms and frowned. "I saw you watching Mr. Henry. Has he done something to upset you? If so, I'll have a word with that young man."

"It's not him. It's me. So much has happened since you left on your honeymoon, and it's left me in a bit of a quandary." She told Gladys about the letter from her father, the offer Stuart had made after she read it and her pending court case.

"Well now, that's a fine kettle of fish. In two weeks' time, you've decided to take a stand against your father, received a proposal from a man you don't love and driven a wedge between you and the one you do. My question is, what are you going to do now? Give up on your dreams or follow your heart?"

"I can't follow my heart. I love Henry, but he doesn't love me."

Gladys gave an unladylike snort. "What do you mean

he's not in love? It's as plain as the wrinkles on my face that he's head over heels for you."

"Perhaps, but he hasn't said anything. I asked him outright if he could give me any reason not to consider Stuart's offer, and he didn't have one."

"Oh, he does, all right, but I reckon he's gone all gallant on you. Either that, or his pride's acting up."

Lavinia shook her head. "I don't understand."

"What I'm saying is that Mr. Henry doesn't want to stand in your way. He knows the kind of life you've been used to, and he can't provide for you like Mr. Worthington can."

"I don't need all that anymore. I just want…" Her lips trembled and she sniffed. She couldn't cry. Not here. Not now.

"Say it, Lavinia. What do you want?"

"To be with Henry."

"Then you know what you have to do, so go out there and do it." Gladys pulled back the sheet.

"I can tell Stuart I won't marry him, but I can't tell Henry how I feel."

"You don't have to tell him. Turning down Mr. Worthington will show him."

She hoped Gladys was right, but she had her doubts.

Chapter Sixteen

Watching Lavinia talk with Worthington tested Henry's resolve. He fought the urge to march across the room and ask the fancy-dressed fellow to leave. If it weren't for his nieces and nephew, who were busy perusing the dessert table again, he might not have been able to stop himself. Lavinia deserved more than a loveless marriage. Standing up to her father and dealing with his outrage would be better than sentencing herself to a lifetime of lost hopes and dreams.

She gazed at Worthington, graced him with one of her beautiful smiles and accepted his offer. Or so it appeared, judging by the answering smile on the encroacher's face.

The scene sickened Henry, and he forced himself to look away. He didn't even know why he was letting himself get riled up. After all, Lavinia was out to destroy him, because that's what taking the children would do. Not that she would win her case and get him ousted as their guardian. Even if he'd unwittingly neglected some finer points of the law due to his grief-stricken state, surely a judge would grant him some leniency.

If he was honest with himself, he admired her dogged

determination to wrest the guardianship from him, especially now that her eyes had been opened and she was acting on her own behalf instead of carrying out her father's wishes. Her resolve proved how much she loved the children. She'd do a wonderful job of mothering them, but the thought of Worthington filling the role of their father soured Henry's stomach. That honor was his, but he'd be happier if Lavinia was by his side, helping him bring up their nieces and nephew.

The trouble was that he had so little to offer, although the conversation he'd just concluded with Mr. Nichols had given him hope. The price the buyer of his hotel up in Marysville had offered, albeit low, would enable him to pay off Jack's mortgage. If all went well, he'd even have enough left over to meet his needs until he could establish a business, at which time the banker would help him secure a loan of his own.

Emery Staples sidled up to Henry and chuckled. "Looks like you've got it bad, son."

"I don't understand."

"Miss Lavinia. You can't take your eyes off her. Not that I can blame you. She's a fine-looking young lady. Hardworking, too. Preparing for this party took some doing." Emery shifted his gaze from Lavinia to Henry. "Gladys tells me you helped with the baking."

"I gave Lavinia a few pointers, but she did most of the work herself." He couldn't have asked for a more eager or enthusiastic student. Watching her learn a skill she enjoyed so much had been rewarding.

"And a fine job she did. I've sampled a number of her confections. Might even have to try another one or two, provided my wife doesn't catch me. Gladys has a mind to trim me down a bit." He patted his rounded stomach and let loose with a good-natured laugh. "The things a man will do for his ladylove."

"It sounds like marriage agrees with you."

"That it does. I highly recommend the institution."

A tall man in an alpaca coat much like Henry's stood in the doorway of the mudroom scanning the crowd. He studied the newcomer. Although he wasn't a local resident, something about the elderly gentleman was familiar.

Lavinia gasped. "Father?"

Shock froze her to the spot, but it set Henry in motion. He took a step, only to be stopped by a firm grip on his shoulder.

"Not to meddle, son, but I reckon Miss Lavinia can fight her own battles."

Emery had a point. She wasn't one to accept help easily, but Henry was prepared to offer it if need be. For now, he needed to get to the children, who were apt to be frightened by the unexpected appearance of their grandfather.

Worthington, to his credit, stepped in front of Lavinia, but she marched across the room to face her father. "What are *you* doing here?"

The room had quieted, with most of the guests riveted on the drama playing out in front of them. Some slipped out, a wise move, since things were likely to get even more heated.

Paul Crowne cast his daughter a disapproving gaze. "Come now, Lavinia. Is that any way to greet your father? I've traveled all the way from Philadelphia to see you and my grandchildren. Where are the little tykes?"

Henry reached the children, who stood wide-eyed and openmouthed. He pulled them to his sides. "It's all right. I'm here."

Dot and Marcie clung to him tightly. Alex put on a brave front, but his hands were shaking.

Lavinia lifted her chin. "If you'd shown even the slightest bit of interest in them, Father, I would be happy to introduce them to you, but that's not the case, is it? All you care about is how they can benefit you."

"Nonsense, my dear. This wild accusation of yours is uncalled for. I've come to take the children back with me."

"You're not taking them. I won't allow it."

Crowne mimicked Lavinia in a sardonic tone. "You won't allow it." He barked out a bitter laugh. "How droll—and shortsighted. I can give them a better life than they can get here in this rough-and-tumble town."

She took a step back and stared at her father, her brown eyes as dark as Henry had ever seen them. He watched her, his muscles tensed. If he wasn't protecting the children from Crowne, he would have been in the bully's face, telling him just what he thought of the cruelty he was inflicting on his only remaining daughter. No wonder Pauline had left home and never looked back.

Emery and Gladys arrived, offering welcome support.

"Thank you for coming to watch the children," Henry whispered. "I can't let Lavinia deal with this on her own."

"I know it's hard," Emery said, "but give her another minute, son."

She cast a glance around the room and returned her attention to her father. Her voice rang out clear and strong. "You've maligned me for years, but I won't stand by and let you speak ill of these good people. They might not measure up to your standards, but they're my friends."

Crowne shook his head. "I knew it. You've gone soft. That's what I was afraid of and why I came. I'm sure it's all that Hawthorn fellow's doing. He's probably convinced you the children are better off here with him, a no-account blacksmith like his brother."

Lavinia fisted her hands. "Don't talk about Henry that way! He's the finest man I've ever known, and he's wonderful with the children. He's their legal guardian, so you couldn't get them anyway."

"A technicality easily overcome by a good lawyer."

"You're wrong. I hired a good lawyer, and he says no jury would find fault with Henry. I agree. The children belong with him, and that's where they're staying. If you attempt to challenge him, I'll go before the judge and tell him what kind of father you've been. I doubt he'd look on you favorably."

"Why, you little—" Crowne dropped the hand he'd raised to his side, as though he'd just realized he had an audience.

Worthington crossed the room and addressed Crowne in an authoritative voice. "I think you'd be wise to leave now, sir."

"I believe you're right. I have some pressing business to attend to anyhow." He turned to Lavinia. "I've chosen my heir—" he inclined his head toward Worthington "—so there's no reason for you to come back."

To Henry's surprise, Worthington addressed Crowne in a firm but decisive tone. "I won't be accepting that position, sir. I refuse to work for a man who treats his own daughter this way."

"Stuart! No! This is the opportunity you've been waiting for. I won't let you give it up on my account." Lavinia attempted to step between the two men, but Worthington motioned for her to stay back.

"It's fine, Lavinia. I have other offers pending. I'll

take one of them." He spun to face Crowne. "You'll have my letter of resignation in your hands as soon as I can locate pen and paper."

Crowne's face reddened, and he jabbed a finger at Worthington. "I don't need a letter. You're fired."

The younger man shook his head. "I feel sorry for you, sir. You're too busy building your empire to see what's right before your eyes. You have a remarkable daughter and delightful grandchildren. It's not too late to—"

"Don't you lecture me, young man! I'll conduct my affairs the way I see fit." He whirled around to face Lavinia. "As for you, young lady, I'll see that you have enough to get settled someplace, but that will be the extent of my benevolence."

"I understand. Goodbye, Father." She rose on her toes, kissed his cheek and turned away.

Crowne stormed out of the room. Worthington and Lavinia carried on a whispered conversation. She nodded and reached out a hand, and he shook it. The formality of the exchange gave Henry hope.

Henry couldn't believe what he'd just witnessed. Not only had Lavinia defended him, but she'd given up her fight and bested her father, sacrificing everything for the sake of the children in the process.

Emery leaned close. "Looks like your sweetheart loves you, too, son. I'd say it's time to stake your claim, before it's too late."

"Yes, sir. I intend to." He glanced at the children, and a plan began to take shape. It might fail miserably, but he had to try.

Would it be enough?

"Come, children," Lavinia said. "It's time to go."

They darted out the door ahead of her, clutching their

new toys and whispering among themselves, no doubt trying to make sense of what had happened. She followed, each step an effort.

Despite her weariness, she felt a sense of peace at odds with her situation that could only have come from the Lord. He'd upheld her through the ordeal with her father. Surely, He had a plan for her future. She'd just have to wait for Him to reveal it.

Hopefully, things would work out for Stuart, too. If the investors at his preferred firm in San Francisco would be willing to grant him a year to find a wife, he was prepared to accept their offer. He deserved to be happy, even if things hadn't worked out for her. At least she was finally free of her father and his unceasing demands.

Gladys's help putting the schoolroom to rights after the last guests headed home couldn't have been more welcome. At long last, Lavinia could leave.

She needed to get the children to bed as soon as possible. Only then could she bury her face in her pillow and give way to the tears that had been threatening ever since she'd seen Henry bolt out of the building an hour ago. He'd witnessed the ugly scene with her father, and yet he left without so much as a word. She'd thought he would be happy. After all, she'd made it clear she wasn't fighting him for guardianship anymore.

They reached Church Street, and Lavinia trudged up the hill. Marcie fell in step beside her. "Your father isn't a nice man, is he?"

"No. He's not."

Alex joined them. "He wanted to take us away. Did you know that?"

"I did. That's why I came here. He'd asked me to take

you back to Philadelphia, but I realized that wasn't right. Sutter Creek is your home."

"What will you do now?" Marcie asked.

Lavinia drew in a deep breath of the cool night air and slowly released it. "I don't know."

"You won't leave us, will you, Aunt Livy?" Dot asked, her voice wavering.

"Not right away." She summoned the cheeriest tone she could muster. "We have a Christmas to celebrate first, and it will be special."

"Yes, it will, because you'll be here with us." Alex took hold of her hand. He didn't welcome displays of affection, and he rarely initiated them. Lavinia relished the unexpected gift.

The children had claimed her heart. She dreaded leaving and watching them grow smaller as the stagecoach pulled away, but she couldn't stay here forever. Henry would be eager to move out of the boardinghouse and reduce his expenses.

She blinked back tears. Somehow she reached the house without shedding any. Alex flung open the gate, and he and his sisters headed up the path to the front porch. Lavinia closed the gate behind them, the wrought iron cold to the touch.

"Lavinia!" Henry called. "I'm out back. Could you come here, please?"

The urgency in his voice sent a jolt of energy through her. He'd mentioned earlier that evening that he'd planned to carry in some firewood after the party. Had something happened to him? She broke into a run. The children's hurried footfalls echoed hers.

She flew down the side of the house, rounded the corner, paused and scanned the area. Henry stood under the large oak tree where he'd rescued her from the downed branch the night he'd arrived back in Sutter Creek. A lantern sat at his feet, casting a warm glow. He motioned her forward.

She approached, scanning him from head to foot. "You're all right. I was afraid you'd been hurt."

"I'm fine."

"What is it then?"

"Look up, Aunt Livy."

She did as Alex requested, and her mouth gaped. Someone had tied lots of red ribbons on the large clump of mistletoe overhead.

"Please tell me you didn't climb all the way up there in the dark, Alex."

"He didn't," Marcie stated gleefully. "It was Uncle Henry."

Lavinia slowly lowered her head, a sense of excitement taking hold of her. "You did this? Why?"

Henry's mouth lifted in a lopsided smile she found irresistible. "Because I enjoyed that kiss you gave me and would like another."

The girls giggled.

"Henry, please," she whispered. "The children."

"They know all about it, but they promised to keep my secret."

She glanced at them. They were grinning. She faced Henry again. The lamplight illuminated his fine features. The attraction she'd seen before was back in full force. Could it be he did care about her after all?

He gazed into her eyes. "You're a remarkable woman, Lavinia, and have a heart of gold. You saw to it that every child at the party tonight received a gift. I think it's only fair that you get one, too." He reached behind his back. "It's nothing fancy. I made it myself."

Her breath hitched. Henry had made something just for her.

"Close your eyes and hold out your hands."

She obliged. He placed a long slender object in them. It was cool to the touch, like the gate she'd just closed, and heavier than she'd expected.

"You can open your eyes now."

"Oh, Henry, it's beautiful." She studied the wrought iron shoehorn. His fine workmanship was evident. "I love the decorative twists in the handle and the little leaf here at the top."

He raised the lantern. "Look at it closely."

"There's an *L* and an *H*, for Lavinia Hélène." She looked more closely. "There's no *C*, though, or did I miss it?"

"There's no *C*. And the *H* isn't for Hélène. I didn't know that was your middle name, although it's beautiful, just like you are."

The girls heaved noisy sighs. Lavinia had been so engrossed in his amazing gift that she'd forgotten the children were there.

"If it's not for Hélène, then…" She inhaled sharply. "Is it…?"

"Yes. The *H* is for Hawthorn. You're part of this family, Lavinia. It wouldn't be complete without you. I know I'm not the kind of man you had in mind. I'm not cultured or wealthy, and I'm not well-versed in all the rules of etiquette."

"That doesn't matter. You're good and kind and wonderful just the way you are."

"I can't give you all the things you're used to. Could

you be happy without dresses from French designers and dinners at fancy restaurants?"

She nodded. "Those things are nice, but they're nothing compared to love and family. I'd like very much to be part of this one."

"I'd hoped you might feel that way. In that case…" Henry hung the lantern on a branch and dropped to one knee.

A tingling sensation swept over her.

He took the shoehorn from her and set it down. "I love you, Lavinia."

"You do? But you never said anything."

"I was a fool. I'd convinced myself I wasn't good enough for you. I'm not, but you seem willing to overlook that."

"Don't you dare discount yourself, Henry Hawthorn. You're the finest man I've ever known."

Marcie laughed. "You said the same thing about him to your father."

"I did because it's true."

Dot chimed in. "Uncle Henry is wonderful."

He cleared his throat and chided the girls playfully. "If you young ladies could keep from interrupting me, I could propose to your aunt."

"Go ahead, Uncle Henry," Alex said.

"Very well." He lifted his face to Lavinia, his eyes filled with love and admiration. "My dearest Lavinia, I'd be honored if you'd marry me and take my name. You already have my heart."

"I love you, too, so very much."

"Then you'll accept my offer?" His voice contained a blend of hesitancy and hope.

"Yes, Henry! Yes!"

He stood, pulled her into a hug and held her tightly. She slipped her arms around him and rested her head against his broad chest. This was where she belonged.

The children's whooping and hollering roused her.

Henry loosened his hold and drew back but didn't let her go. "Sounds like we have their approval."

She smiled. "That it does."

"You're under mistletoe, Uncle Henry," Alex pointed out. "You have to kiss her."

"Gladly." He leaned toward her and pressed a kiss to her lips, pulling away far too soon for her liking.

The gate clanged shut.

"Goody! Grandma and Grandpa S. are here." Dot raced off to meet them with Marcie right behind her.

Alex sauntered over to Henry and Lavinia. "There's a whole lot of mistletoe up there. You need to give Aunt Livy a better kiss than that, Uncle Henry."

"Don't worry. I will, once you and your sisters are inside."

Alex nodded his approval and dashed off to join his sisters.

A shiver of anticipation shimmied up Lavinia's spine. She'd never been so eager for the children to head to bed.

Concern furrowed Henry's forehead. "You're not cold, are you?"

"No. It's not that." She focused on his lips.

"How interesting." His voice took on a deep, intimate tone with his rolled *R*'s more pronounced than ever. "You like my kisses, do you? I'm glad, because there are many more to come."

"Well, if that isn't a beautiful sight." Gladys had rounded the corner of the house with Emery on one side of her, the children on the other. "Your aunt and uncle have gotten together at last. So, when's the wedding?"

"Tomorrow, if my bride-to-be is agreeable."

She shook her head to clear it. "Tomorrow? Really? But it's Christmas."

"That it is. One of the most special days of the year. Marrying you would make it even more so."

"It would, but there's no time to plan anything."

Henry shrugged. "What's there to plan? The house has been decorated, we have a tasty feast planned and the guests have already been invited."

"So are you getting married on Christmas or not?" Marcie asked.

The prospect of becoming Henry's wife in a few short hours sent a shiver of anticipation skittering up Lavinia's spine. She slipped her arms free, took Henry's hand and turned to their eager audience. "Yes. We are."

The children rushed over, enfolding her and Henry in a family hug.

Alex was the first to break away. He grinned. "Frankie was right about the mistletoe. It really works."

"That it does," Henry said, his eyes twinkling in the lantern light.

Gladys approached and beckoned to the children. "Come now. We've got a busy day tomorrow, so your grandpa and I will get you tucked in and give your aunt and uncle some privacy."

The children chorused their good-nights, tromped up the back steps and went inside, followed by Gladys and Emery.

Lavinia picked up the shoehorn. "This is what you made the day you worked in the smithy with Mr. Dealy, isn't it?"

He nodded.

"But you didn't plan to propose back then, did you? And yet you used an *H*. Why?"

"You were on my mind, and I added the letter without thinking. I'd meant to replace the leaf, but I couldn't bring myself to do it." He took the shoehorn from her and set it down. "A part of me secretly hoped you'd become my wife one day, even though my sensible side knew I'd never be the kind of man worthy of you."

"I'm the one who isn't worthy of you. You're everything I've ever dreamed of—and more."

Henry held her hands and pressed his lips to the back of them. "You have no idea how much it means to me to hear you say that. I was afraid you wouldn't be willing to give up the life you had. I can meet your needs, but you'll have to learn to live with less."

"That's fine. This last month has shown me that I don't need as much as I thought I did. I might buy some fabric with the money I have left, though, and ask Gladys to help me make a few simple dresses. I like the ones I brought, but red and green were Pauline's favorite colors. I prefer blue and purple."

"Make yourself as many as you need, at my expense. I can give you dresses, but—" he smiled apologetically "—I'm afraid our budget won't cover matching footwear. Can you survive?"

"I do like my boots, but I don't need to have a pair for every outfit."

He slipped his arms around her waist and gazed at her with unbridled love. "If I could provide them, I would."

"I appreciate that, but we have so much already—three wonderful children, a fine house for them to live in and a town filled with some of the nicest people I've ever met."

"About the house—I spoke with Mr. Nichols at the party tonight and told him I'll be in on Monday to pay off the mortgage."

"We could use the money my father's giving me instead and save yours for—"

He put a finger to her lips. "I'm not surprised that you want to help, but the adjustments you'll be making could be difficult at times. I'd like you to keep your money and use it to get the things you might want."

All she wanted at that moment was the kiss he'd promised her. She lifted her chin and stepped closer, but Henry kept on talking.

"I spoke with Mr. Price after the party and asked him what Mr. Benedict might be willing to take for his building. As I expected, he wants more than the place is worth. Mr. Price thinks he might be able to convince Benedict to take less, though, since the place has been vacant for so long and I could offer a portion of the price up front."

Henry had accomplished a great deal in an hour, but he was a man of action. "Are you planning to open another hotel?"

"It would make sense. I have experience, and you have a great deal of knowledge in that area, too, but I won't proceed unless you agree."

She wasn't used to a man asking her opinion, but Henry wasn't like other men. "I do agree, but only if the hotel includes a restaurant. You're excellent chef, and I feel certain you'd earn a stellar reputation in no time. We could call the hotel Hawthorn House, and the restaurant could be Henry's Place."

He chuckled. "You're full of plans, aren't you, and keeping my hobby a secret doesn't seem to be one of them."

"It would be a shame to keep your talents all to ourselves. The Lord expects us to share them. Which reminds me... I'd also like to offer the meeting room to the congregation for our services until we can afford to have a church built. What do you think?"

"I think a man could go far with a woman like you at his side. No one's ever believed in me or my dreams the way you do."

"And no one's ever loved me the way you do. You've made me happier than I thought possible. Now, if you don't mind—" she splayed her hands on his chest and gazed at the incredible man God had given her "—I'd like that kiss you promised me."

He grinned. "And you shall have it." He pulled her into his arms, tilted his head and leaned toward her. Her eyes slid shut.

This kiss was nothing like the others he'd given her, which had been sweet but tentative. He claimed her lips with the assurance of a man in love, firm but tender. She'd never felt as cherished, as appreciated for who she was as she did then.

He pulled away slightly, whispered her name against her lips and kissed her again. She didn't think things could get any better, but they did. Time seemed to stand still. She wasn't aware of anything but Henry and the delight of being in his arms.

Until a distant knocking began. It continued, growing louder and more insistent.

He brought the kiss to an end, and they turned toward the sound.

A lantern illuminated Marcie, Dot and Alex, who stood at the girls' second-story bedroom window. Their nieces and nephew waved and smiled. Lavinia and Henry waved back.

He chuckled. "It appears we've finally satisfied our mistletoe matchmakers."

"So it does. I didn't realize we had an audience, though."

Gladys appeared at the window, shooed the children away and closed the curtains.

"No one's watching now, my love, so I can show you how just much you mean to me."

His endearment was as sweet as the kiss that followed.

* * * * *

If you enjoyed Their Mistletoe Matchmakers,
look for these other books by Keli Gwyn:

Family of Her Dreams,
A Home of Her Own,
Make-Believe Beau
and
Her Motherhood Wish.

Dear Reader,

I'm a December bride, so when my editor asked if I'd like to write a Christmas story, I responded with an enthusiastic yes. This time of year thoughts turn to love—of our families, our friends and, most important, our Lord, who came to earth as a baby. Creating a love story set during this wonderful season was special.

I enjoyed writing Henry and Lavinia's story and hope you've enjoyed reading it. This couple has experienced heartache, but they find solace in caring for their nephew and nieces. They also find a love of their own as they work together to make Christmas special for the children.

I strive to make my stories as historically accurate as possible. As I did my research, I learned a lot about Sutter Creek, a Gold Rush-era town not too far from where I live that has a rich history. I did take a bit of fictional license. The first church wasn't built until two years after the story takes place. There was a congregation in the late 1850s, but I don't know where they met. I chose to use the schoolhouse.

I love hearing from readers. You can contact me through my website at www.keligwyn.com or write to me at PO Box 1404, Placerville CA 95667.

Warmly,
Keli Gwyn

Get 2 Free Books,
Plus 2 Free Gifts—
just for trying the Reader Service!

Love Inspired HISTORICAL

"I brought you up here because I have a couple of dogs I'd
especially like to introduce to Harper and Hudson," he said.

She flashed him a surprised look. He couldn't possibly
think that with all she had going on, she'd want to adopt a
couple of dogs, or even one.

"I appreciate what you do here," she said, trying to buffer
her next words. "But I want to make it clear up front that I
have no intention of adopting a dog. They're cute and all,
but I've already got my hands full with the twins as it is."

"Oh, no," Simon said, raising his free hand, palm out.
"You misunderstand me. I'm not pulling some sneaky stunt
on you to try to get you to adopt a dog. It's just that—well,
maybe it would be easier to show you than to try to explain."

"Zig! Zag! Come here, boys." Two identical small white
dogs dashed to Simon's side, their full attention on him.

Miranda looked from one dog to the other and a light
bulb went off in her head.

"Twins!" she exclaimed.

Simon laughed.

"Not exactly. They're littermates."

He helped an overexcited Harper pet one of the dogs and, taking Simon's lead, Miranda helped Hudson scratch the ears of the other.

"Soft fur, see, Harper?" Simon said. "This is a doggy."

"Gentle, gentle," Miranda added when Hudson tried to grab a handful of the white dog's fur.

"Zig and Zag are Westies—West Highland white terriers."

Zig licked Hudson's fist and he giggled. Both dogs seemed to like the babies, and the twins were clearly taken with the dogs.

But she'd meant what she'd said earlier—no dogs allowed. At the moment, suffering cuteness overload, she even had to give herself a stern mental reminder.

She cast her eyes up to make sure Simon understood her very emphatic message, but he was busy helping Harper interact with Zag.

When he finally looked up, their eyes met and locked. A slow smile spread across his lips and appreciation filled his gaze. For a moment, Miranda experienced something she hadn't felt this strongly since, well, since high school—the reel of her stomach in time with a quickened pulse and a shortness of breath.

Either she was having an asthma attack, or else—

She was absolutely not going to go there.

Don't miss
TEXAS CHRISTMAS TWINS
by Deb Kastner, available December 2017 wherever
Love Inspired® books and ebooks are sold.

www.LoveInspired.com

Love Inspired®

Inspirational Romance to Warm Your Heart and Soul

Join our social communities to connect with other readers who share your love!

Sign up for the Love Inspired newsletter at **www.LoveInspired.com** to be the first to find out about upcoming titles, special promotions and exclusive content.

CONNECT WITH US AT:

Harlequin.com/Community

 Facebook.com/LoveInspiredBooks

Twitter.com/LoveInspiredBks

LISOCIAL2017

Looking for inspiration in tales
of hope, faith and heartfelt romance?

Check out **Love Inspired**®,
Love Inspired® **Suspense** and
Love Inspired® **Historical** books!

New books available every month!

CONNECT WITH US AT:

www.LoveInspired.com

Harlequin.com/Community

 Facebook.com/LoveInspiredBooks

Twitter.com/LoveInspiredBooks

www.ReaderService.com